DESPERATE SILENCE

MARK PETTINGER

Desperate Silence
Copyright © 2025 by Mark Pettinger

All rights reserved. No part of this publication may be reproduced, distributed, or transmitted in any form or by any means, including photocopying, recording, or other electronic or mechanical methods, without the prior written permission of the author, except in the case of brief quotations embodied in critical reviews and certain other non-commercial uses permitted by copyright law. For permission requests, contact info@markpettinger.com

All characters and events in this publication are fictitious and any resemblance to real persons, living or dead, is entirely coincidental.

ISBN: 979-8-3136-5111-8

DESPERATE
SILENCE

ALSO BY MARK PETTINGER
DCI Priest Series
The Decalogue
Tick Tock Time's Up
Paper Soldiers
Where Darkness Lies

PROLOGUE

May 2011

Hayley Findlay was wrapped up tight, her ochre-yellow padded coat providing sufficient protection against the elements. It was mid-May and the promise of summer was threatening to reveal itself, but for the moment it was being strangled and held hostage by a lingering winter chill.

'I'm nine years old,' she had proclaimed to her mum, as the latter had insisted on the coat being accompanied by a set of gloves and scarf.

'You need to keep warm, Hayley, it's bitter outside.'

It's bitter outside wasn't a phrase that resonated with the average nine-year-old. It was either warm or cold; the thought of introducing *bitter* was an unnecessary adjective that young people had shown no desire to understand.

Hayley had won her personal battle in respect of the hat and glove set, and having kissed her mum goodbye she proceeded to skip merrily towards the park. Despite the years having advanced swiftly through her adolescence, she was still attached to a doll, her favourite doll, her Hettie, and had taken her to the park clasped tightly under her arm.

Hettie had been a birthday present, received on her sixth birthday. Hayley had pestered her parents for the doll almost daily, since her disappointment at not receiving one from Santa at Christmas. Her dad had openly said that she was getting too old for dolls, but Mum had swiftly moved to shut him up and told him that they should let her have her childhood, for soon enough she would grow up and it would be gone forever.

The park was no more than two hundred metres from their family home, and her parents had no reservations about letting her play there. Sometimes she would meet up with other children and play on the swings or the slide, other times she would play on her own, but Hettie would always accompany her.

It was early on Saturday afternoon when Aileen Findlay kissed her daughter and saw her off down to the park.

'Make sure you stay on the path all the way down to the park.'

'Yes, Mum, I will. See you later.'

'See you later, sweetheart.'

After watching Hayley until she was out of sight, Aileen retreated inside the house and recommenced the cleaning that she had started before battle had commenced over the hat and gloves.

A couple of hours had passed by in the blink of an eye, and Aileen had stepped outside to take her husband, Callum, a cup of coffee. Callum was to be found in the front garden on his knees, picking out the chickweed that had lain dormant throughout the harsh winter months, but that had now woken from its floral hibernation and was starting to flourish again, much to Callum's loudly vented disgust.

'These bloody weeds get everywhere, it's a full-time job just to keep on top of them.'

'Aye, and it's not even summer yet.'

Callum was startled and turned around to see Aileen standing behind him with a hot mug of fresh coffee.

'You made me jump.'

'Ah, so you were talking to yourself then?'

'Don't be daft, of course not,' he said as he took the mug from her hands, 'thanks. No, I was just thinking out loud.' She smiled.

'How was work this morning?'

'Yeah, busy. Well, I kept busy all morning.'

'And him?' The *him* to whom she referred was Callum's boss, Michael McGrouther. McGrouther had started to be a pain in the arse over the past couple of months, especially towards Callum. He would pick up on every little detail and highlight where Callum had made mistakes or was taking too long to complete a task. This was generally unwarranted as Callum was, by all other accounts from both colleagues and customers, a very good vehicle mechanic.

'Quiet this morning. He didn't say anything, I think he had his head stuck in a Jaguar for a couple of hours.'

Aileen couldn't help but laugh out loud.

'No, not literally. I meant he was just concentrating and focussed on the job in hand, although getting physically stuck in a car for a couple of hours might have been amusing. Yes, I've got the image in my head now.' He laughed too.

He took another sip of his coffee, placed the cup on the ground next to him, and returned to grasping at the weeds between his index finger and thumb.

'Eh, you're doing a grand job there, Callum.'

Callum looked up; Jennifer McGovern was standing on the other side of their four-foot privet hedge at the front boundary to their garden. 'Hello there, Mrs McGovern, how are you?'

'I'm grand, thanks. You can come and do my garden when you've finished here.'

'He'll be cutting the lawn after he's finished weeding, Jen,' said Aileen, 'maybe I'll hire him out to you.' The women smiled.

'How does ten pounds an hour sound?'

'Like daylight robbery, Aileen, like daylight robbery. Anyway, you shouldn't pay tradesmen by the hour.'

'Really,' asked Callum, 'and why might that be?'

'Well, if you pay a man by the hour, he'll drag out a

small job all day long. Morning break here, long lunch break, stopping every two minutes for a cigarette whilst leaning on his spade like the proverbial council worker.'

'Aye, fair comment,' Callum conceded.

'You need to crack on with cutting this lawn, never mind sitting on your arse drinking coffee.'

'I've only just stopped for a quick break,' protested Callum.

'Aye, that's what all the men say when they've been caught.' She shared a smile with Aileen.

'Anyway, if you get this lawn trimmed then Hayley will be able to play outside.'

'She already is, Jen, she's down at the park.'

Mrs McGovern's eyebrows dropped. 'No she isn't, Aileen. I mean, I walked past the park about five or ten minutes ago on my way up here. I couldn't see her.'

'Are you sure, Jen?'

'Well, yes, fairly sure. She might have been hidden somewhere, or playing out of sight, of course; but I usually see her when she's in the park. She has that favourite spot...'

'Underneath the climbing frame,' Aileen finished her sentence, 'yes, she likes to sit there and play with Hettie, when no-one else is out to play.'

'I'm sure she's fine,' said Callum as he looked to reassure his wife, accompanied by a smile.

'Me too,' chipped in Mrs McGovern, 'anyway, must be off, toodle-oo.'

'Bye, Jen, see you anon.' Aileen put her mug of tea

down on the paved pathway, 'I'm just going to go to the park, Callum, just to check on Hayley.'

'Sure, okay. Don't worry,' said Callum, 'she'll be there, probably chasing Hettie under the slide, or the climbing frame.'

'I know. I'll be back soon. Oh, and I want that lawn cut for when I get back.'

'You're having a laugh,' he protested, 'you'll only be gone ten minutes, I'll still be here, on my arse, pulling weeds out of the ground.'

Aileen set off for the park, with just a hint of trepidation and an expeditious step. Hayley had been allowed to walk to the park and back on her own since last summer, although the darkness of the winter months had curtailed this activity. Her parents, living in a small rural community, had weighed up the pros and cons of this decision, and after advising Hayley that she must never stray from the route either there or back, had decided that their nine-year-old could be trusted, and that there was almost zero chance of Hayley coming to any harm. She was literally only two minutes away, both parents had agreed.

Aileen rounded the corner, and the park came into view. It wasn't a vast expanse of play area by any stretch of the imagination, barely twenty metres by twenty metres. The local parish council had negotiated the purchase of the area from the landowner just over eight years ago, and the local residents had pooled their finances, plus had raised some external funds through a National Lottery grant to purchase some play equipment, and to have it professionally installed: swings, a slide, climbing frame, merry-go-round and a spring rider.

Aileen's brisk walk came to an abrupt halt; her jaw dropped, and her heart sank. She couldn't see Hayley. Her eyes quickly scanned left to right; swings, slide, climbing frame, merry-go-round, spring rider. Nothing. She extended her vision to the outskirts of the play area, the fence towards the south and west, and the hedge at the north and east. Nothing.

She moved forward again, and picked up the pace, running towards the metal gate that provided the entrance to the park. Having quickly negotiated the kissing gate, she ran into the central grassy area. She stood still and pivoted three hundred and sixty degrees, eyes as sharp as a hawk. Nothing.

Where was she? *Fuck!*

'Hayley,' she shouted, 'Hayley. Hayley, where are you, sweetheart?'

No reply. Nothing.

Aileen started to run towards each piece of play equipment in turn; she didn't know why, she could see them all from where she had been standing. After the swings she ran to the slide; after the slide she ran to the spring rider, and after that she ran towards the climbing frame, Hayley's favourite.

Upon reaching the climbing frame, Aileen fell to her knees and let out a wail that would only resonate with another mother. On the floor lay Hettie, her favourite doll that never left her side, never left her clutches. She hastily picked up the doll and pulled it close to her chest, the faint smell of Hayley's aroma present within the doll's hair, the familiar comforting scent that lingered on the soft fabric. For a moment Aileen was transported back to the tender moments of her daughter's infancy, the scent evoking memories of lullabies, cuddles and quiet nights. A fragrant connection that transcended time. A reminder of the love and closeness they shared.

Aileen stood. 'Hayley. *Hayleeeeey.*' No reply.

She spun around, eyes quickly scanning every inch of the immediate area, but there was no sign of her.

'Hayley,' again she shouted, the emotion clearly breaking through in her voice, as her words stuttered slightly on her trembling lip.

Hayley wasn't here. Aileen clutched the doll to her chest and made her way back through the gate and out of the playground. She stood for a moment contemplating what she should do, where she should go. Should she run back to the house and tell Callum or press on and continue to look for Hayley? But where?

The harbour, she thought, *she could be at the harbour.* She had no idea why. She couldn't immediately rationalise why Hayley might have gone to the harbour, but she wasn't at the park, that was for sure. As a forced walking pace became a gentle jog and turned into a purposeful run, Aileen rounded on the harbour some five minutes later.

It wasn't an expansive area, and it took less than twenty seconds for Aileen to scan the area for signs of Hayley. Nothing.

As she stood at the harbour edge, staring into the waters of Loch Fyne, she heard footsteps, quick footsteps approaching. She turned around to see Callum had caught up with her.

She sobbed, 'I can't find her, Callum, I can't find Hayley.'

CHAPTER 1

July 2021

Paul Calvert checked his watch, nine am; he carefully placed the medium-sized suitcase into the boot of his car and returned up the driveway to the front door of his house. His daughter Lisa was standing in the open doorframe.

'Are you sure you'll be okay?' he asked.

'Dad, I'm twenty-two years old, of course I'll be okay.'

'Yes, sorry. I forget sometimes that you're not my little princess any longer, you've matured and grown up so much, especially over these last six months.'

She leant in to hug him. 'Dad, I'll always be your little princess, whatever age I am, and wherever I am.'

She kissed him on the cheek and gave him what he had described many times as *one of those award-winning smiles.*

Her smile spread across her face, subtle yet radiant, as if the world brightened in its wake. It started at the corner of her mouth, a soft upturn that deepened into something full of warmth, her eyes sparkling with a quiet joy. There was an almost imperceptible pause before it bloomed, as if the smile was too big for just her lips, and spilled into her entire being. The kind of smile that felt like a gentle embrace, one that filled the air around her with a sense of calm and happiness, leaving anyone who saw it with their own sense of peace and connection.

'Are you excited? And are you sure that you don't want me to come with you?'

Lisa had suggested a few weeks ago that he spend a week away to relax and unwind, to find some time for himself. She had offered to go with him for company, if he wanted, or had needed. She was a little despondent to learn that he neither wanted the company nor the week's break apparently. However, once he had finally been convinced that it might be a good idea, he had moved fairly swiftly and booked a seven-day break.

'I wouldn't go as far as to say excited, but I am looking forward to some time away; and no, I don't need you to accompany me. Not that the company wouldn't be welcome of course.'

'Okay. So, remind me again, where exactly are you going, Dad?'

'Kelvedie.'

'Kelvedie; where is that?'

'It's a small place in Argyll, Scotland.'

'Argyle? And how far is that, exactly?'

'Sandra says it's three hundred and sixty-five miles,' he confirmed.

Now Lisa looked somewhat perplexed. 'Who's Sandra?'

'Sandra satnav.'

'Sandra satnav,' she replayed, 'you muppet. I've never driven that far. Three hundred and sixty-five miles, that's insane, how long is that going to take?'

'Between six and seven hours, I think.'

'Are you sure that you wouldn't rather take the train, Dad? I'm not comfortable with you driving almost four hundred miles.'

'Don't be daft, I'll be fine. Anyway, it will give me plenty of time to think.'

'Yes, I know, that's what I'm worried about.'

'Right, I'm off,' he gave her a big hug, 'I've left the address of the bed and breakfast on the table in the kitchen. If you need anything, just call me. Failing that, just call Carl, I'm sure he will help with whatever emergency you have.'

They looked at each other and smiled. 'Hmmm…well, maybe not,' he conceded.

Carl was Lisa's brother, and Paul's eldest child. He had chosen to move out of the family home when he was just nineteen years old and had struggled to keep his head above water for the subsequent six years. He had been adamant that he had to be *independent*, that he wanted to be free from *parental interference*, and had, in the main, succeeded in this, although extended periods of sofa-surfing had pretty much exhausted his stay at the home of most of his friends. Six months ago, Carl had found a flat and a girlfriend and a job, all within the space of a three-week period. He didn't do half measures, did Carl, when he eventually set his mind to something, there were generally few equals to be found in terms of his steadfast focus and determination.

'Don't worry, I'll be fine. And, yes, I'll call Carl if there is an emergency,' she paused, 'like World War Three breaks out, or the tectonic plates under East Yorkshire undergo a seismic shift and create a sinkhole two miles wide across West Hull; you know, that kind of emergency.'

Her quip didn't elicit a response from her dad.

'Bye.'

'Bye, Dad, love you. Drive safely.'

It was a good three hours before Paul decided to take a break. It had been a number of years since he had spent so much time behind the wheel of a car. Paul was five years from planned retirement from the Humberside Police Force, and had twenty-five years' service under his belt, during which time his career could be segmented into three distinct phases, or *chapters* as he had liked to refer to them. His initial five years had been spent in uniform as a beat bobby, the next five as a traffic officer; and the last fifteen years he dedicated to CID, where his current tenure saw him promoted to detective inspector.

After pulling into the motorway service station and buying a coffee and a Cornish pasty, he sat outside on one of the wooden A-frame tables. It had just tipped midday, and the positioning of his little table was proving to be a nice suntrap; he closed his eyes and lifted his face upwards. There were few better feelings than the relaxation brought by the heat of the sun warming your face.

The sun's rays felt like a delicate embrace, spreading a comforting heat that sank into his skin, relaxing his muscles. There was something grounding in the way the light touched him, as though time slowed down for a moment. His eyes closed briefly, just to take in the sensation; a peaceful, almost meditative feeling as the world around him continued to buzz.

His mind drifted to thoughts of his wife, Melissa, as it often did. He wondered what she would have made of this: a seven-hour drive, over three hundred and sixty-five miles, to spend a week in a remote fishing village in Scotland.

You must be bloody mad, he expected she would have said, and *make sure you have plenty of breaks.*

Melissa had died earlier that year, January the third, and Paul was working his way through the various stages of grief. These seven stages were all documented and agreed by medical professionals and psychologists, but for most of those grieving the loss of loved ones, they simply morphed into a single sustained period of numbness. By his own admission, he was nowhere near the final phase of acceptance and hope, nor if he was honest, was he ready to touch the penultimate stage of reconstruction and working through, but he was sure that he had started to turn the corner on the depression stage, and had started to think, at least think, about life without Melissa.

After the pain and anguish of the immediate loss, followed by the whirlwind of visitors and the organisation and emotional intensity of the funeral, Lisa had suggested that he take some time out for himself. Perhaps he needed to recharge his batteries, perhaps he needed some quiet time for contemplation, perhaps he simply needed some time to grieve, on his own, in isolation, and without feeling as though his entire family and wider social circle was watching him, waiting for him to falter, and being there to pick him back up. Yes, this short break had been Lisa's idea, and he was open-minded as to how it might pan out. After all, what could one do for seven days in rural Argyll?

Back on the road, one hundred and fifty-two miles done, two hundred and thirteen to go. The scenery, whilst enjoyable, was becoming somewhat indistinguishable from one mile to the next; open rolling grassland with the occasional copse or woodland area on the immediate horizon.

There was an underlying loneliness to the drive that Paul finally admitted to himself. He had never been afraid to spend time in his own company, and was often alone, but seldom lonely. He reached across and placed his hand on the vacant passenger seat.

It was either Sergeant Samantha "Sam" Brewster, his long-standing partner and sidekick in the Humberside Police Force, or his wife Melissa who generally occupied the passenger seat. He cared for them both in differing ways, but they would both take responsibility for taking the sweets from the glove compartment and handing them to him. His wife would remove the wrappers and either place the sweet in his hand or pop it straight into his mouth. Sam would generally just throw it in his general direction.

It dawned on him that the journey to date had been silent. Yes, he had the radio playing, but…it was still silent.

Melissa was his self-proclaimed *driver-helper*, the helper he didn't know he needed. She would be kind enough to let him know when the traffic lights had turned to green, she would tell him to be mindful of cars waiting to pull out on the main road, and of course, she would constantly tell him how far over the speed limit he was driving.

Oh yes, Melissa was a *driver-helper* alright. He didn't know how he ever managed to drive a single mile without his little *driver-helper* by his side.

But now, there was just…silence.

The difference, Paul thought, between being alone and being lonely, was conversation, or the obvious lack of it. Many times during the journey Paul would have remarked on something he heard on the radio or something he saw out of the window, and this would have sparked conversation or a debate that might have lasted minutes, or hours. But there was to be no conversation. Not today.

Paul had opened up the Audible app on his phone and selected an audiobook that he'd purchased a couple of months ago – *Managing Grief and the Loss of a Loved One*. The synopsis had sounded promising, and he had hoped to get some practical takeaways on methods to help deal with his grief. What he didn't want to hear was that *time is a great healer*, although after persevering for almost thirty-five minutes he gave up. It sounded a little too preachy, and he was unsure if he was getting any value from it.

In its place he opened up *Cilka's Journey* from author Heather Morris. He had immensely enjoyed her first book *The Tattooist of Auschwitz*, and was certain that this follow-up would hold his attention too. It certainly couldn't be any worse than the codswallop unfolding in the *Managing Grief…* book. Yes, for the remainder of the journey he would immerse himself in a veritable feast for and symphony of the senses.

Each word, carefully chosen, became a note in a melody flowing smoothly from one to the next, resonating with meaning. The cadence of the narrator's voice danced through the air, rising and falling in rhythm with the story. Dialogues crackled with life, sharp quick exchanges or hushed lingering pauses painting pictures in the mind's eye.

The deeper he went the more he realised that it wasn't just the words that filled the air, but the spaces between them, the pauses that allowed you to breathe with the characters, to feel their weight, their joy, their losses. It was a feast that nourished the soul, a banquet that left you hungry for more, yet completely satisfied in the present.

As the audio played out from his speakers, the rest of the journey was fairly mundane, different landscapes rolled into a single perspective, until he hit the south side of Glasgow where rolling hills and fields were met head-on with sprawling urbanisation. It was a collision of nature's quiet majesty and humanity's relentless expansion. Thankfully he was to be spared the hectic M8, which was now challenging the M25 as the largest car park across the United Kingdom. Skirting the M8, he headed north-west, and would soon, he hoped, arrive at his destination.

CHAPTER 2

After passing through the nearby town of Tarbert, Paul arrived at his destination some five miles later; Kelvedie. He checked his watch; four pm, the journey had taken six and a half hours in total, which had included one brief stop, so he was pleased. Tired, but pleased.

The postcode that he had taken from the booking confirmation, and that had been carefully entered into the satnav, had taken him right to the bottom of the driveway of the bed and breakfast, his lodgings for the next week.

The online photographs of Shallowbrook Lodge had been impressive, as had their website in general, and Paul wasn't disappointed with his first view of the property as he pulled off the main road and onto the gravel driveway that led towards the house. Shallowbrook Lodge was originally built in 1842 and looked as though it had retained many of those original features like its steep gabled roof and decorative wooden fascia boards; its external rendered walls were tastefully painted in an almond white, which itself highlighted the building against the rather bland backdrop of meadowland behind which it stood. The light grey slate roof complemented the almond walls like tartare sauce does to battered cod, and now catching the re-emerging sun after a brief rain shower, glistened as incandescent droplets waited to be burned away. Having observed a small sign with an arrow pointing forwards, he drove to the rear of the property where he found a small number of parking spaces, enough for six cars. His was the second car parked.

There was a rear entrance to the B&B, and Paul wheeled his suitcase behind him through both the narrow outer and inner doors and into a small reception area. He waited patiently for a minute or two, then started to look around the desk for a bell. Perhaps the receptionist needed to be summoned from one or more of the other tasks that they were currently engaged in. Visions of John Cleese's *Basil Fawlty* immediately sprang to mind, and he half expected to see a middle-aged man in an ill-fitting single-breasted brown suit come rushing around the corner chasing a small Spanish waiter with a wooden broom aloft, shouting *it's okay, Sybil, I've got it all under control.*

Alas, Basil Fawlty didn't appear, but a sharply dressed middle-aged man did.

'Good afternoon, sir,' he said, his exuberant welcome

only eclipsed by the size of the grin on his face, 'and you must be Mr Calvert?'

'Correct. Good afternoon.'

'Yes,' he continued, 'I could tell who you were by the clothes you are wearing.'

Paul looked somewhat perplexed and was searching for a quick response, which he didn't find in time.

'Yes, your clothes, they easily identify you as an Englishman you see.' Paul was a little shocked and wondered if he should be offended. 'My other guests are all Scottish you see, and you clearly stand out as an Englishman.'

Paul was still a little shell-shocked, when the man announced, 'I'm only joking with you, and I can no more tell an Englishman from a bloody Ghanaian from their clothes. No, you see, all of my other guests have arrived and checked in, so on balance of probability, what with you standing next to a suitcase, I assumed you were my remaining guest.'

'Yes, quite.' An outstretched hand was offered and Paul took it firmly.

'My name is Brian, and I am one of the co-owners. Welcome to Shallowbrook Lodge.'

'Thank you, Brian.'

'Good drive?'

'As good as seven hours in the car can be, I guess.'

'Oh dear, did you hit any traffic?'

'Traffic? No, it's been an easy journey all the way,' he replied, 'I've driven almost four hundred miles from East

Yorkshire, that's just how long the journey took.'

'Right, I see, you must be gasping for a wee snifter or two?'

Brian's Scottish accent wasn't as broad as it could have been, and the trilling of his R's was softened by the adjacent vowels. Paul wasn't immediately familiar with the phrase *a wee snifter,* but he took an educated guess that Brian was referring to a whisky, or another alcoholic drink.

'A drink? Aye, I would na mind a wee dram of Talisker,' Paul confirmed in his best Scottish accent.

'I see what you did there, Paul, I see what you did. You'll fit in fine here, just fine. Now, let's get you checked in and I'll show you to your room.'

As Paul was signing the guest register, he enquired as to the other guests.

'There are just three of the six bedrooms occupied at present, you in one, we have lovely elderly couple in another, and then a gentleman on his own completes the set.'

Brian handed Paul his room key, which was a small brass key attached by a key-fob style connector to a wooden baton about six inches long with the words 'Shallowbrook Lodge' burnt into the wood. Paul held up the key/baton combo and looked at Brian.

'Aye, I know what you're going to say, probably the same as every other guest over the years. We've had so many guests lose their keys, we had to attach them to something that they wouldn't lose.'

'Never mind,' said Paul, 'if I lose my key and get locked out of my room, maybe I can use this as a battering ram to break down the door?'

They shared a smile, but no further words on the subject.

Stepping out from behind the small reception area, Brian urged Paul to follow him. 'Right, your room is upstairs on the first floor, as are all the bedrooms, but down here we have three public areas, the dining room, the bar and the snug.'

He opened the door to the snug, and they both stepped inside. It was reassuringly traditional. The wall to their left-hand side was brimming with books, the floor-to-ceiling chunky oak shelving had to be holding several hundred. The snug, with its comprehensive makeshift library, needed two further items in order to deliver a relaxing environment to the weary traveller, and there they both were: a set of four armchairs that looked as though they would hug your body as you collapsed down into them, and the pièce de résistance, an open fireplace with a roaring log fire, all too willing to diffuse the kind of heat that one only gets upon passing the *one hundred million kilometres to the sun* marker.

As Paul was absorbing the splendour of the snug, he heard rushed footsteps behind him, and in bounded another gentleman. He was smartly dressed, like Brian, but with his olive complexion and medium length curly hickory brown hair, he looked more of a Mediterranean heritage.

'Oh, Brian, I have messed up.' His carefully enunciated soft tone and his posture immediately put Paul in mind of an effeminate man. Then it clicked.

Brian introduced him. 'Paul, this is my partner, Antonio.'

'Nice to meet you, Antonio.'

'Charmed.' Antonio held out his hand, and found it was taken with a rather firmer grasp than he had expected. 'Well, aren't you strong?'

'What's wrong?' asked Brian.

'Well, I think I've messed up the drinks order. We might be receiving one hundred barrels of beer tomorrow, instead of ten.'

'Ah, man, yer heid's full o' mince,' noted Brian, returning to a much broader dialect. Paul would later discover that Brian turned on the broad dialect and colloquialisms to annoy Antonio, as he clearly had no idea what Brian had said. It was Brian's way of swearing at his partner, without the profanity.

'I had better go and sort this mess, Paul. Anyway, the stairs are over there,' he pointed back towards the entrance hall, 'and the only two other things that I wanted to say are, firstly, the pub and the harbour are about a fifteen-minute walk down the hill.'

'Okay, thank you.'

'And, the second thing was, welcome, and enjoy your stay.'

'Thank you, Brian, I intend to.'

CHAPTER 3

'*Slàinte Mhath*,' proclaimed Brian as he held his glass tumbler aloft, 'the first drink for the weary traveller is always on the house. It's a tradition in this area that dates back to the eighteenth century.'

'Cheers,' replied Paul somewhat tentatively as he held his glass aloft too, 'I assume what you said could be translated as cheers?'

'Aye, that's correct, it's a local Gaelic toast.'

Paul took a sip of the Talisker whisky; the smoky, peaty flavour of the guaiacol was like liquid gold as it slowly travelled over his tongue and trickled down his throat. He looked back into the glass at the liquid not consumed, as it returned to the bottom in its own ponderous manner like waiting for the one hundred and nineteen seconds for a Guinness to settle.

'Now that was worth the three-hundred-and-sixty-five-mile drive from East Yorkshire.'

'Aye, can't argue with that, although you must be able to get Talisker in, where was it?'

'Hull,' confirmed Paul.

'Yes, Hull.'

'Yes of course, but it's psychological. It's like Guinness.'

Paul looked to the draft pumps, and pointed towards the Guinness one as though Brian needed any help in identifying which pump provided it, or the very fact that his B&B served the black stuff.

'Guinness is served in thousands of pubs up and down the country, but it's generally accepted that a pint of Guinness tastes better when taken in Dublin.'

'Really?' challenged Brian, 'I haven't heard that. Perhaps that's the myth peddled by the pubs on Temple Bar trying to peddle their *authentic draft* for eight euros a pint.'

'I agree. I've had a pint of the black stuff in each of the four countries that make up the United Kingdom, and I've also sampled a considerable number in Ireland. Of course, it tastes the same in bloody Manchester and Hull as it does in Dublin, it's psychological like I say, your thoughts and emotions are governed to a certain extent by your environment. You're in Dublin, having a Guinness, it *must taste better* than any other comparable pint that you've had.'

'Sounds plausible, Paul. Us Scots tend to focus on the Tennent's beer, or the hundred or so brands of pure Scotch whisky.'

'Hundreds?' Paul immediately realised how ridiculous his challenge was just by looking at the shelves behind the bar in this rural B&B, dominated by two dozen different bottles.

'Aye, Johnnie Walker, Glenlivet, Macallan, Bell's, Teacher's, Whyte & Mackay, Chivas….' Paul felt that given half a chance Brian would probably list them all, whatever the total number was.

'Yes, I get the point, Scotland is synonymous with whisky.'

'Aye, it trickles and dances through our veins like the tributaries of the River Spey,' affirmed Brian.

Paul, quite taken by Brian's poetic articulation on the whisky, looked at the tumbler and threw the remainder down this throat. 'By 'eck, bloody good stuff that.'

'So, what does tonight look like?' asked Brian.

Paul took a few seconds before his brain absorbed the words and interpreted them into a language he was familiar with. 'What am I doing tonight?'

'Aye, that's what I said.'

'Nothing too strenuous, I would have thought. I saw online that there is a local pub, The Plough, is it?'

'Aye, quick walk down the road, to the end of the drive and turn right, walk towards the harbour and you'll come across it.'

'Will there be one or two in on a Wednesday night?'

'Aye, one or two is about right to be honest, it'll be a wee bit hushed tonight. Anyway, Gordon and Angie will see you right.'

'Gordon and?'

'Angie. Gordon and Angie, the landlords of The Plough. Let them know that you're staying with me, here at Shallowbrook Lodge, and you might even get a free pint.'

'Really?'

'Nah, I doubt it, but it'll be interesting to see what Gordon says if you tell him that I promised you a free pint though.' Brian had a brief chuckle to himself. 'Anyway, enjoy yourself, you've got your key I assume?'

Paul extracted the six-inch-long wooden baton, attached to which was the ever-so-diminutive brass key. 'Oh yes, I've got it.'

Paul checked his watch as he exited the front door of the B&B; eight forty-five pm, the night had yet to take hold and the light remained good. As he trudged through the deep pebble drive, over to his right-hand side and running adjacent to the building he saw a brook. The water was flowing fairly quickly, rippling over the smooth pebbles that lay on the riverbed, and the noise of the running water was soothing. He stood for thirty seconds immersed in the relative tranquillity before he pulled himself away. He imagined walking, with Melissa's arm tucked tightly into his, passing comment about the beauty of the place where they would be spending some quality time together over the next few days. Yes, Melissa would have liked this.

The Plough was to be found exactly where it had been promised after a leisurely ten-minute stroll. The frontage was facing the harbour and the south wall was adorned with two large hanging baskets of bright and colourful flowers, their heads flowing over the edges of the basket. Reds, ambers, yellows, lavender and pink – a veritable smorgasbord of colour and visual stimulation. In between the two hanging baskets and fixed above the door was an illuminated *Tennent's* sign, and with the natural light starting to fade it had sprung to life and radiated its red neon glow for all of, well, about five metres beyond its fixings. It looked as if it needed a bloody good wash down as most of the light was being supressed by the outer dirt and grime clinging to the acrylic frame.

Bolted to the floor either side of the entrance were five wooden A-frame tables, three of which were occupied by people enjoying a refreshing drink in the warm evening, watching the setting sun.

'Evening.' He was ignored by two of the tables as he strode forward towards the entrance door, which he assumed was either because the two young men and a couple were either deep in conversation and didn't hear him, or his broad English accent was enough for them to bury their heads further into their own affairs.

'Good evening, lovely evening, isn't it?' the elderly couple on the far table responded.

'Indeed, it is, yes.' He made his way inside, to the left a door with a sign that said *lounge*, and to his right a door that indicated *snug*. He swung open the door to the snug.

It was fairly busy, with a dozen or so people creating a disproportionate noise for their number, but it was a welcome and mirthful sound and clearly a good atmosphere. Paul walked up to the bar where he surveyed the options: the pumps provided a choice of either Tennent's or Brewdog IPA, whilst the shelves behind the bar stocked a seemingly endless array of different whisky brands.

He had been noticed, and a portly middle-aged gentleman approached from the other side of bar that connected to the lounge.

'Evening, what'll it be?'

'Evening. Well, let's see. I'll have a pint of Tennent's please.'

'Pint of Tennent's coming right up.'

'Brian at Shallowbrook Lodge sends his best by the way, he says his guests are generally offered a free pint on their first visit to The Plough.' Paul managed to keep a straight face; he wasn't angling for a free drink, but thought that he would test out Brian's throwaway comment from earlier, if only to feed back what the landlord said.

'He did, did he?'

'He did, yes.'

'Free drink, you say.'

'That's what he said.'

'Well, if that's what he said, then I'll have to honour it, I guess.'

'Really? I'm sure he was just winding me up,' confirmed Paul.

'No, a free pint it is,' the pint was placed on the bar, 'there you go.'

'Thank you.'

'You're welcome. Anyway, I'll just add the price onto his tab. That'll bloody teach him.' They both smiled.

'I'm Gordon, Gordon McKie. Landlord.' He held out his hand across the bar.

'Paul Calvert, nice to meet you.' His hand was taken.

'You too. So, let me guess. A few days R&R, a bit of walking perhaps, peppered with a wee dram or two and an evening's entertainment in a bustling vibrant local hostelry?'

'That'll do for me, Gordon. That sounds like a plan.'

'How long are you staying for?'

'Just a week. A week should be long enough to relax and recharge those batteries,' he said as he patted his stomach.

'Let me introduce you to the wife.' Gordon disappeared, no doubt to try to locate his wife.

Now perching on a bar stool, Paul swivelled around slightly to look around the room. The fixtures and furnishings were fairly traditional and in keeping with a rural pub. There was navy blue fixed upholstered seating on two sides of the room, with a dozen or so mahogany effect chairs with matching upholstered seats, each evenly allocated to the six small tables in the room. The main feature on the far wall was an open fire which was, despite the relative warmth of the summer month, roaring away having recently been fed with two substantial logs. Above the fire was a mantelpiece, which itself was an interior design masterstroke, although quite probably unintentional. The wooden beam that formed the mantelpiece was about five feet long, with half of the depth having been embedded onto the wall. Its uneven and jagged weather-worn or sea-battered edges prompted thoughts and images of a piece of timber found beached a hundred years ago from a shipwrecked vessel in the Irish Sea. Upon said mantelpiece stood a sole ornament, a clock. Again, the untrained eye might take one look at the clock, Roman numerals adorning a pearl-effect face, encased in a rather battered and unimaginative wooden case, and be fooled into thinking that the modern-day reproduction that would be churned off the manufacturing lines at the rate of a couple hundred per day, was in fact a nineteenth-century clock, perhaps a commission from a bespoke craftsman based in Edinburgh or London.

The walls were furnished with a number of black-and-white framed photographs, some depicting farmers walking behind sturdy shire horses pulling a wooden plough, whereas the other images looked as if they were taken from the harbour just outside the door of the pub. Fishermen were hauling their catch of day over the harbour wall, or enjoying some down time in the sunshine, repairing fishing nets with needle and thread.

There was a small number of people in the room. Having never been there before, Calvert didn't know whether to interpret the current occupancy as a landlord's disappointment, or an overly busy night. Although, personally, he thought it was a half decent turnout for a Wednesday evening.

A middle-aged couple sat immediately across from him, appearing to argue although almost inaudibly as though they were both embarrassed for their argument to be heard by anyone else. Adjacent to them, save for one table in between, was a more elderly couple, who didn't appear to have two words to say to each other. The only other two tables occupied were done so by a younger and livelier bunch. Both tables Calvert assumed were families, the first family of four with two teenage children, and the second a younger couple with a young boy.

Gordon appeared again with a woman who Paul assumed must be his wife. She was not much shorter than Gordon, and with a slender frame and a mane of fiery copper hair, at a first glance you could be forgiven for thinking that she was the physical embodiment of the animated sexpot in *Who Framed Roger Rabbit*. Although in her mid-fifties, Paul guessed, the fresh-faced beauty and alluring sultry lips that had Roger's cartoon heart thumping over a certain Jessica Rabbit, had clearly packed up and deserted this lady many years since.

'Angie, this is Paul, he's staying in the lodge with Brian for a week. Paul, this is the trouble and strife.' They both extended a hand and shook.

'Don't mind him,' said Angie, 'he was born an arsehole and just grew bigger.'

Paul chuckled.

'I always say that marriage is a three-ring circus, don't I, sweetheart? Engagement ring, wedding ring, and suffering.'

'Hilarious, Gordon.'

'When we were married, I promised to take Angie to places she never seen before, you know, like the kitchen.'

'Do you know, he asked me once if I thought that time flies during sex; I looked at my watch and said no, it's still only one minute.'

These two were hilarious, thought Paul, playing off each other with witty one-liners that made Morecambe and Wise look like amateurs. They had obviously been at it for most of their married lives and it appeared to be effortless, and more importantly, neither of them appeared to get the least bit offended.

'Nice to meet you, Paul,' said Angie, 'you'll enjoy your stay up at the lodge. A lovely wee couple are Brian and Antonio.'

The overly theatrical wink advised Paul that there was more than a hint of light humour in her comment. He responded with a knowing smile, and Angie was called away to serve in the adjacent lounge bar.

Gordon cleared his throat. 'Listen up.' The room quickly fell silent and almost without exception everyone turned to face him. 'This is Paul, a visitor from England, although let's try not to hold that against him, he's here for a few days so let's make him feel welcome, eh?'

The warm but unnecessary introduction appeared to

have fallen on deaf ears as everyone immediately returned to their conversations without further acknowledgement. Gordon too returned his focus elsewhere in the bar.

As Paul was settling into the bar stool, he heard his name called. 'Paul, come and take a seat with us.' He turned to find a couple in their late thirties looking their way; they had a child with them, a boy who looked to be around seven or eight.

He stood up from the bar stool and made his way over to their table.

'Thank you,' he said, 'that's very kind of you. Paul Calvert.' He held out his hand, which was taken in turn by both the man and woman, and then the young boy when offered.

'I'm Danny and this is my wife Shona.' He was about to introduce his son too but was interrupted by the young man himself.

'What's wrong with your leg?' asked the boy.

'Fergus, that's rude. Enough,' his mother chastised him, 'sorry, Paul, don't mind the wee one, you know what boys are like, opening their mouths without thinking.'

'He's fine, don't worry about it.' Fergus had had been watching as the man had approached their table, and his limp was too defined to shrug off as short-term cramp. His parents had noticed it too across the six or seven steps, but were clearly too polite to mention it, as most decent adults were. Anyway, he had only been at their table a matter of twenty seconds.

Paul leaned into Fergus. 'What do you know about the British army, Fergus?'

'Quite a lot actually.' His quick retort surprised Paul. 'My uncle Fraser is in the army, he's in the Black Watch.'

Paul looked towards Fergus's father, who immediately nodded his confirmation.

'Aye, the Black Watch are 3rd Battalion of the Royal Regiment of Scotland, and my Uncle Fraser fights with his mates.'

'Oh right.'

'Aye, he's got a big gun and everything,' the adults chuckled, much to the confusion of Fergus who hadn't a clue why they were laughing, 'he has, he's got a gun. And he shoots people.'

'I'm sure that he does have a gun, Fergus. I used to be in the army too.'

'Did you have a gun?' asked the boy.

'Yes, yes I did.'

'Did you ever shoot anyone?'

'Fergus! We've told you before, haven't we? You don't ask soldiers that question.'

'Yes, Mum. Sorry.' Fully chastised, he slumped back into the back of his chair. Paul beckoned him forward again.

'I was in the army a *looooong* time ago, way before you were born, perhaps around the time that your mum and dad were born.'

'Wow, were you in the army with Napoleon Bonaparte?'

They all let out a raucous laugh, again except Fergus.

'We've been learning about Napoleon at school,' he confirmed.

'I'm very impressed that you know about Napoleon, but no, I wasn't in the army with him. He was French, and became Emperor in 1804, just a little before my time, Fergus.'

'Ah, okay.' Fergus shrugged it off like he had been out on the dates by a couple of years.

'Anyway,' Paul continued, 'there was a war in 1982 in a place a long way away called the Falkland Islands. The Argentinians had invaded the island, which was part of the British sovereignty, so me and few mates went down there to sort them out.'

'Really?'

'Yes, really. Well, me and a few thousand mates.'

'How old were you when you were deployed to the Falklands, Paul?' asked Shona.

'Eighteen. I was eighteen years old, and I had joined the Parachute Regiment about twelve months earlier.'

'Gosh, that's terribly young to be going off to war.'

'It was, but if you think back to World War One and World War Two, young men were being conscripted at the same age.'

'Yes, I guess so. Sorry, I didn't mean to interrupt, carry on with your story.'

'So, during this war there was battle on a hill.'

'A hill?' replayed Fergus.

'Yes, well, I'd like to say mountain but it couldn't really have been categorised as a mountain. Let's just say it was a *reaaaaally* big hill. Anyway, history would look back and call it the Battle for Mount Longdon.'

'Mount…'

'Longdon, Mount Longdon. Anyway, the battle in June lasted twelve hours, during which time I caught some shrapnel in my leg.'

'What is shrapnel?'

Paul looked to the boy's parents for confirmation that it was okay to elaborate. He received a nod.

'Well, Fergus, when a bomb or grenade lands close to where you are, it explodes and lots of pieces of metal are thrown into the air. If one of these pieces of shrapnel hits your body, then it hurts.'

'Did you die?'

Shona didn't know whether to chastise him further or just laugh with the others at yet another absurd question that could only come from the mind of a primary school child.

'No, I didn't die, but I did have to be airlifted in a helicopter back to a hospital ship.'

'Wow.'

'And that, Fergus, is why I walk with a limp.'

'Do you still have it, you know, the shrapnel in your leg?'

'No, it was taken out by the doctors on the hospital ship,' Paul confirmed.

Fergus was a little confused. 'Why was there a hospital on a ship?'

'Well, we sailed eight thousand miles from the UK to the Falkland Islands, and we had to make sure that we took everything with us, and that included taking our own hospital.'

'Wow!'

Calvert smiled at Fergus.

'Does it still hurt, Paul, you know after all this time? Can you not get it looked at again?'

Paul waited until Fergus's attention was elsewhere, then said, 'can I let you into a secret, Shona?'

'Aye, of course.'

'The leg has long since healed, and my wife tells me that it's the gout that makes me limp now.' They shared a smile.

Danny had been to the bar, and Gordon had refreshed their glasses. Paul pulled a crisp note from his wallet, only for Danny to tell him to put his money away.

'Are you married? Is your wife not with you?' asked Shona. The first of the two questions was asked rhetorically as she had already clocked the gold wedding ring on his finger, although seemingly having just forgotten that Paul had just mentioned his wife.

'My wife isn't with me, no,' Paul quickly moved to change the subject before the inevitable follow-up question, 'so what's the story with Gordon and Angie? They're like a comic tag team.'

'They have always been like that,' replied Shona, 'we

moved to the village just after Fergus was born, but I believe that they have been here running the pub for twenty years or so. By all accounts they have been light-heartedly bickering at each other with one-liners for twenty years.'

'Right, okay.'

'I think that both Gordon and Angie have been in the village since they were born, in fact Gordon's parents ran the pub before him. And Angie, well she was born here too. Childhood sweethearts they were, neither of them ever wanted to move away from Kelvedie.'

'Children?'

'No,' confirmed Shona with a hint of a sombre tone, 'I don't think that they were able to have kids, well that's what I heard anyway. Village gossip, you know.'

After another pint, Paul proclaimed that he was going to call it a night. Shona and Danny had taken Fergus home, and he had been sitting at the bar chatting to Angie for a while.

'I might pop my head around the lounge door and have a quick look on my way out.'

He downed the dregs of the pint and stood up. 'See you all later, and thanks for the hospitality.'

'You're most welcome, Paul. Will we see you tomorrow?'

'Quite probably, Angie. Goodnight, all.'

As he had alluded to, Paul pushed open the door to the lounge and stuck his head through. It was as he had expected. In the centre of the room was a pool table, a good quality one, slate bed with quality red cloth and a chunky mahogany frame. The far wall held a dart board with a chalk scoreboard either side. The edges of the room had fixed upholstered seating, and a scattering of small tables completed what was a fairly typical pub lounge.

The room was empty, as probably expected for a Wednesday evening. Paul imagined it bustling with noise on a Friday or Saturday evening, probably filled with a number of younger villagers huddled around the large screen television hung on the wall, watching football.

The door closed behind him, and he started off back up the hill towards the B&B.

CHAPTER 4

Calvert was up early. Awake, showered, dressed and out of the door before eight am. The weather forecast on last night's news had promised plenty of sunshine, with temperatures in the late teens and not a cloud in the sky.

The weather forecast was known to be less than reliable though, and he would be prepared for balmy tropical sunshine, or freezing snow blizzards, or pretty much anything in between.

He had been woken well before he threw open the curtains at seven-fifteen; the flimsy light cotton curtains did nothing to hold back the morning sun penetrating into the room. He didn't mind, it was a natural and pleasing way to wake up, and far better than being startled by the da-da-da-da, da-da-da-da of an alarm clock.

Today, he had decided, he would get to know Kelvedie and its surrounding areas, and armed with a sturdy pair of walking boots and a light rain jacket he set off to explore. It wasn't that he didn't trust the news forecast, but they had been known to be wrong many times before, and as he had often noted to his wife over the years, the weather presenters on the national news only have about fifty or sixty seconds to narrate through a script covering sunrise and sunset times, temperature, pollen count, prevailing winds and wind chill factor for England, Scotland, Wales and Northern Ireland. The forecast was pitched at such a high level that pockets of localised weather could never be picked up, even if they had three hours to talk through it all. It might just be Paul's bad luck that today Kelvedie was going to experience its own little climate ecosystem, and whilst Glasgow might well be basking in near Mediterranean temperatures, Kelvedie could be lashed with driving rain. Anyway, he had his rain jacket, and would tie it around his waist like those young and trendy Generation Z types attending the Glastonbury festival.

The decision to get away for a week might have been made on a whim one evening, or perhaps it would be more truthful to say that he had finally acquiesced to Lisa's suggestion. However, once his mind was made up, Paul had undertaken some research and had gathered some basic knowledge about Kelvedie and what to expect when he arrived. *A quant old fishing village* was a common headline to be found across a number of websites, so Paul decided that he would start at the harbour. He didn't have a map, why would he? This was a village after all. What was the worst that could happen? He would wander aimlessly through the village streets before he found his way back to where he had started, perhaps after no longer than an hour. Anyway, he had the pub as a reference point, his anchor, and he knew that the pub was facing the harbour.

As he walked towards the harbour, he recalled further reference information from the website that he had studied. Apparently, the village had one hundred residents as noted at the last census, and with very little in the way of commercial businesses, the houses were all generally within half a mile of the harbour.

He paused upon reaching The Plough and looked at the houses that could be seen. Some were stone built with dark slate roofs, whilst most were rendered and painted white with red tiled roofs. Quite a few were built to three storeys. With his back to the harbour, he was struck by the beauty of this very picturesque setting, and it reminded him of certain views of Whitby, North Yorkshire, where he had spent many a day. Initially in his early twenties with a group of friends, interested more in the pubs on a bank holiday than the scenery, but as he grew older, met his wife and had children, days at Whitby would be less about the pub crawl and more about eating fish and chips, sitting on the harbour wall trying to fend of the seagulls, or climbing the one hundred and ninety-nine steps up to the famous Whitby Abbey. Although he thought that he had deserved a beer by the time they had descended the steps sometime later.

The harbour was much bigger than he had expected; the adjacent road had parking bays for twelve vehicles and there were two slipways for transporting trailered boats from water to dry land, and vice versa. The heavy-duty winch had seen better days and was no doubt inoperable these days, but it wasn't hard to imagine visions of lifting heavier vessels in and out of the water. Paul could easily imagine a busy harbour many years ago, with fishing boats and trawlers of all sizes setting off in the early hours of the morning and returning later that day, or even a couple of days later, laden with baskets of cod, plaice, haddock, pollock and turbot, all to be sold to fishmongers in the local area.

The village had ceased to be an active fishing harbour around twenty-five years ago and all that remained in the harbour was one old trawler that looked as if it hadn't moved for a decade, and three small pleasure boats probably moored by local residents.

Paul noticed a round metal plaque embedded into the stone wall, a little weather-worn but still readable.

In honoured memory of the crew of Wild Rose fishing trawler, stationed here at Kelvedie which foundered with the loss of all eight hands on 9th January 1948. James Hardy. Davey Gilbraith. Paul Johnstone. Archie Soanes. Stephen McNeill. Stuart Tavistock. Walter O'Brien. John Ballantyne.

Paul brushed his index finger across the raised text as he thought not only of the lives lost, but also those that remained. Families and friends left to grieve. He wondered if any of the current village residents were related to those men remembered on the plaque, perhaps there were a number of grandchildren. And then, probably inevitably, his thoughts turned to his own life and the recent loss of his wife. He reflected for a few minutes not only on his loss, his grief, but that of their children, Carl and Lisa. Yes, they were adults themselves now, living their own lives. One had flown the nest already and the other was no doubt itching to do so, but the loss of their mother and their grief and emotional state preyed on Paul's mind more than his own loss.

He left the harbour and walked back past The Plough, up the hill and towards the church. The relatively steep gradient quickly reminded him that he wasn't at his physical peak any longer. He was pleased that the Humberside Police Force didn't mandate an annual fitness test for all of its officers, for he was sure he would fail, and having pondered on it for a few seconds he thought that most of the officers that he served with in CID might struggle too. A police force bereft of officers because they couldn't run for more than thirty seconds. Oh dear!

The fourteenth-century church had seen better days, that was obvious. Paul had read on Wikipedia that it had been used as late as 1950 but it had since fallen into disrepair and was now unsafe.

The building itself was not large, imposing or apparently gratuitously arrogant of itself, like some churches; it had no spire protruding into the sky, nor a turret that dominated the skyline. Instead, a humble structure stood in front of him, one that he imagined would struggle to accommodate more than a dozen parishioners.

The walls of the medieval building were a layer of stone with a mixture of sand, stone and rubble used to fill the gaps between the layers, and mortar, as it would later become known, wasn't to be used until some four hundred years later. The walls of the church were in relatively good condition, still standing, still vertical and without any gaping holes, testament to both the quality of the materials and the craftsmanship back in the day.

The roof however was a different story. There were more tiles missing than were still in place, and the exposed oak beams had been weather-worn since the roof had opened up, and there was a central section of the roof that sadly appeared to have collapsed in on itself.

As expected, the window glass was broken and mainly gone, but they had not been boarded up. The lead window framework was all still in situ, and the intricate patterns that would have held small delicate pieces of coloured glass provided a glimpse of the once beautiful and ornate windows that stood five feet from the bottom to the top of the arch.

He cast his mind back to his native Hull and immediately thought that if that lead was visible and accessible, someone would have had it away and sold it, *but that's Hull for you* he thought.

Calvert cast his eyes across the adjacent graveyard, the floor of which hadn't seen daylight for many a year. It had become overgrown with a sea of thick prickly brambles, and what grass was to be seen was long and matted with weeds. There was no doubt that there would be a number of gravestones within the grounds but these were now barely visible through the tangle of wild flora.

'It's a bit of a mess, isn't it?'

Slightly startled, he turned around to see who had crept up behind him without him being aware. He turned to see an elderly woman dressed in light hiking gear: Merrell walking shoes, nylon knee-length khaki shorts and a long-sleeved fleece top.

'A mess? Yes, rather,' he replied.

'It's a shame really.'

'Yes, I guess so.'

'The last Sunday service was back in the fifties.'

'Oh, right. I think I read the same, yes.'

'Apparently the vicar was redeployed to another parish and not replaced. As a result, and shortly afterwards, the funding for the general upkeep was withdrawn by the diocese. The villagers tried fundraising in the seventies, but the renovation costs were too high, and the community back then was not much bigger than it is now, so they fell someway short.'

'I guess fundraising only really works if people from

outside of the immediate community contribute, otherwise it tends to be those with a vested interest just putting their own money in, and it's less fundraising and more direct contributions.'

'Yes, I guess you're right.' She pondered for what Calvert thought was an uneasy period of time then asked, 'so, are you walking or hiking?'

He was unsure as to the difference between the two options.

'Neither, well not really. I'm staying locally, in the village at the B&B for a few days. Just looking to relax and recharge the batteries as they say. I'm Paul, Paul Calvert.' He held out his hand, which was taken.

'Hello, I'm Morag Simpson.'

'Hello, Morag, nice to meet you.'

'Well, there isn't much to do locally unless you've a pair of walking boots and a desire to trek for a few hours. The nearby town of Tarbert is quite nice and well worth a visit though.'

'Thanks, yes I heard that, I'll bear that in mind. Do you live locally, Morag?'

'Me? Yes, just down the road.' She turned and with an outstretched arm pointed in the general direction of the village centre.'

'Have you lived here all of your life?'

'Oh, yes. Third-generation resident. My parents and my grandparents both lived here.'

'Did they work in the fishing industry?' asked Paul.

'They did,' she confirmed, 'that was a good guess.'

Paul held his tongue, not wanting to appear rude and pointing out what was the bleeding obvious, and a fifty-fifty at best.

'Yes, my father and grandfather worked on the fishing boats, and my mother and her mother before her worked two jobs, both the same jobs. They worked in the village shop.'

She paused for a second; 'it's long gone now, you know…the village shop.'

'Yes, I assumed it must be. And the second job?'

'Oh yes. They both repaired the fishing nets.'

'Ah right. Did that keep them busy?'

'A few hours every week apparently. You'd be surprised how much time the women spent repairing fishing nets.'

'You'd have thought that the men would take better care of them?'

Paul's high-level sarcasm didn't register and fell on deaf ears.

'Well, I must be on my way,' Morag said, 'enjoy your time in Kelvedie.'

'Thanks, I will.'

After two hours and having explored most corners of the fairly limited village, Calvert found himself back at the harbour where he saw Gordon on a pair of stepladders watering the hanging baskets.

'Morning, Gordon.'

'Ah, morning, Paul. You're not waiting for me to open up, are you?' he asked.

Calvert checked his watch; eleven am exactly. 'No. I'm not that desperate for a beer. I'm just walking through the village, trying to get my bearings.'

'Aye, it's not big, but it can be quite scenic, you know, in the right light.'

'Yes, I agree.'

Calvert pointed at the round metal plaque embedded into the stone wall, that had caught his eye a couple of hours ago.

'Did you know any of those fishermen?'

'Aye, they were all regulars in the pub. My dad used to run the pub before me, years and years ago. Davey Gilbraith was my uncle. He was only twenty-four years old when he died. I was just a wee nipper back then, so I don't really remember them all too well.'

'Tragic accident.'

'Yes, it was, but to be honest with you, Paul, it happened all too often back in the day. Every fishing village up and down the coast of West Scotland will have a similar story of loss at sea. The fishing boats back then were not as big and sturdy as those you see these days, many of them were primarily made of wood too. You get yourself in the middle of a storm at sea, and you're pretty much buggered.'

'I guess so.'

'Add to which, back in the day the onboard

communication was a bit primitive, and there was no such thing as satellite or GPS, nothing like that. If you got in trouble out there, the skipper knew where he was, but no-one coming to your aid would have a clue on your location.'

'Yes, I can see that.'

'Yes, technology has made fishing a lot safer these days, both in terms of the boat design and structure and also the onboard communications, but technology also heralded the end of the industry.'

Paul was a little unsure on the point he was making. For sure, he wasn't an expect in commercial sea fishing, but surely years and years of overfishing combined with cheaper imports of fish from the EU had contributed more to the decline of the Scottish fishing industry. But what did he know?

'Right, I'll leave you to your hanging baskets, Gordon.'

'Aye, see you anon.'

CHAPTER 5

The car had no sooner pulled up at the side of the road than Florence opened the door and ran up the path towards the house. School was out for the weekend.

'I'll sort your school bag then, shall I?' moaned her mum as she was left to retrieve the schoolbook bag, lunch box and PE bag from the rear seat.

It was four o'clock on Friday, and the afternoon sun was radiating through a cloudless sky. It was the kind of afternoon where you sit in your garden with a glass or two of Pimm's, engrossed in a good book until the sun set. There weren't many summer days like this in Northwest Scotland and they were to be savoured and enjoyed, although Aileen Findlay had a mountain of ironing to get through before she would start dinner, let alone have time for such indulgences as patio recliners, chilled drinks and a good Mills & Boon.

At least Florence was outside enjoying the sunshine. Aileen checked on her before returning indoors to commence the ironing.

Paul was walking towards Shallowbrook Lodge, enjoying the sunshine and in no particular hurry to return to his lodgings. His mobile phone rang, and he retrieved it from his rear trouser pocket. It was Lisa.

'Hi, Dad, it's me.'

'Hello, me. Are you okay?'

'Yes of course. I haven't burnt down the house just yet.'

'I should hope not, you're twenty-two years old.'

'I'm just checking in with you, making sure you're okay. What are you doing?'

'Well, it's a glorious day here, the sun is shining, and right now, I'm walking back to the B&B.'

'You're not spending your time alone in some two-bit ramshackle room with mould growing up the walls?'

'No, sweetheart, I'm not, anyway the B&B that I'm staying at is very nice actually. I showed you the pictures before I came away, right?'

'Yes, you did.'

'Well, the pictures didn't do the place justice. It's a lovely place, in a wonderful setting, and a stone's throw from the centre of this charming little ex-fishing village,' he paused for a second, recalling the second part of her question, 'and no, I'm not spending time alone. I've met some of the local villagers…'

'In the pub?'

He laughed, 'yes, in the pub. I've been out walking, had one or two shandies, and just generally tried to relax.'

'Good. As long as you're not drinking too much.'

'Bloody hell, you sound just like your mother.'

'Well, yes, someone has to keep you on the straight and narrow, Dad.'

'Your mother tried and failed for twenty-seven years so I'm not sure how much more successful you are hoping to be. Anyway, I've had to cut down.'

'What do you mean, had to?'

'Like I said, I have been walking and drinking, and the more I walked, the more I spilt. So, I've cut down… walking that is. Now I find that if I stand still, I spill less.'

'Not funny, Dad. Anyway, you've not got yourself wrapped up in any crimes in the last couple of days, have you?'

Paul laughed, a little louder than he perhaps should have. 'No, not this time.'

Paul had laughed at Lisa's words, but for her it had been asked as a genuine question. Paul had a knack of being in the right place at the wrong time, or the wrong place at the right time, dependent upon how you viewed it. This had served him well during his time as a police officer and on duty, but on three consecutive family holidays Lisa recalled how her dad had somehow got caught up in a street robbery, being a witness to an assault, and most notably a large-scale theft of motorcycles on the Greek island of Corfu when Lisa was fifteen years old. Paul had noticed something strange when seeing three men cutting chains and loading motorcycles into a van. He had observed the same men two days later in a different location near to their resort hotel. Paul had called to notify the police and several days later it was discovered that this gang had been responsible for the theft of fifty-seven motorcycles in the previous three-week period.

'Okay, got to go. Love you, chat later.'

'Okay, love you too. Bye.'

'Florence, there's a glass of lemonade here.' Aileen placed the half-full glass tumbler on the patio table and returned inside. She didn't see Florence, but she heard an out-of-breath, 'thanks, Mum,' after she had gulped down the lemonade before she took off again.

With the ironing completed, Aileen's attention turned to the evening meal. Her husband, Callum, would be home from work around six o'clock and they would eat together shortly afterwards, but she would make something for Florence beforehand.

Standing over the kitchen sink Aileen could see out of the rear window. Immediately beyond the twenty metres of their back garden there was an arable field where the most gorgeous golden-headed barley would grow every summer. It was wondrous to see tens of thousands of golden heads gently swaying to and fro in the summer breeze, and she always thought it looked like an amber sea into which she might plunge on one of the rare hot summer days. That was until harvest arrived, then it looked as if the apocalypse had happened overnight; a sight that was compounded even further if the farmer felt it necessary to burn the remaining stubble. Despite the practice being effectively prohibited for a few years, many local farmers ignored government instructions not to burn the stubble, due to the increasing return of black-grass which occurred at high density and competed with the crop for water and nutrients from the soil. The seeds had a short period of dormancy and viability, and the numbers could be reduced by surface cultivation or burning after harvest; this was the solution favoured by local farmers and *to hell with what those ignorant buggers in Westminster said*.

Beyond the field was open pasture as far as the eye could see. The same farmer also had a couple of hundred head of Ayrshire dairy cattle that roamed fairly freely across several hectares of land behind their house. With their distinctive red and white markings, they could easily be spotted throughout the pasture.

The family back garden extended twenty metres from the house to the boundary of the field, and they had a small patio area large enough for a table and chairs, beyond which was a paved path that meandered through a cut lawn towards a shed at the bottom. Opposite of which was a trampoline, bought for Florence's eighth birthday and from which it would generally take a battalion of soldiers to prise her away on even the coldest of days.

Aileen couldn't see Florence on the trampoline or in the garden, and a quick glance into the field beyond proved fruitless too, but she wasn't too worried. Florence would be around somewhere, she thought.

She was looking forward to this weekend. Callum had promised to take them both to the cinema and on to Nando's tomorrow afternoon. Disney's *Cruella* was to be the movie of choice. It had been a while since they had been out for the day as a family. The school summer holidays were only one week away, but the forecast for next weekend didn't look too good, so they had promised Florence that this weekend they would treat her.

'Florence,' Aileen shouted from the back door, 'your tea is on the table.' She waited for a minute, but not having seen her daughter appear or heard any verbal acknowledgement, she returned to stand in the rear doorway.

'Florence. Florence, where are you? Your tea is getting cold.'

No reply, and no sign of her.

'Florence…FLORENCE….'

'Eh, what's all this commotion?' Sandra Carruthers popped her head over the fence from next door, 'is that daughter of yours giving you the runaround again, Aileen?'

'Aye, that's about the measure of it. I've no bloody idea

where she is. She was here not so long ago.'

'She'll be playing in the back field no doubt,' said Sandra, referring to the field of barley that would be about waist-height on Florence.

'I'll tell you what, I'll take a walk into the field, why don't you check with Pauline?'

'Okay, will do.'

Pauline was Aileen's neighbour on the other side. Before she went to see her, Aileen quickly checked in the garden shed, under the trampoline and in a couple of other places favoured by Florence during previous games of hide and seek. Needless to say, she wasn't to be found.

'Oh, hiya, Aileen, come in, love.'

'Thanks, Pauline.' They both wandered through to the kitchen.

'Will you have a coffee?'

'Thanks, but I won't. To be honest I'm looking for Florence. You haven't seen her, have you? She isn't playing here, is she?'

'I don't think so, well, I haven't seen her.'

Pauline and John's house was always open to Florence, and on some weekends she could be found more at *Aunty Pauline and Uncle John's* house, than at her own. Their door was always open, and Florence was free to come and go as she pleased. She could generally be found in one of three places: in the back garden helping John with his fledgling allotment area, trying to grow carrots and onions; in the lounge sitting on the sofa playing draughts with John; or possibly raiding the kitchen pantry for cakes and biscuits.

'John…John, are you there?'

John came trudging through from the lounge, after pausing *Racing on Four* on the television. 'The five o'clock from Sandown is just about to... oh, hi, Aileen, are you okay, love?'

'Hi, John, yes, I'm fine thanks. I'm just looking for Florence. I don't suppose that she is sitting with you watching the racing, is she?'

'No, sorry, love, she isn't.'

'Ah, okay. Have you seen her since she got back from school?'

'No, I don't think so.' He pondered for a few seconds. 'Tell a lie, I saw her about thirty minutes ago, she was running from your kitchen back into the garden.'

'Yes, she came back for some lemonade, then she ran off again. That's the last time that I saw her.'

'Why, what's up? Has something happened?'

'No, nothing is wrong, as such. Her tea is on the table, and I can't find her, that's all.'

'Not to worry, she can't have gone far,' reassured Pauline, 'I bet she's in the back field.'

'That's what Sandra said, in fact Sandra is looking in the back field now.'

'There you go then,' said John, 'I'll tell you what, I'll go into the field and give her a hand, and I'll double-check our garden as I pass through. She'll be playing in the field, Aileen, you know how big it is, and you know the two dips at the far side could hide an army without being seen.'

'Aye, I guess so,' agreed Aileen.

After a fruitless twenty minutes, during which all three houses and gardens were searched and re-searched, and the back field had been scoured as thoroughly as a twenty-acre field of waist-height barley could be with just three people, Aileen started to get more than a little worried.

'Well, I'm sure she's around somewhere, Aileen,' reassured Sandra.

'Sandra's right,' said Pauline, 'she'll turn up, probably when she's hungry.'

'Aye, I guess so, but it's not like her though. She is different to…' she paused for a second '….to Hayley.'

'Now then, you can stop all those thoughts right now,' said John, with his tone of assertive empathy.

Aileen forced an acknowledging smile, but thoughts of Hayley had come hurtling to the forefront of her mind like a juggernaut.

'Not again,' she said, 'this can't be happening all over again.'

'Now, now, we'll have none of that talk,' Pauline said in a reassuring but dismissive manner.

Aileen knew it was incredible to think that Florence could go missing, never to be seen again, just like Hayley, but that didn't stop the heart-pounding emotions resurfacing and overpowering any rational train of thought.

'Here's what we are going to do,' said John with a degree of authority and decisiveness no doubt taken from his time as shift supervisor at McLennan's Pipe Manufacturers, 'I'll go back into the field and have another search there, God knows she spends so much time running around that field, that's where she'll be I bet you. Pauline, you go down to the park, just in case she wandered there to play or meet some friends. Sandra, can you look in and around the gardens again, I wouldn't put it past her to be right under our noses.'

'And me?' asked Aileen, 'do you think I should call Callum?'

'No, there's no need to worry him. Anyway, there's nothing to tell him yet, is there?'

Aileen shrugged her shoulders like an adolescent being berated by the school headmaster for writing on the back of the locker room door.

'I think it might be worthwhile if you called her friends and check that she hasn't gone to one of their houses to play.'

'But...' protested Aileen, 'she would have asked first.'

'Yes, in all probability, but why don't you check with them anyway,' said Pauline, 'I know John thinks she'll be in the back field, but for me, I think the likely outcome is that she has gone to a friend's house.'

'Okay.'

As they dispersed, Aileen reached into the rear pocket of her jeans and retrieved her mobile phone.

'Oh, hi, Jackie, it's Aileen...yes, I'm good thanks. Listen, do you have Florence with you, playing with Sophie?... you don't…no it's okay. Have you seen her since school ended?...okay, no it's fine. I'll come back to you if needed. Thanks, Jackie.' She ended the call.

'Hi, Shona, it's Aileen, is Florence playing with Catherine?...ah, okay…no, I can't find her at the minute and I assumed that she had probably walked to one of her friends' houses to play. Never mind, thanks anyway...yes, I'll call you to let you know when she's been found. Bye, Shona.'

Three further calls were made to the mothers of Annie, Bethany and Isabella, all with the same outcome; Florence wasn't playing with their daughter, at their house.

Aileen had been so focussed on ascertaining if Florence was physically at a friend's house, she had forgotten to ask if any of her friends had heard from or spoken to her in the last hour or so. A quick text message to each of the mums rectified that, although her heart sank that little bit further upon receipt of each reply confirming that their respective daughters had not had any form of call, text or social media engagement with Florence since their return home from school.

'Callum,' she said in a somewhat faint and desperate voice, 'I can't find Florence.'

Instinctively, Callum knew the importance to which Aileen would have attributed the call. After Hayley's disappearance ten years ago, and the subsequent birth of Florence, they had both agreed that a fine balance needed to be struck in her upbringing. On the one hand, having lost one daughter they knew that it would be natural for them as parents to be excessively overprotective with Florence. Yet on the other, they had been advised by numerous counsellors and therapists over the last few years that this potential approach of wrapping their arms around her until she had reached the point of maturity, and even potentially right up until she had found a husband and left home, was likely to prove more detrimental in terms of her personal growth, social skills, and general mental health.

A call noting that Florence was missing and could not be found was the very last thing either of them expected to hear down the other end of a phone line.

'Okay, calm down, Aileen. Where have you looked?'

'Everywhere. In the house, in the garden, at Sandra's, at Pauline's, in the back field,' she paused, 'at the park, literally everywhere, Callum.'

'She will be at a friend's house.'

'I've called all of her friends; she isn't there and they haven't seen or heard from her since school.'

'Right, okay, well she'll be around somewhere,' said Callum, trying to remain positive and optimistic, 'she can't have just disappeared.'

As soon as the words left his mouth he regretted it and wished that he could roll back the last three seconds. 'Sorry, I didn't mean that, you know what I mean. Sorry.'

'I'm really worried, Callum.'

'I know, that's understandable. Look, I'm on my way home, I should be back in about ten to fifteen minutes.'

It had just tipped past six o'clock when Callum walked through the back door into the kitchen. Florence's meal of poached eggs on toast was still sitting on the table, cold and untouched, accompanied by a glass of blackcurrant juice.

Aileen came running through, and flung herself sobbing into his arms.

'Oh, Callum, where is she? Where is she?'

'She'll be fine. She is fine, trust me. Now, where did you say you had looked for her?'

Aileen recounted where she and their neighbours had been looking for the past hour. Callum checked his watch.

'It's nearly ten past six now, and you say that you saw her last just before five?'

'Yes.'

'Okay.'

'Do you think that we should call the police?'

'No, I bloody do not.' Callum's short shrift shocked Aileen for a second. 'It's been an hour and half, that's all. I know that we don't know where she is, and that we have been looking, searching, for her, but it is less than ninety minutes, Aileen. Let's not panic, and let's not try to worry too much.'

'I know, Callum, but…'

'But what?'

'I…I just have a feeling…you know.'

He pulled her close again. 'I know that you are thinking

about Hayley as much as you are Florence.' He kissed her forehead.

'Right,' he said assertively, 'let's round up the troops and go out and continue to look for her.'

Six o'clock quickly marched through to seven-thirty when Callum strode purposefully through into the lounge of The Plough. He bounded through the door with such a commotion that everyone immediately turned to look at him, which was just as well as he wanted their attention.

'Has anyone seen my daughter Florence?'

'Not today, Callum,' said the landlord, 'why?'

'We can't find her. She has been missing for two or three hours.'

The immediate silence surprised Callum a little, and he started to turn around and walk out. His hand reached the door handle, when Gordon said, 'I'll come and help you look for her.'

'Thanks, Gordon.'

Paul, who had been sitting at the bar in front of Gordon, placed his half empty pint on the bar. 'I'll come too.'

Within twenty seconds, six diners and four drinkers had left their unfinished meals and drinks, stood up, and were walking out of the door behind Callum, hastily pulling on jumpers and coats.

The search party now stood at sixteen people, and dispersed to all four corners of the village: harbour, loch shores, play park, the old abandoned church, and up and down every street. Aileen, Sandra and Pauline returned to their respective homes to check once again that Florence wasn't hiding there, or perhaps she had found her way back home again in the preceding hour or so.

'Anything?' Aileen asked desperately, as Callum walked back in through the door.

'No, nothing,' he replied, cutting his own desolate and forlorn figure.

Aileen checked her watch; it was nine pm. 'I'm calling the police now, Callum. They have the resources to organise a proper search, you know, with those night vision infrared camera thingies.' She moved with her hands in front of her eyes as if she was playing charades, trying to silently articulate what those *thingies* were.

The darkness had not yet descended on the Scottish summer evening, but dusk was certainly settling in, and it wouldn't be too long before they would need more than their eyes if they were to find Florence that night.

The caller was certainly persistent, thought PC Davidson as he heard the phone ring for a third consecutive time. Not wanting to be interrupted from making his cup of coffee, he had ignored the first call, and although he had attempted to reach the second, he was too late. Having returned to the kitchen, he heard the phone ring again.

'Hello, Lochgilphead Police sta…' He was cut off mid-sentence by a female voice whose hysterical utterings over the next few seconds couldn't be deciphered.

'Okay, madam, please try and calm down for me. Can you start again please, a little slower.'

'Florence, my daughter, is missing. I can't find her, we've looked everywhere.'

'Okay, Florence, you say?'

'Yes,'

'And her surname?'

'Findlay, Florence Findlay.'

'And you are her mum, correct?'

'Yes, Aileen Findlay.'

'How old is Florence, Aileen?'

'She's nine years old.'

'Okay, and when was the last time that you saw her?'

'About five o'clock.'

'That's today, I assume, five o'clock today?'

'Today, yes, of course today.'

PC Davidson checked his wristwatch, nine pm. 'Okay, that's only four hours ago. Are you sure that she isn't with someone else, her dad perhaps, or probably with one of her friends? Perhaps she has lost track of time and is out playing somewhere?'

'You're not taking this seriously,' roared Aileen, 'my nine-year-old daughter is missing.'

'I understand that, Mrs Findlay, and I know that you

are worried and anxious, and I'm not playing down the fact that you don't know where she is, but I'm sure she'll turn up. Where do you live?'

'Kelvedie,' she confirmed.

'Listen, I recommend that you go back to her friends, and check with everyone that you know. In the meantime, I'll speak to the inspector. Why don't you leave me your contact number and I'll come back to you shortly, and of course it goes without saying, if there are any updates, please call me back.'

'Really? Is that it? Is that all you are going to do?'

'As I said, let me speak to the inspector and we'll come back to you.'

'Okay.'

'We'll be in touch.'

Aileen hung up the phone feeling more worried and emotionally strained than she had at the start of the call. The gut-wrenching fear mixed with an overwhelming sense of helplessness had now been compounded by feelings of frustration and anger. The police's apparent lack of urgency added to her sense of isolation.

'What did they say?' asked Callum.

'Bugger all. I don't think that they are bothered, to be honest.'

'Of course they are, she's nine years old and been missing for hours now, they have to be taking it seriously.'

'He said that he would speak to the inspector and call me back.'

'Okay,' Callum started to pull on his coat, 'you wait here by the phone, I'm off back out again.'

Callum felt a formidable responsibility that searching for his daughter had fallen squarely on his shoulders. He wouldn't give up until she was safely back home.

PC Davidson took his handwritten notes through to Inspector Mason. He knocked on a half-opened door. 'Do you have five minutes, inspector?'

'Aye, come on in. What can I do for you?'

The young constable handed the note over. 'I've just taken a call from a woman reporting her daughter as missing. She was emotional and distraught as you might expect, but her daughter had only been missing for four hours. I advised her to check with all the family, friends and neighbours that she could, and that her daughter would no doubt inevitably turn up at one of those locations. I just thought that I should make you aware.'

The inspector looked up from the note, towards the constable. 'You know who this is, don't you?'

The constable looked slightly puzzled. 'Err, Mrs Findlay I think she said. Aileen Findlay. Is that what I have written down?'

'Correct, but you know who this is? Mrs Findlay from Kelvedie?'

'No, should I?'

The inspector paused for a second. 'Actually, it was ten

years ago, and you were probably still in short breeches. Anyway, Callum and Aileen Findlay had another daughter called Hayley, she went missing about 2011 if I recall correctly.'

'I don't recall that, mind you, as you say I wouldn't have been a police officer at the time.'

'No, but you watch the news, don't you?'

'I guess. Although to put it into perspective, inspector, I would have been twelve years old.'

'Okay, fair enough. I was a sergeant at the time, and I recall we questioned both Callum and Aileen over Hayley's disappearance. In fact, we pulled Callum in several times for questioning.'

'Any joy?'

'No, nothing. We suspected the parents were involved in her disappearance in some way, but we had no evidence, and sadly we never found Hayley either. It remains an open case.'

'Right, and now the mother is calling to report the disappearance of another daughter, that's…'

'Yes, that's one hell of a bloody coincidence, and I don't buy it if I'm honest. I didn't buy it back then, and I don't buy it now.'

'So, what do you want to do?'

'Well as you say, it has only been four hours, and I fully agree with your assessment that the young girl…' she checked the note '…Florence, will turn up, probably within the next couple of hours. However, based on what we know, or what we think we know about the disappearance of Hayley, can you get yourself over there?'

'Yes.'

'And take PC Crossman with you.'

'Okay, will do. What exactly do you want us to do? I mean, we aren't going to start organising full scale searches yet, are we?'

'No, not yet. I'm sure that the parents will have rallied a few friends and neighbours to help look for their daughter. Just add a degree of pragmatism and organisation to what they are doing, and make sure that they have checked all of the obvious places where she might be. I'm sure she will turn up in the next couple of hours, but if she hasn't been found by midnight, give me a call and we'll be ready to mobilise with a larger search team.'

'Sure, understood.'

'Whilst you're out, I'll call the chief inspector and put him on notice that we might be needing a couple dozen bodies for a missing person search.'

CHAPTER 6

Upon hearing a knock at the front door, Aileen almost fell over herself rushing to answer it. As swiftly as her heart had quickened, it immediately sank once again when her hopes of seeing Florence being returned home were replaced with a view of two uniformed police officers.

'Mrs Findlay?'

'Yes.'

'I'm PC Davidson, and this is PC Crossman. We spoke on the phone earlier. May we come in?'

'Aye, of course.'

Aileen ushered them through to the lounge where she beckoned them to sit. PC Davidson regarded the lounge with interest; a welcoming and homely room adorned with many photographs, clearly portraying happier times for family life.

'I don't suppose there have been any updates since we spoke, have there?' A silly question, thought PC Davidson, but one best asked anyway.

'No, nothing,' replied Aileen, 'my husband Callum is still out looking for her, as are a few of the villagers.'

'I understand,' he replied. Looking at the many photographs, he asked, 'which one is Florence?'

Aileen stood and took a silver photo frame from the bookshelf. 'This is the most up-to-date one we have, well one that we have printed anyway, I might have more on my phone.'

'When was it taken?'

'Last autumn, so about eight or nine months ago I guess,' she confirmed.

'And has her appearance changed in any significant way since this picture was taken? You know, perhaps a change of hairstyle?'

'No, no, not really.'

'Then this one will be fine, Mrs Findlay, thank you.' PC Davidson looked at the photo. It was a photograph taken at school, and Florence was dressed in a white blouse and a navy school cardigan with the school logo embroidered on the left-hand side. Her smile looked false and somewhat forced, although PC Davidson guessed that this was probably due to the awkward seating position and pose that the school photographer had made her adopt. He recalled that all too well from his own school days.

'Can I ask, what was Florence wearing when you saw her last?'

'Pretty much what you see in that photo to be honest. We had returned home from school earlier in the afternoon, and she had run out to play without changing her clothes.'

'Okay, that's useful, thank you. And, what about the bottom half?' PC Davidson indicated that the school picture was showing Florence from her waist upwards.

'Errr…' she paused for a second, 'grey pleated knee-length skirt, white socks and black shoes. Is that what you meant?'

'Yes, exactly, thank you.'

PC Davidson looked at his colleague, who was frantically scribbling in his notebook. They exchanged a brief acknowledgement.

The next fifteen minutes was spent with PC Davidson asking, and Aileen recounting, all the areas where she, Callum and the other neighbours and volunteers had been searching for Florence, all to no avail so far.

'Does Florence have any illness or take any medication at all?'

Aileen confirmed that she was a fit and healthy young girl.

'Is there any reason to think that Florence might have run away?'

'No. No,' Aileen was adamant, 'no, definitely not.'

'Okay. Have there been any arguments recently?'

'No, we don't argue, we have a great relationship.'

'What about with her dad?'

'What are you implying?'

'Nothing at all, Mrs Findlay. I'm just trying to ascertain if there has been any event, any trigger that might have contributed towards Florence's current disappearance.'

'No. We have a loving relationship with Florence, both me and Callum. She's only nine years old, she hasn't reached those teenage tantrum years yet.'

'Look, I know this is of little comfort until Florence is found safe and sound and back home with you again, but I'm sure she will be fine, she'll be back with tales to tell of her adventures no doubt. I have a couple more questions for you, if that's okay?'

'Sure.'

'Has her character changed recently? Perhaps you've noticed changes in her mood? Has she appeared somewhat withdrawn; you know, from her usual self?'

'No, not really, not that I can say I have noticed.'

'Okay, thank you.'

PC Davidson ventured out into the village, leaving his colleague back at the house with Aileen Findlay. He didn't wander far before he saw someone. It was Paul Calvert.

'Are you one of the residents looking for the little girl?'

'Yes, sort of,' said Paul, 'I'm not one of the residents here in Kelvedie, but I am helping to search for her.'

'Okay, well we appreciate your support, but now that we have police officers on the ground, let's let the professionals take control, shall we?'

Paul extracted his warrant card from his rear pocket and presented it to the young officer. 'The professionals have been here a while, constable.'

This had the desired effect as the young constable proffered his apologies. 'Sorry, I didn't recognise you. Detective…?'

'Calvert. Detective Inspector Calvert. It's fine, you wouldn't recognise me, I'm not local, I'm part of the Humberside Police Force based in Hull.'

'Hull? Aye, you're a long way from home, sir. What are you doing here? Wrong place, wrong time?'

'I'm spending a week's leave here, just relaxing. And it's probably the wrong place, at the right time. I'm here, and available, to offer my services, constable.'

'Okay.'

'Who's your SIO? Have you one assigned yet?'

PC Davidson informed him that a senior investigating officer had not yet been assigned due to the relatively short period that the girl had been missing. He confirmed that there were two uniformed officers in attendance, and that his inspector was aware of the situation, and had requested to be kept up to date with any developments over the next couple of hours.

'Have you had many missing persons around here?' Paul was referring primarily to hikers, visitors, who might had lost their way and had perhaps needed the assistance of the local mountain rescue team.

PC Davidson knew where his thought train was at. 'One or two, sir. Hikers if I recall correctly, got caught out in bad weather.' He paused for a second, wondering whether he should elaborate further, and then his youthful exuberance got the better of him. 'Although I am told that we had another missing girl a few years ago.'

'Really?'

'Yes, but it was before my time as a police officer, so I don't really know any details.'

'Right, okay.'

'Suffice it to say that the missing girl was the daughter of Mrs and Mrs Findlay.'

PC Davidson had a broad, smug look on his face, but the surname had not registered with Paul. Davidson was about to elaborate for the obvious benefit of a bemused Paul when a man came strolling past.

'Evening,' said PC Davidson, 'any luck?'

The man paused, clearly confused by the question. 'Any luck with what?'

'The search. Where have you been looking?'

'I'm sorry, I've got no idea what you are talking about.'

'Right. Sorry. I just assumed that you were one of the villagers out looking for the missing girl.'

'No,' came a rather curt reply from the man eager to continue his walk.

'I don't think we've been introduced,' said Paul, 'I'm

Paul Calvert.'

'Why would we be?'

'No, sorry, of course not. I'm spending a few days here recharging the batteries, but now this poor girl has gone missing. Do you know her, Mr....?'

'Macaulay. Michael Macaulay. No, I don't know her. Sorry, I have to go.' And with that he turned away and continued on his direction of travel.

'Couple of things that stood out for me with that encounter, constable. Although, I'm not here to tell you how to do your job.'

'But clearly you will.'

'Firstly, it might not be uncommon, especially in this area where I have to admit it might be a daily occurrence, but to see someone out walking at eleven o'clock at night would strike me as unusual.'

'Unless they are walking a dog, or walking back from the pub,' noted Davidson.

'Correct. And the second, more important, thing is when asked if he knew the missing girl, he said that he did not.'

'Correct, and?'

'And I never mentioned who the missing girl was.'

'True, but he must have heard about it, it'll be all over the village by now, and half of the village have been out looking for her. He's probably picked up the name of the girl through another one of the villagers.'

'Yes, probably. Although that does then beg the

question why he answered your first question with, *I've no idea what you're talking about.*'

PC Davidson looked at his watch. 'Midnight almost. I propose we call off the search and resume again at first light. If I nip back to the Findlays', can you tell all the villagers out there to stand down for the night?'

'I'll try of course, but I'm not expecting many to heed your request. I expect the dad and one or two others may be out all night.'

'Understandable of course, but try and impress upon them that we will need the numbers tomorrow morning when we resume at first light. Perhaps I should tell them.'

'Constable, I'm a DI, I'm more than capable.'

'Yes, of course, sir, sorry. In the meantime, I'll speak to my inspector and ensure that this gets upgraded to an official missing person investigation now.'

'I assume you have family liaison officers?'

'Yes, sir, but not at Lochgilphead. There are a couple of FLOs attached to Greenock station about eighty miles from Lochgilphead. I'm not sure that we'll get them out at midnight on a Saturday.'

'Of course you bloody will, are your FLOs not on twenty-four-hour call?'

'I don't know, possibly, the inspector will sort that.'

'Make sure he does. You need family liaison here through the night.'

'She.'

'Sorry?'

'She. My inspector, she's a female.'
'Right. Make sure that she sorts it.'

After a quick knock at the door, PC Davidson re-entered the Findlay home twenty minutes after midnight. His news that he had instructed all villagers to call off the search for the night was greeted by Aileen as expected, with anger, disappointment and an understandable degree of worry. She couldn't comprehend why they would choose to stop looking for her missing nine-year-old daughter. PC Davidson empathised and advised that the search would resume at first light under the control of the police, and that the intervening period would see significant resources mobilised in readiness.

PC Davidson called Inspector Mason.

'Just a quick update, ma'am.'

'Okay, go on.'

'There has been no sign of the girl. There are still a small number of residents out looking for her; I guess some might be out all night.'

'Okay. Can you log it as an official misper? I'll arrange for an FLO to be assigned and to be there first thing tomorrow morning.'

'What shall I tell the residents that are still out looking for her?'

'Ideally, tell them to stand down, get some rest, and we'll start again tomorrow morning. It'll no doubt fall on deaf ears anyway. In the meantime, I'll arrange for some resource to commence a formal search tomorrow morning.'

'Okay, ma'am.'

'What time does your shift end?' she asked.

PC Davidson looked at his watch. 'About two hours ago.'

'Alright, stay on as long as you feel necessary. I'll sort the overtime out, but make sure that you leave at a decent hour to get some rest yourself as I'll be wanting you and Crossman as part of that search team tomorrow morning.'

'Sure, will do. Oh, one more thing, ma'am…'

'Yes.'

'Whilst in Kelvedie, I met a detective inspector who had joined the villagers in the search.'

'A DI? Who?'

'Well, that's the thing, he was a DI from England. He did say where, but I can't recall. He said he was here on holiday and just offered to join the search.'

'Okay, thanks for letting me know.'

CHAPTER 7

The police had requested that anyone who wanted to volunteer should make themselves available and gather outside of The Plough at seven o'clock. However, people had started gathering since just after six, and there were a good twenty to twenty-five there when Paul Calvert rounded the corner and came upon the meeting place.

Gordon and Angie McKie were serving hot drinks into disposable cups from a large urn resting on an A-frame table at the front of the pub.

'Coffee, Paul?'

'Yes, thank you, Gordon,' said Paul as he accepted a small polystyrene cup with piping hot coffee. He added milk and two sugars from those available on the table.

'Thanks for volunteering, Paul, I know you're a visitor

and only been here a couple of days. I'm guessing this is not what you had in mind when you booked your short break?'

'No, probably not. Happy to help out. Anyway, to be honest it would probably be expected of me.'

'What do you mean?'

Paul paused for a second trying to remember if, in their brief engagement so far, he had told them of his occupation. He thought he must have, but perhaps it never came up in conversation.

'I'm a police officer.'

'Really?'

'Yes, did I not mention it before?'

'I'm not sure, I don't think so, or I'm sure I would have remembered.'

'Yes, I'm a detective inspector with the Humberside police force, based out of Hull.'

'Oh, right,' said Gordon, 'this must be like a bloody busman's holiday for you then?'

Paul's smile broke briefly into a laugh, although he tried to hide it from the crowd. It wasn't really the kind of gathering to be cracking jokes or laughing. He had immediately recalled the television programme of the same name from the late eighties and early nineties. Paul remembered watching Julian Pettifer hosting two competing teams in an occupation-based quiz, where the winning team would be whisked away to some far-flung resort at the other side of the world, just to see how their exact same jobs were undertaken by workers in said far-flung resort.

'Now there's a blast from the past, *Busman's Holiday* indeed.'

There were two or three others waiting behind, so Paul took his polystyrene cup and wandered off towards the harbour wall where he perched himself. He had time for two or three sips before two police squad cars and a marked van arrived, pulling up at the side of the road. He recognised PC Davidson as he exited, and to Paul's surprise he started to walk over to him accompanied by a female officer.

'Sir,' he gestured with a hand towards his colleague who, apparently, was already fuming that PC Davidson had called him *sir*, 'this is Inspector Mason.'

'Inspector Mason.' Paul held out his hand which was met in return with a leather-gloved version. The strength of Mason's handshake belied her small hand.

'My officer informs me that you're a DI from Yorkshire.'

'Correct, Hull to be precise.'

'Hull. Not sure I've heard of it, or perhaps I have, is it a town in Yorkshire?'

'No, it's a city. Population of over three hundred thousand,' he confirmed, knowing that she was trying to imply that he was a DI from a quiet part of the country, and couldn't possibly know much about major crimes. The irony, standing here in a fishing village in rural Argyll, was laughable at best.

'Right. Well, nice to have you here,' she paused, 'in the capacity as a member of the public of course.'

Paul could see a smirk appear on the face of PC

Davidson, out of sight of Inspector Mason. 'Of course. I'm happy to help in any way I can whilst I'm here.'

'Thank you.'

Paul wasn't in the slightest peeved that she hadn't had the professional courtesy to recognise and respect his rank and call him *inspector*. Although he instinctively knew that she would have been aggrieved if he had not done so during their conversation.

'Ladies and gentlemen, gather round please, gather round.'

Inspector Mason was joined by the balance of the police contingent, albeit a few paces behind. There were ten police officers in total; Inspector Mason, Sergeant O'Brien, and Constables Davidson and Crossman, all from the nearest station in Lochgilphead, plus six other officers drafted in from Campbeltown and Strachur stations.

'Firstly, thank you for turning out this morning, I know that many of you know Florence Findlay and her parents, Callum and Aileen. Looking around I can see that we probably have thirty to thirty-five of us.'

'It's not very many, is it?' noted one of the volunteers, 'where are all the police officers? A wee lassie is missing, has been all night, and you arrive with a handful of officers. It's not enough, is it?'

'I understand your frustration, really I do, but we have sufficient numbers to undertake a thorough search under the supervision of myself and my colleagues.'

'Aye but…'

'It's fine,' interjected Paul, 'there are plenty of us, let's just crack on, shall we? It's been light for over thirty minutes now, and we should get moving as soon as possible.'

'Thank you. As you know we are searching for Florence Findlay, aged nine. She was last seen yesterday afternoon by her mum at around five pm heading out of their kitchen door and into the back garden. She was wearing a white blouse and a navy school cardigan with the school logo embroidered on the left-hand side, also a grey pleated knee-length skirt, white socks and black shoes. PC Crossman is going to hand out a copy of a photograph of Florence.'

Right on cue PC Crossman worked his way through the assembled crowd, ensuring that everyone had a copy of the colour photo that had been printed.

'Thank you. Right, in an attempt to cover as much ground as possible, we will be splitting into three groups. The first group will be led by myself, the second by Sergeant O'Brien, and the third by PC Davidson. We'll split you all up in a few minutes.'

'What do we do if we find something?' asked an eager volunteer.

'You stand still, exactly where you find the item, raise your arm and shout towards your group leader. They will come to you and take it from there. Clearly, we are still hopeful of finding Florence alive and safe, but if you do come across any piece of clothing that I mentioned earlier, or any other item that you think we might want to see, follow the process as outlined.'

The next fifteen minutes was spent busily dividing the group into three, introducing them to their group leaders. There were a number of volunteers that had arrived together, husbands and wives for example; they had dropped their children off at The Plough and a couple of other mothers had agreed to look after them for as long as they were out searching.

Gordon, Angie, a couple of mums and a handful of children retreated inside The Plough. Promises of bacon butties and cups of tea from Gordon fell on deaf ears with the children, but when these promises were replaced with chocolate-covered pancakes and some orange juice by one of the other mums, they soon settled down in eager expectation of their early Saturday morning breakfast treat.

Paul looked at his watch as he set off with his group; 7.23. Florence had now been missing for over fourteen hours.

Just after nine am, two plainclothes detectives arrived at the Findlay home. After being shown through to the lounge and offered a cup of tea, they introduced themselves.

'Mrs Findlay, I'm Detective Constable Taylor and this is Detective Constable Waller. As you know our uniformed colleagues are organising and leading a search this morning, for your daughter Florence.'

'Yes, my husband is with them,' she replied.

'Okay, great. We have a couple of things that we need to go through with you, Mrs Findlay, if that's okay?'

'Sure.'

'Firstly, you will be assigned a family liaison officer. The officer will be here in the next couple of hours and will remain with you for most of the day today, and for as long as is necessary moving forward.'

'Will they sleep here?' asked Aileen somewhat naively, but also out of genuine concern that she had no spare bedroom for this officer to stay.'

'No, Mrs Findlay, the officer won't need to sleep here. She will leave early evening, or may perhaps come and go throughout the day, but she will be on call and available to you twenty-four hours a day.'

'Oh, right, I'm sorry, I didn't really…' She tapered off without finishing her reply.

'That's okay. The other update that we have for you is that we have confirmed that no-one matching Florence's description has been admitted to hospital since she was reported missing.'

'Right,' said Aileen, drawing out the word over a much longer time as though her mind was elsewhere, and her voice was simply going through the motions. Her thoughts were indeed elsewhere; she had wondered if Florence not being located at a hospital overnight was good news or bad. On the one hand, finding her in a local hospital would mean that they knew where she was, and that she was safe, despite any injuries sustained that resulted in her being taken to hospital. On the flip side, as she hadn't been located in a hospital, she must still be local, nearby, and the police search this morning must surely locate her unharmed. Wouldn't they?

'Try not to worry, Mrs Findlay, we all remain hopeful and very optimistic of finding Florence safe and well.'

Aileen forced a smile.

'The final thing that brings us here is Florence's mobile phone.'

'What about it?'

'We need to take it away with us, we'll get one of our techs to look at it in the hope that it might provide some clues as to her whereabouts.'

'How?'

'Well, we'll take a look at her call history, any text messages, but mainly her social media accounts, especially chat rooms.'

'Chat rooms.' Aileen paused for a second until it clicked. 'You think she's been groomed, don't you?'

'Not necessarily, Mrs Findlay, no. We maintain an open mind, and this line of enquiry looks to rule things out as much as it might look for avenues to pursue.'

His explanation wasn't met with any response.

'Does Florence have access to a personal computer, laptop or tablet at all?'

'Not her own, but yes, she uses the family laptop.'

'And tablet?'

'Yes, we have an iPad that she uses sometimes.'

'Okay. We need to take those too, I'm afraid.'

'But you can't. We use those, Callum and me.'

'I'm sorry, really I must insist.'

Aileen Findlay took five or six minutes to gather the three electronic items and handed them to the detective. 'When do we get them back?'

DC Taylor was a little taken aback by her misaligned focus away from her missing daughter and took the opportunity to remind her of exactly why they were taking the electronic devices.

As the discussion was coming to a natural ending, there was a knock at the front door, and DC Waller offered to see who it was. Recognising the caller, he closed the door behind her and led her through to the lounge.

'Mrs Findlay, this is PC Jackie Macallan, the family liaison officer that we mentioned.'

'Hello, Aileen, may I call you Aileen?'

Aileen Findlay nodded.

Jackie Macallan was a softly spoken woman in her early forties who had spent almost all of her eighteen years in the police force as a family liaison officer. And whilst the black-and-white of the job description clearly noted that the role was an investigative one, to gather evidence and information from the family to contribute to the investigation, it was the family support element that she enjoyed. Her natural sensitive and compassionate manner ensured that she had no problems in securing the confidence and trust of the families of victims of crime, in most instances quite serious crime. She found immense job satisfaction in both informing and comforting families during their ordeal. Her role was not without its ups and downs, but in the main, the instances of good outcomes had so far outweighed those with tragic endings. Those she continued to find difficult despite her substantial years of experience. The time when she was to feel little or nothing for the family and for their loss; the time when this didn't take a huge personal toll on her own emotions; that would be the time to move to a new role, or perhaps even a whole new career.

'As DC Waller noted, I'm PC Jackie Macallan. Please call me Jackie.' She received a smile, but little more.

'I assume that you were expecting me?' PC Macallan looked towards the two detectives, expecting them to confirm so, which they did with a brief nod.

'Yes,' Aileen replied, 'the detectives were just telling me.'

'Okay. My role here, Aileen, is to support you and your family, to answer any questions that you might have, and also to pass on any important information to you from the investigating team, and vice versa. It makes sense that I'm here with you, at home, a lot of the time, but I won't get in your way. You have a family life to maintain during this period. Your husband...'

'Callum.'

'Yes, that's right, sorry, Callum. And other children?'

And that was where PC Jackie Macallan's failure to be fully up to speed, or more accurately the failure of the senior management to ensure she was fully briefed, delivered the cruellest of body blows to Aileen Findlay.

'No, it's just myself, Callum and Florence. We had another daughter, but…' She tailed off.

Sensing that there was a vital piece of information that she had not been given, or that she was not yet privy to, PC Macallan moved the conversation on. As she did, the two detectives made their apologies and left.

'Right, Aileen, let's get that kettle on, shall we?' she said, pointing to an open door off the lounge, 'this way, is it?'

CHAPTER 8

It had just tipped past one-thirty when Calvert's group, led by PC Davidson, came into view of The Plough. There was already quite a crowd of people there, and Calvert surmised that the other two groups had already returned.

As group leaders the police officers had radios, and Calvert assumed that Florence hadn't been found by either of the other groups or they would have heard, although he was unsure of the reliability and range of the police issue radios over the rugged and undulating terrain that they had all been traversing for the past few hours.

Florence had now been missing for twenty hours.

Gordon and Angie had resurrected their refreshment station outside of The Plough and were busy handing out hot mugs of coffee, bottles of water and sandwiches. As

Calvert took his coffee from Gordon, he overheard a conversation between handfuls of other volunteers.

'Sorry, did I hear you correctly,' interjected Calvert, 'Inspector Mason has had an accident?'

'That's right,' confirmed one of the group, 'we think that she has broken her ankle.'

'How did that happen? Where is she?' asked Calvert.

Just as he asked the question his eyes were drawn to a vehicle that pulled up; on the side were the words *Mountain Rescue*. He quickly scanned the volunteers milling around the area, searching for Inspector Mason.

'Is she here? Did she come back with you?'

'No, she is still out there,' replied one of the group.

'Is she…'

'No,' anticipated another, 'she's not on her own. Davey stayed with her whilst we returned here to raise the alarm.'

'Okay, so what happened?'

'I'm not sure to be honest as we were spread out, you know, walking in a line across an area adjacent to the loch. I heard that she had fallen over. We all thought that she had twisted her ankle. I mean, she tried to stand up and put pressure on it, but soon collapsed to the floor again. Someone helped her take her boot off and you could tell that it was a little more serious than a sprained ankle.'

'Right, okay. The mountain rescue boys will have her down and on her way to hospital shortly,' said Calvert. Changing the subject, he asked, 'obviously no-one found Florence, was there anything else found?'

'Such as?'

'You know, clothing. Any of the clothes that she was reported as wearing?'

'No,' confirmed one of the group, 'certainly not in our team led by Inspector Mason.'

'Nor ours,' said another, 'ours was the Sergeant O'Brien group.' And with Calvert having been part of the PC Davidson group, that was a blank across the entire search party. Still, Calvert knew that a search of a few square miles around the local area was just one avenue of enquiry, and the investigative team would now focus their efforts elsewhere.

'Shouldn't we be using those mountain rescue teams, and maybe some of the underwater search teams?' asked one of the volunteers, clearly having watched too many episodes of *Taggart*.

'Not at this stage,' advised Calvert, 'those specialist units are generally used as more of a retrieval team rather than a search team.'

'A retrieval team, yes, that what we are trying to do,' said one of the group, then as soon as she had finished, she added, 'ah, you mean retrieval of the body?'

'Correct. The police will still be hopeful of finding Florence alive, so they will be focussing their resources on activities other than those, for now anyway.'

Calvert was approached by Sergeant O'Brien. 'I guess you've heard, then?'

'About Inspector Mason? Yes, I've just been brought up

to speed by some of those that were in her group.'

'Yes, the mountain rescue team will bring her back down to the harbour and there is an ambulance on its way to take her to hospital.'

'Can I ask a question?' asked Calvert.

'Sure.'

'Appreciate that Kelvedie is a small rural village, and without wishing to be disrespectful, why are there no CID involved in the case, especially as SIO?'

'I think you answered your own question. This is a small rural area, and we don't have an abundance of CID officers. There are two, DCs Taylor and Waller who visited Aileen Findlay earlier this morning, they were drafted in from Greenock station. As for seniority above inspector, of course there are more senior officers but I'm not sure that any have been assigned SIO for this case.'

'Okay, I wonder if I should look to lend some support, in a more formal way?'

Calvert's question was mostly rhetorical, and one he was asking of himself rather than Sergeant O'Brien, but one that received an unexpected reply nevertheless.

'Funny you should say that. Well, not that I'm privy to the thoughts of Superintendent Talloch, but she wants to meet you this afternoon. When we've disbanded this search, I've been asked to drive you to Greenock station. Or...' noting that he might have been a little presumptuous, 'you could drive yourself there. Sorry, I didn't know if you have a car, or not.'

'I do, sergeant, but if you're going to chauffeur me there, and back I assume, then I'll hitch a ride, Thanks.'

Sergeant O'Brien gathered the volunteers. Whilst his speech was short on detail and quick on brevity, he did remember to thank them for their efforts over the last few hours and confirmed that the police would be working on numerous lines of investigation to ensure the safe return of Florence Findlay to her parents.

'Tell me…' started Calvert, sitting in the passenger seat of Sergeant O'Brien's squad car, 'Inspector Mason hasn't been senior officer on a misper before, has she?'

'To be honest, I don't know. What I do know is that we don't really get any missing persons here. I've been stationed locally for fifteen years, and I only recall one other. You've got to travel the hundred or so miles to Glasgow to see any real stats for mispers. Why do you ask?'

'No reason, just a feeling I had. Anyway, tell me about your super.'

'Talloch? She is the divisional commander for quite a large area covering Argyll and West Dunbartonshire. She has been superintendent for the past three years, and a bit of a high-flyer so I hear, fast-track path through the ranks in Edinburgh. I believe she was promoted to inspector at twenty-six, and chief inspector not long after her thirtieth birthday. She is very hands-on and likes to spend more time out in the field rather than behind a desk.'

'Good, I like her already,' replied Calvert.

'Me too. She has a decent reputation for some high-profile arrests. She has always been in uniform but must have been seconded for a spell to the vice squad as she worked on Operation Hades.'

'Hades? The Greek god of the underworld. Let me guess, some kind of operation to take down an organised gang?'

'Kind of. Operation Hades targeted the organised gangs that used to traffic young girls from Eastern Europe to work as prostitutes in Edinburgh and the wider Lothian area.'

'Was she the SIO?'

'I don't think so, but I'm not sure. If not, she must have played a pivotal role in the investigation as she received a Commissioner's Commendation.'

'You seem to be well informed about her career to date, are you some kind of closet fan? Although, less closet and more overt.'

Sergeant O'Brien smiled, 'a fan? Not quite, but I guess you would say she is our *poster girl* within Police Scotland. She is always on the news, on the telly, in the papers, and her profile has been documented and retold dozens of times. So, it's not hard to recall some of her career highlights, everyone in the force must bloody know.'

The rest of the journey passed fairly uneventfully and

devoid of further substantive conversation, and soon they arrived at Greenock station. Sergeant O'Brien advised Calvert that he would be waiting in the canteen. Despite his shift having finished a couple of hours ago, he would hang around and give him a lift back and be grateful for the three hours' overtime that would be approved.

'Afternoon, how can I help you?'

'I'm here to see Superintendent Talloch.'

'And you are?'

'Detective Inspector Calvert.' The desk sergeant looked him up and down before pointing towards an adjacent door and pressing a button to allow access.

Calvert was shown through to an office at the rear of the building; a knock at the door and he entered.

His mind had created a picture of what he believed Superintendent Talloch would look like, and apart from the fact that he could never have pictured her face, he was right on most areas of her physical appearance. She looked to be in her early forties, slender athletic build, short layered blonde hair and impeccably dressed in her uniform, minus her jacket which was hung on a coat hanger to her left-hand side. In that first immediate glance, Calvert couldn't help thinking that she bore a striking resemblance to the actress Anna Carteret who played the part of Inspector Kate Longton in the BBC police drama series, *Juliet Bravo* in the eighties.

'DI Calvert?'

'Yes, ma'am.' He took her hand as it was extended.

'No need for the ma'am, I know that you're on holiday at present, so let's keep it informal. May I call you Paul?'

'Of course, ma'am. Sorry...' He paused for a second.

'Isobel,' she confirmed.

'Isobel.'

'Please take a seat.' Calvert settled into one of the faux-leather office chairs that had seen better days.

'I've taken the liberty of asking one of the officers to bring in two cups of coffee. Is coffee okay?'

'Perfect, thank you.'

'Thanks for agreeing to meet me. Quite fortuitous that I was here really, fairly local to Kelvedie. Well relatively local anyway. I'm out on the road all week visiting a number of the local stations.'

'I'm guessing it's not quite like police headquarters?'

'Ha, no. My usual office looks more like the head office of KPMG or Accenture, or something of that ilk. Multiple floors, glass fronted, Starbucks in the foyer. You know that kind of thing.'

'It's a tough life,' noted Calvert, with tongue in cheek.

'But someone's got to do it, eh?'

They shared a smile.

'Paul, let me get straight to the point. I'm conscious that you are only temporarily in our neck of the woods, and despite your welcomed involvement this morning with the search, you might be eager to return to your holiday activities, or even go back home again.'

'I think we both know that I'm willing and able to support further as required.'

'I hoped you might say that. I wanted to sound you out about stepping into the role of SIO, at least for the next three or four days.'

'Are there no other senior officers available?' Calvert asked, somewhat surprised.

'Well, it's a bit embarrassing to be honest, Paul. Experienced CID officers are a bit thin on the ground in that area. Our two most senior officers, DCI Mason and DCI Geary, are both on annual leave. Not together, I might add, although I don't think so. Anyway, I'm not sure how their concurrent annual leave was approved and signed off, that's something to be looked at another time.'

'Will they cut short their leave and return early?'

'Is the million-dollar question…We've been trying to contact them for the past eighteen hours. We can't reach Mason, and Geary is in Jamaica. He can change his return flight, but still wouldn't be back for another three days.'

'No DIs available?'

'DI Cochrane is on long-term sick.'

Calvert raised his eyebrows, which didn't go unnoticed by Talloch. 'I know, you couldn't make this up, could you? Neither of my DCIs are available, or in the country for that matter, a DI on long-term sick leave, and another DI who simply doesn't have the experience in managing a misper. It's not his fault, we just don't have many cases across this region. Then to cap all that, my uniformed inspector lands herself in the hospital and no doubt bed-ridden for a couple of weeks at least.'

'Yes, I see your point. Okay, so are there any practicalities with regards to working for another force?'

'Yes, and no. As I'm sure you know, police officers are seconded to other forces on a frequent basis. Your powers of arrest will be restricted, but I'm not sure that will be a problem for the brief time that you'll be with us.'

'And the Chief Superintendent in Humberside?'

'Ah, Donny,' she smiled, 'Donny and I go back a few years. Yes, I spoke to him a short time ago, that's why I know that you're exactly the man for the job, even if it is for a brief interim period. Your chief super tells me that unfortunately mispers are fairly common in East Yorkshire, and that you've been SIO on quite a few of them.'

'Yes, thirty-five in total, not that I'm counting, eh? Thirty-four of them were found, thirty of which were alive and well, and four found deceased. One still remains missing.'

Calvert looked pensive and paused for a second or two. 'James Harvey, aged ten when he went missing, and we're still no closer to finding him.'

'Still, that's an impressive recovery record, Paul.'

'Just luck really, most of the thirty had not ventured out of East Yorkshire, so we didn't need to scour the country, and as I'm sure you know, those that don't want to be found, won't be found, but all others will have retained some ties with family or friends.'

'Nevertheless, that's a good recovery record. Anyway, if you're up for it, I'd like you to step into the role of SIO, at least for the next three days. You can set yourself up at Lochgilphead station, it's not the biggest station but it does have a room that you can designate as your special operations room. Unfortunately, we have no station at Kelvedie, and our station at Tarbert was closed just over two years ago.'

'Thanks, I'm sure it will be fine. We won't need much space for the SOR.'

'Lochgilphead is only about twenty miles from Kelvedie, so it's not too far. What about transport, do you have a car?'

'Yes, I travelled up from Hull in my car.'

'Would you like the use of a CID pool car whilst you are here?'

'No, thank you, that won't be necessary. I'm happy to use my own. Thank you anyway. What about local support and resources?'

'Anticipating your acceptance, I've already spoken to Inspector Daley and asked him to provide you with as much resource as possible, and all the support needed over the next seventy-two hours.'

'Thank you. What's the latest news on Inspector Mason?'

'She was transported to the Inverclyde Royal Hospital and confirmed she had sustained a broken ankle. I believe she will be sent home later today and will return for surgery in a few days once the swelling has gone down. After that, a couple of days in hospital, then no doubt a few weeks convalescing at home. I think that she'll be off active duty for six to eight weeks.'

'Right, okay,' Calvert took to his feet, 'well, I hope she recovers quickly.'

'Indeed.'

Calvert was halfway out of the door.

'Oh, Paul…'

He stopped and turned.

'…find that little girl and bring her back to her parents.'

'We'll try our best, ma'am.'

CHAPTER 9

Lochgilphead police station was, in the main, what Calvert had expected. A relatively small building of stone and tile construction, in keeping with the style and architecture of the town; no floor-to-ceiling glass, no shiny chrome, no new decals and certainly no immediate kerbside appeal.

The front counter was without presence when Calvert walked through the door with Sergeant O'Brien, although the latter did confirm that it was usually manned. O'Brien showed him through to a room on the first floor.

'So, this is your base, sergeant, your local station?'

'Yes, sir, this is where I am based.'

'And what is the staff compliment here?'

'Well, there's Inspector Mason, who you met this morning. I'm the only sergeant. We have Constables Davidson and Crossman, again you met both of them this morning. We have two PCSOs, Hayter and Greaves, then Constable Muggen, our local SOCO.'

'No CID?'

'No, not based here. All CID covering the local area are based at Greenock station.'

Calvert looked around the room. It looked as if it had at one time been used for operational purposes; there were two desks, half a dozen chairs, and a large whiteboard on the wall to his left.

'When was the last time this room was used for anything other than dumping stuff?' asked Calvert as he surveyed the endless boxes and buff files piled high on the desks, the overflowing waste bin in the near corner, and two overhead projectors thick with dust, both of which had seen better days, probably back in the 1980s when that type of technology was last being used.

'I was posted here about four years ago, and in that time, I don't recall us using the room for anything,' confirmed O'Brien.

'Okay, well...' pondered Calvert, 'it's usable, might just take an hour or three to clean it out and make it habitable.'

The shuffle of feet was heard as others approached the open door.

'Ah, perfect timing, muck in, will you?' said Sergeant O'Brien as he stacked another box in the corner of the room. He paused, noting that introductions were probably a good idea at this point.

'This is Constable Davidson, Constable Crossman, both of whom you might recall from Kelvedie earlier today, and PCSO Hayter.'

Calvert took each of their hands offered in turn and introduced himself but notably without his rank.

'I remember you from the Kelvedie search this morning,' said Crossman, 'have we recruited you to tidy our station as well now?'

Calvert chuckled, 'not quite, but I have been recruited, as you put it, just for a few days.'

'Right,' replied Crossman, the inflection in his single word response clearly expecting further elaboration.

'I'm not sure if you are aware, and to be honest I don't recall it being mentioned this morning in Kelvedie, but I'm a detective inspector with the Humberside Police Force. I have been asked by Superintendent Talloch to step in as senior investigating officer for the next two or three days.'

'That's a little, well, unusual isn't it, sir?'

'Yes, I'll give you that. But I understand through one reason or another there is a lack of experienced senior officers on the ground at present. Anyway, my sole focus will be the case of the missing girl, Florence Findlay. I won't be involved in day-to-day operations, nor any other investigations.'

The next forty-five minutes was spent completing the tidy-up of the room; it was a little cramped with all five of them, but Calvert was appreciative of their help. With the boxes and files all stacked on top of each other in one corner, the tables and chairs were now more accessible and there was room to walk around. PCSO Hayter, who had only just come on duty, promised to try to catch the night-time cleaner and ask her to give the room a bit of attention with the duster and vacuum cleaner.

It had been a long day and Calvert was glad when Sergeant O'Brien dropped him back the twenty miles into Kelvedie just before six pm. Calvert's mind was awash with things that needed doing, but most importantly, where was nine-year-old Florence Findlay? Was she safe? Had she been taken by a stranger and whisked out of the area, or had she been taken by someone she knew and was still within the locality? The crucial initial twenty-four hours had passed, but Calvert remained upbeat about finding her alive and well.

Despite waking just after six am, and the fact that today had been a long one, Calvert decided that he would go out for the evening. Irrespective of the terrible circumstances in which the village found itself, especially the Findlay family, he had decided that after a long soak in the bathtub he would go to The Plough for a couple of hours. After all, were it not for the present circumstances, there was no doubt where he would be on a Saturday evening. Freshly pressed Farahs and a clean shirt, topped with a splash of the latest Ralph Lauren Polo Sport, and he was on his way.

'Ah, good evening, Paul.'

'Evening, Gordon, are you well?'

'Me? Of course, never better. Well…' he looked over his shoulder, 'be a damn sight better if the missus would run off with the milkman, but hey ho, we can but dream.' He smiled.

'Usual?'

'I've only been here three days. I have a usual, do I?'

'Of course. Everyone has a usual, and a good landlord will remember.'

'Aye and a better landlord, better than you, Gordon McKie, will have the drink poured and just settling, ready and waiting for when the customer walks through the door,' interjected Angie as she came up behind him. 'How are you, Paul?'

'Fine thanks, Angie, and yourself?'

'Fair to middling. I can't help thinking about that wee lassie.'

'Terrible isn't it,' agreed Calvert, 'but I'm sure it will all end up fine. She'll be found safe and well. Sooner rather than later hopefully.'

'This one is on the house,' remarked Gordon, as he placed the pint down on the bar, 'for helping out with the search this morning. I know you're only here for a few days' break, but the community really appreciate your help.'

'Well, that's very kind of you, but not necessary. Thank you anyway.'

'You're welcome. Enjoy.'

Calvert, sitting on a stool at the bar, listened for the next fifteen minutes to the conversations of some of the others in the bar. Danny and Shona, minus their son Fergus tonight, were chatting to a couple in their mid-sixties. Calvert hadn't met them yet.

'Isn't it terrible about that wee girl, and such a young age,' remarked the older woman.

'I know, I can't imagine what Aileen must be going through right now,' Shona replied.

'They had the whole village out looking for her this morning.'

'Yes, I know, Betty, Danny was one of the volunteers that joined the police search.'

'Oh, Danny, good for you. John would have joined too if I'd have let him, but it's his hip, you know.'

John smiled, which was his usual contribution to a conversation where he generally couldn't get a word in edgeways, or where Betty talked about him as though he wasn't actually sitting right next to her.

'If you ask me, the police need to be looking closer to home.' Andrew Hamilton's first foray into the conversation was met with stern gaze from some within the room.

'That's enough of that kind of talk, Andrew,' brusquely interjected Gordon, who had been nearby drying glasses and listening as the discussion unfolded.

'It's only what people are thinking, Gordon,' said another, Michael Macaulay.

'That may be, Michael, but there was no evidence last time and as far as I'm aware none this time either.'

'Once is bad luck, twice is coincidence, and three times is a pattern.'

'What are you talking about, Andrew, there hasn't been a third time, has there?'

'No, but…'

'No but nothing. Stop with the malicious rumours, Aileen and Callum are a lovely couple and they adore Florence,' there was the slightest pause, 'and Hayley.'

Calvert's ears pricked up and he decided to join the conversation.

'Sorry, can I just ask a question?' Despite his rhetorical question, he waited a couple of seconds for their approval. 'Am I correct in understanding that Aileen and Callum have two daughters, and from what I think I overheard, their other daughter went missing also?'

'That's correct.'

'Who are you, and why do you want to know?' asked a rather curt Hamilton.

Hamilton was in his late thirties, of medium build with scruffy unkempt hair that looked as though it hadn't met a dollop of shampoo let alone seen a pair of scissors for the best part of a year. He was wearing a pair of jeans and a retro Scottish national football team shirt. A fairly unremarkable man that you might pass on the street without a second glance, save for the large C-shaped scar that cut through his stubble. The gouge across his cheek had not diminished or faded over the years since he had obviously been on the wrong end of a broken glass several years ago.

'Andrew!'

'It's fine, Gordon, it's a fair question. My name is Paul Calvert. I am, was, just here for a week's holiday, a bit of rest and relaxation. I volunteered to join the search for Florence earlier this morning;' he paused, 'I don't recall seeing you there.'

'Errr, well…' Hamilton stuttered but failed to fully respond.

Calvert, not wanting to get off on the wrong foot, gave him an out. 'Although there were lots of people there, split into different groups, so I might have missed you… Andrew, was it?'

'Yes, that's right.'

'I am also a detective inspector with the Humberside Police Force, and due to a strange set of circumstances, I've just been asked to support the search for the missing girl, Florence Findlay.'

His comment, whilst not the most earth-shattering of news, drew little if any response from those seated in the bar, until the usually quiet John Coulson piped up, 'good for you, son, I hope you find her safe and well.'

'Thanks, that's exactly what I intend to do. Now, what was this I overheard about a second disappearance?'

Between Betty and Shona, with intermittent and sometimes unhelpful comments from Andrew, Calvert discovered that Callum and Aileen Findlay had another daughter who went missing ten years ago in similar suspicious circumstances.

'She would probably be around nineteen years old now.'

'That's right, I believe she was just nine when she went missing, poor wee lassie.'

Calvert pressed for more detail. He knew that he could, and would, read the police reports in the morning back at the station, but the perception and views of a handful of the villagers would aid his understanding now, and fill in some of those background gaps.

'She was playing in the park by all accounts, and when Aileen went to check on her, she was gone. The police came and there was a big search, not too dissimilar to the one this morning, but the poor girl was never found.'

'He was questioned,' said Hamilton, 'more than once, I might add.'

'He?'

'Yes, the dad, Callum. The police took him in for questioning several times. Held him for weeks, they did.'

Calvert knew that Callum would not have been held in custody for weeks, not unless he had been charged, then for whatever reason, subsequently released.

'And Hayley, you said, correct?'

'That's right, Hayley Findlay.'

'And Hayley's body hasn't been found, and she hasn't been seen since?'

'Again, correct,' confirmed Danny.

Calvert looked at the middle-aged man sitting at the corner table, one hand holding a half-empty pint glass, the other resting on his lap. He was staring, trance-like, into nowhere.

'And what about yourself, Mr Macaulay?'

Macaulay was initially surprised that Calvert knew his name, but quickly recalled that he was with the uniformed officer last night around eleven o'clock, when he had been stopped and asked a couple of questions.

'What about me?'

'You've been a little quiet, do you have any thoughts or opinions on the disappearance of Florence Findlay?'

'Me? Not really. I hardly know the family if I'm honest. I'd seen the wee girl playing in the village, perhaps in the park once or twice if I was walking by, but no, I've got nothing to add over what the others have told you.'

Calvert chatted to the group for another hour as conversation swung from life in Hull compared to Kelvedie, to the highs and lows of *Britain's Got Talent*, before bidding everyone goodnight and setting off back to the B&B.

CHAPTER 10

Calvert had one foot on the stairs when he heard his name being called from within the bar area; he turned around and entered the room to see Brian and Antonio sitting and cradling a glass.

'Join us for a wee dram, Paul? A nightcap?'

'Yes, why not, go on then.'

Calvert took a seat across from where they were sitting and placed the wooden baton, with his room key attached, on the table.

'I'm impressed that it's still in one piece.' Calvert knew what he meant and gave a knowing smile.

'Most people have detached the key and left the bloody baton in their rooms.'

'Well, in my line of work it's always good to have a large piece of wood handy.'

Brian took to his feet, walked behind the bar and ran his fingers across the bottles of whisky until he found the one he wanted, Talisker. He poured a healthy measure.

'Ice?'

'I'd love to say yes, but I bet you'd frown upon that, wouldn't you?'

'Aye. Whisky is best enjoyed neat at room temperature, and the ice only serves to distil the flavour as it melts. But each to their own.'

'I'll take it neat, thanks.'

'So, what is your line of work?' asked Brian as he returned to the seating area and placed the glass on the table, before lifting his own in a toast. '*Slàinte Mhath*.'

'I'm a police officer, a detective inspector.'

'Oh right, good for you. I didn't see you leave this morning, but I heard that you joined the search for wee Florence this morning.'

'That's right, unfortunately we came up empty-handed.'

'Must be like a busman's holiday for you, this week?'

Calvert smiled, 'that's the second time I've heard that today. Yes, I guess so.'

'Have you found much time to relax since your arrival on Wednesday?'

'Yes, some, although I don't see much relaxation over the next few days.'

Calvert proceeded to tell them both about the request from Superintendent Talloch, and his acceptance of stepping into the role of senior investigating officer for two or three days.

'Do you have family back home, Paul?'

'Yes, a daughter, Lisa, and son, Carl. Both grown up now, well in the eyes of the law they're grown up, although I'm not so sure about their maturity, especially the lad.'

'And a wife?'

Calvert paused, long enough for Brian to know that it wasn't a simple answer. 'Sorry, maybe a husband?'

Calvert smiled, 'no, a wife. She passed away earlier this year.'

'Oh, I'm sorry. I didn't mean to pry, ignore me.'

'That's fine,' replied Calvert. Then he had an unexplained urge to continue, to open up and divulge his life story to these two relative strangers.

'Her name was Melissa. She was initially diagnosed with breast cancer about seven years ago, she was only forty-four. At the time she had a double mastectomy followed by an intense course of chemotherapy. All appeared well for a number of years, life returned to normal, and she went back to her job, but last year we were advised that the cancer had returned. She fought a tough six-month battle, but in the end, cancer won.'

'How old was she, Paul?'

'Fifty-one.'

'That's no age at all, is it?'

'She passed away in January this year having spent the Christmas and New Year period in palliative care at the Dove House Hospice.'

'It sounds like it took its toll on you too.'

Calvert forced a smile. 'It was difficult watching her deteriorate over time. She had been fit, energetic and super healthy. She always did the 5K park run every Saturday morning, and although she stopped after her surgery, she did pick it back up again when she had recovered. But her final days in the hospice, well let's just say, it was still the Melissa that we all knew and loved but the life had all but drained away.'

All three took a sip from their glass tumblers in almost perfect synchronicity. Calvert looked to change the subject.

'So,' he started as his eyes moved from Brian to Antonio, then back to Brian, 'tell me, how did you two meet?'

Brian looked at Antonio with a look of a man who had only just left the wedding ceremony, and clearly the eleven years since had done nothing to dampen their love.

'In Majorca.'

'Majorca?'

'Yes, I was on holiday. Ten days in the sun. I went on my own, well…because I was single, and well…one night I got chatting to this gorgeous barman at an ultra-trendy club on the beach front. I remember he had a linen white shirt with enough buttons open to reveal his toned physique, a fantastic mane of hair, and chiselled Mediterranean features.'

Brian paused for a second to look at Antonio; 'then after he left the club, I met Antonio.'

Brian laughed, Calvert smiled, but Antonio failed to

see the funny side, or perhaps didn't quite understand. His English was good, but sometimes Brian's dialect would catch him out. The usual words that were easy to understand and comprehend would morph into a language that Antonio thought might as well have been Swahili.

'I have something to do, I'll be back in ten minutes,' announced Antonio as he stood and exited the room.

'To be honest with you, Paul,' Brian leant in towards him, 'I'm a little surprised we've lasted all these years.'

'Why do you say that?'

'Well, I'm fifty-seven years old now, and he's coming up thirty-nine next birthday. I thought the magic might have worn off, I thought he might have got fed up with me by now and gone back home. Add to which, Kelvedie couldn't be further away from Majorca both in terms of distance and climate. There's no sunbathing in your budgie smugglers here in summer, I don't mind telling you.'

'Age is just a number, Brian. Can I give you some advice? From someone who has recently lost their soulmate.'

'Of course.'

'Plan as though you'll live forever but live every day as though it's your last.'

'Very true. One of your own pearls of wisdom?'

'Good God, no. A slight rewording of a quote from James Dean, I believe.'

'Well, I'm dating a hot Spanish waiter who is twenty years my junior, and I'm running my own successful business, so I would say that I'm not doing too badly.'

'I agree, good for you.'

'I'm hungry,' said Brian, 'would you care to join myself and Antonio for a snack? The kitchen is closed, obviously, but I can rustle up something.'

'I didn't know that you did food, to be honest, well lunch or dinner.'

'We are predominantly a bed and breakfast, we don't provide lunch, but we do offer a dinner service for those that request. You just need to book with twenty-four hours' notice.'

'Okay, thanks, that's good to know. I'm okay, but thanks for the offer. And with that, I'll bid you a good night.'

'Goodnight, Paul.'

CHAPTER 11

For most families, Sunday morning would be a lazy affair. A later alarm, if there were one at all, and relaxing in pyjamas reading the newspaper whilst drinking your weight in coffee, perhaps wondering if your own *lazy good-for-nothing teenagers* were going to surface this side of noon. Not for Callum and Aileen Findlay.

Aileen had been awake and downstairs sitting at the kitchen table since five am, although she was lucky if she had an hour of deep sleep at all during the night. She was joined in the kitchen at six am by Callum.

'Morning.'

Aileen smiled at him but didn't respond.

'I heard you get up in the night, a couple of times actually.'

'Yes, sorry, I couldn't sleep. I came downstairs at two,

and probably back up to bed about three. I'm not sure that I slept much.'

'Me neither.'

Aileen looked at him with a stern but playful scorn. 'You lying sod, I heard you snoring for most of the night. It was one of the reasons that I came downstairs.'

They smiled at each other.

'Well at least you managed to get some sleep.'

There was a brief pause in conversation, then Aileen asked in a soft, sullen, and almost heartbroken tone, 'I wonder what my baby is doing right now? Where she is, is she safe? Is she with someone that she knows, someone that we know?'

'I don't know, sweetheart, I really don't. I know it probably sounds terrible, but I hope that wherever she is, she is with someone that she knows. It might be...' he paused '...the best thing we can hope for at the minute.'

'But why haven't they brought her home, Callum? Why haven't they brought her home?'

'I don't know,' replied Callum, dejected and despondent at not being able to reassure his wife, and to provide her with the answers that she was so desperately seeking.

Aileen broke down in tears and he moved closer to wrap his arms around her.

'What do you want to do today?' he asked almost nonchalantly as though they might consider a day trip to the seaside, or browsing at the nearest shopping mall, were this a normal Sunday. Aileen knew that wasn't what he meant.

'I want to see the family liaison officer…' She looked as though she was struggling to recall her name.

'PC Jackie Macallan,' said Callum.

'Yes, Jackie. Is she due to come today?'

'I'm not sure to be honest, it's Sunday, but if we needed to see her, I'm sure she would come through.'

'I want an update on what is happening. I want to know what the police are doing to find Florence.'

'I'm sure they are working flat out, and doing all they can.'

'Are they though, Callum, are they?'

'Well…' Truth be told, Callum was as unsure as Aileen.

'Why haven't they organised one of those press conferences? You know, the ones that you see on TV when someone goes missing. Appealing for witnesses and…' she paused '…providing telephone numbers for people to call in with details. Surely the more people that know she is missing, the more people will be keeping an eye out for her, or maybe someone has seen her and knows where she is.'

Callum agreed that whilst his knowledge was limited, he was aware of previous press conferences that had been broadcast on television, and the investigation of the missing person in question had become more high profile as a result. He had also seen similar press conferences held when police were trying to locate a known suspect, someone suspected of a crime.

'I also read that we should be posting on social media, and there are lots of dedicated websites where you can leave a post on message boards.'

'Message boards? Who is going to read them? Who trawls through dedicated websites for missing kids, reading messages from their parents?'

'It's not just for children, there are messages left for teenage runaways or adults that are missing too. It raises awareness, and I think that some parents leave messages for their missing child, hoping that they might see it, and asking them to come home.'

'Aileen, she's nine.'

'Yes, Callum,' she replied quite sternly, 'I know. In our circumstance, maybe it will raise awareness and ensure that more people are keeping an eye out for her. What have we got to lose?'

'Well, yes. Perhaps have a look later this morning, although…' it had just dawned on him that the police had taken their laptop and iPad '…I'll speak to Jackie and see when we can get our laptop back. I don't know why they have it, to be honest. She's bloody nine years old. What can there possibly be on the laptop that will help find her? They want to dedicate more resource on the street out looking, knocking on doors, and less in windowless basement rooms staring at fucking laptops.'

The Sunday morning drive to Lochgilphead station was a pleasant one, meandering through the countryside on the road that hugged the shore of Loch Fyne. The sun had been quick to rise a couple of hours earlier, and the clear blue sky signalled its intent to allow the sun to work overtime today, radiating its heat across Western Scotland. It was a far cry from his usual commute in East Yorkshire; once out of his quaint village setting, he quickly set upon the grim areas of the outskirts of Hull, areas that had seen decades of underinvestment from both business and successive local councils. Added to which, the sheer volume of traffic made his journey twice as long as it might without a clear run. Unlike Manchester or even its Yorkshire counterpart Sheffield, Hull had not invested in a tramway system. The light railway transport network carried tens of thousands of commuters towards their city centre jobs every day, and arguably probably removed the same volume of cars from the city roads. No, this morning's commute was one to be enjoyed, to be savoured, to be remembered.

Lochgilphead station was as quiet as Calvert had expected when he pulled into the car park just before eight am. With a total staff compliment of seven, he would be the eighth, even if for a brief period, although today he would find himself and three others. Sergeant O'Brien, Constable Davidson and Constable Crossman were on duty today and had been assigned to support Calvert as and where needed, although as the only police officers on duty in the area, they would still need to be available for anything reactive.

Calvert understood the challenges of policing a rural area with a limited team of officers, but hoped that those that had been assigned to support, would be available to support. He didn't much fancy conducting the misper investigation with *me, myself, and I.*

After the opening pleasantries of the day, Calvert made a brief statement attesting to his commitment concerning what he hoped and expected would be no more than two or three days. Not that his commitment would waver beyond this period, nor be affected by the fact that within three days he was likely to be relieved by the returning DCI Geary from his curtailed Jamaican holiday. No, he was adamant, and optimistic, that they would locate young Florence Findlay within the next seventy-two hours. His optimism was shared by the collective, albeit outwardly anyway.

'Right, let's have a quick roundup on a number of areas,' started Calvert, 'we took Florence's mobile phone and the family laptop and iPad, I believe. What have the tech guys come up with?'

'Nothing so far, guv,' replied Constable Davidson as he opened his notebook for reference, 'we took the electronics yesterday, so they haven't had a great deal of time yet. The tech team have been through the social media accounts; Facebook, Instagram and TikTok…'

'Hang on a minute, Tik what?' asked Calvert.

'TikTok,' confirmed Davidson.

'Never heard of it.'

'You're definitely showing your age there, guv.'

The sergeant and both constables smiled at each other.

'Have you?' asked Calvert towards Sergeant O'Brien, 'heard of TikTik?'

'TikTok,' politely corrected O'Brien, 'yes, guv, but only

because I have a couple of teenage daughters. It's not something that I use myself.'

Crossman advised, 'it's a social media site where you create and share short videos, between a couple of seconds, up to a minute long.'

'Videos of what?'

'Well, anything. Singing, dancing, anything to increase your profile and hope that the video is shared and goes viral.'

'Why?' asked a bemused Calvert.

'Indeed,' replied O'Brien, 'isn't that the overarching question to pose about all social media, just, why?'

'Anyway, the tech team have spent a few hours so far trawling through Florence's social media accounts but haven't found anything that would help us. No messages, pictures or videos that provide any insight into her disappearance. The posts are the usual stuff you would expect from a nine-year-old girl.'

'Don't you need to be a certain age to have these social media accounts?' asked Calvert, partially knowingly and partially winging it.

'Yes, thirteen I believe it is, guv,' confirmed Davidson.

'That's right,' Crossman affirmed.

'Well, how the bloody hell does a nine-year-old set up multiple social media accounts?' he asked, now somewhat naively.

'They lie about their date of birth, you know, when registering for the account on the app.'

'And then…' Calvert stopped '…ah, it doesn't matter. We're digressing.'

'Guv.'

'And beyond social media?'

'They haven't got that far yet.'

'We're running out of time.'

'They promise today, guv. They have got some kind of whizzy software that helps them analyse the files on electronic devices like laptops. So, I'm sure we have further feedback later today.'

'Okay. Keep me updated when we hear anything more. Whilst I don't profess to be an expert on social media myself, my past experience with mispers has shown that social media can give us a valuable insight into a person's mindset prior to their disappearance. Unless they were taken suddenly and without their consent, obviously, then we aren't likely to find anything useful.'

'Is that what you're thinking, guv, that Florence was abducted?'

'It's becoming a stronger probability as each hour passes by. For me, I just don't see a nine-year-old as a runaway. She's just too young. Unfortunately, that potentially leaves us with the stark reality that she is being held against her consent…or even worse.'

There was a brief pause in the dialogue and an emerging sense that the investigation might, just might, take a darker turn.

'Tell me about the door-to-door enquiries from

yesterday.'

'Door-to-door of the full village was done yesterday afternoon,' advised Crossman, 'there was little point doing it first thing in the morning as quite a lot of the residents had joined the search. Half a dozen of us completed it in a couple of hours.'

'And?'

'Nothing, guv. Almost everyone confirmed that they had not seen Florence for a few days, and no-one had seen her on the Friday evening, or earlier in the day yesterday.'

'Aside from the tech, did we ask her parents if Florence kept a diary?'

'We did, guv, and we had a search throughout her bedroom, but didn't find anything.'

'Okay. I'm going to see the parents this morning. There are a number of things that I would like you to crack on with whilst I'm gone. Firstly, can you check the missing persons index for any other misper within a fifty-mile radius of Kelvedie.'

'How far back should we go, guv?'

'Make it five years to start with please,' he paused, 'but, I discovered last night that the Findlays have another daughter.'

'Aye, that's right, Hayley. She went missing too about ten years ago if memory serves me right.'

'Yes. Take the mispers back five years but pull me everything that you can find on the disappearance of Hayley Findlay too.'

'Yes, guv.'

'And finally, I'm not sure what has been done in the preceding twenty-four hours, perhaps this has all be done, but if not, let's close the circle with social services and the local safeguarding team. I want to know if either of the girls were on the at-risk register, or if either the children or parents were known to the authorities. Can we also liaise with the PNMPB, I know they generally gather information from…'

Calvert stopped. He could see the bemused faces of the two constables and wasn't entirely sure about Sergeant O'Brien either.

'…The Police National Missing Persons Bureau?'

'Sorry, guv, not familiar with them,' advised Crossman.

'That's probably answered your question about the last five years' mispers, guv,' noted O'Brien.

'Yes, possibly. Anyway, the PNMPB collects reports of vulnerable mispers which are still outstanding after fourteen days, but also acts as a data point for mispers where the person has still not been found after seventy-two hours. Clearly, we are not at that point yet, but can you give them a call and see if we can submit our report now as our misper falls within the vulnerable person category, plus ask them if they have any other information or data that they can share that might be useful to our investigation.'

'Like what, guv?'

'Well, they have gathered and collated information on thousands of missing persons going back twenty or thirty years. When, or if, the person is found they will also update the information.'

'I get that, they keep the records up to date, but I'm not sure how that helps us?'

'Well, we all know the high-level figures, ninety-seven percent of missing people either return home or are found dead within a week; and within twelve months, this increases to ninety-nine percent. We also know that 0.1 percent of all abductions are by strangers to the abductee. These high-level stats are drilled into us as part of our initial and any ongoing refresher training, but the PNMPB is able to tailor some of the historical data to help with new investigations.'

'Such as?' asked an eager PC Crossman.

'Well, it's not an exact science of course, but the historical data may tell us that X-percent of abductions involving a female minor turned out to be one of the parents, or Y-percent was a family relative, and Z-percent was a stranger. I'm expecting that, based on age and gender, it will give us some probabilities of the most likely places to find Florence.'

'Okay, I guess it can't hurt. We'll get on it, guv.'

Looking at the two constables, Calvert asked, 'can I leave most of these tasks to you if I take Sergeant O'Brien with me?'

Calvert looked towards O'Brien, who nodded his approval.

Calvert and O'Brien pulled up outside the Findlay house just before eleven am. There were five or six cars parked on the roadside, and Calvert's first thought was that he hoped the Findlays didn't have a houseful of guests. As they started up the garden path, the front door opened and out stepped four people. They hugged, offered their best wishes, and turned to walk towards the gate.

'I think we timed that just right,' whispered O'Brien. Calvert smiled his agreement.

'Mrs Findlay.' Calvert withdrew his warrant card from his jacket pocket. Despite being off duty and on a period of leave in what was effectively another country, Calvert like most other police officers tended to carry his warrant card with him wherever he went, holiday or not.

'I'm Detective Inspector Calvert, and this is Sergeant O'Brien. May we come in?'

Calvert and O'Brien followed Aileen through the hallway and straight to the kitchen diner.

Before she offered them a drink, or a seat, she asked, 'you haven't….'

'No, Mrs Findlay, we haven't come with bad news,' confirmed Calvert, having correctly anticipated the back end of her incomplete question.

His response brought a forced smile from Aileen, just as Callum entered the room.

'Hello, I thought I heard voices, well, more voices.'

'You've had one or two this morning, I understand.'

'Aye, they're all well intentioned, but they are distracting us from finding Florence.'

'Well, it's probably time that you left that solely to the police now.'

'Sorry, who are you?' asked Callum, guessing Calvert was a police officer, not least of all because his colleague was a uniformed sergeant.

'Sorry. Detective Inspector Calvert.'

'Ah, at last, a senior officer. Finally, we are being taken seriously.'

'Callum, may I call you Callum?' He didn't receive much of a reply, so he continued regardless.

'Callum, let me assure you that the disappearance of Florence is being taken very seriously by not only the police, but at least half a dozen other services too. There is a significant amount of resource currently allocated to the investigation, and whilst I might be the most senior officer that you have met to date, again let me reassure you that there isn't an officer within a hundred miles who isn't aware of Florence's disappearance, and that includes Superintendent Talloch.'

Again, Calvert didn't receive much in the way of a response or an acknowledgement.

'Is your family liaison officer due today?'

'Yes,' confirmed Aileen, 'I believe so. She's lovely. She has been keeping us up to date with what's going on and what we can expect over the next few days if Florence still hasn't been found.'

'Okay. Let's hope it doesn't come to that, eh. We are

all working very hard to bring Florence back home safe and sound.'

'Thank you, inspector.'

'Make sure you stay engaged with your FLO as much as possible. She is your direct link to the investigation and will be able to provide you with as much up-to-date information as she can. Now, I know that officers have already taken a laptop and an iPad, but are you aware if Florence kept a diary, or a journal, at all?'

Aileen was fairly quick in her confident response; 'no.'

'Okay, are you one hundred percent sure? Young girls, or boys for that matter, are renowned for keeping secret diaries.'

'Yes, I'm sure.'

'I guess it wouldn't be secret if we knew about it.' Callum directed his comment towards his wife.

'I'm sure. Trust me, a mother would know these things. And…she's only nine years old.'

'Right, okay. Thanks for that. Whilst we are here, I would like to have a look around Florence's room. Would that be okay?'

'Yes of course. Shall I show you?'

Aileen led Calvert up the stairs and into Florence's bedroom. Having had a nine-year-old daughter himself, albeit some years ago, Calvert was pleased to see that young girls' bedrooms had remained pretty much the same over the years. Posters adorned the walls: Little Mix, Dua Lipa and Ed Sheeran had replaced the likes of Beyoncé, Britney

Spears and Usher. CD players had been replaced with iPhone docking stations, but a nine-year-old girl's bedroom was still furnished with plenty of books, cute furry cuddly animals and a character-based matching curtains and duvet combo.

Calvert looked through drawers, leafed through books, picked up and put things down, all with the respect and sensitivity expected. He hadn't learned a great deal, apart from that Florence probably didn't keep a personal diary, and that she looked to be a very ordinary nine-year-old girl.

Calvert indicated that he had finished and was about to walk out of the room when Aileen asked, 'can I ask you something, inspector?'

'Yes, of course.'

'I've been reading about these websites where you can post messages about missing people in the hope that they will be read and shared. What do you think?'

'Well...' Calvert sat beside her on Florence's bed, 'firstly, I would say that it is the police force who are most likely to find Florence using the vast resources at our disposal. People, systems, databases. Our reach is extensive, and our knowledge and, as sad as it is to say, our experience in this area is significant. Having said that, the more people who become aware of a missing person, the better the chances are that they will be found. You can start by sending out an email to everyone you know who knows Florence and request they help spread the word, perhaps they can send their own email to everyone they know, and so on. Social media is a great way to communicate with lots of different people and a useful tool when it comes to getting the message out about Florence. Make a post on Facebook or Twitter and include a picture and description of her, and publicise the fact you're looking for her, and ask that people share the post. Are you a Facebook user?'

'Yes.'

'In the case of missing children, Facebook now ensures that posts about high-risk cases appear high up in the news feeds of users who are located within the areas where officials are searching. These alerts are part of the police's Child Rescue Alerts scheme.'

'It sounds worth doing.'

'As a police officer I would say that you should trust the police force to locate Florence and bring her home safely, but as a father myself, I would probably be thinking the same thing, and looking to ensure that the whole country was out looking for her.'

'What about Next Door?'

'I don't know what you mean, Next Door, you mean your neighbours?'

'No, there is another online platform that I read about called Next Door, a social media platform made for local communities. You create a post asking if anyone on the area has seen Florence.'

'In principle I would say it's a good idea, but I would guess that it is targeted at large towns rather than small rural communities like Kelvedie. Firstly, how many people here will have heard of this social media platform? And secondly, from what I have seen so far, almost all of the community are already aware of Florence's disappearance, and would, I assume, have come forward to either yourself or the police if they had sighted her since Friday evening.'

'Yes, I suppose you're right. I'll leave that one alone then.'

'I would, Mrs Findlay, I would.'

'Did you learn anything from that visit, guv?' asked O'Brien during the drive back to the station.

'Not a lot, to be honest. I really just wanted to meet the parents, to put faces to names. But the one thing I do know for sure is that irrespective of her relatively young age, Florence did not run away from home. I'm one hundred percent sure that we are looking at something more disturbing, sergeant.'

'Yes, I thought that you might say that. I agree. Someone has taken young Florence, and the outcome looks bleaker with every passing hour.'

'It does, although truth be told, there is a high probability that she is already dead.'

Calvert didn't mince his words and had said out loud what some of the officers had been starting to think. Still, they were hopeful and optimistic and would remain that way right up to finding Florence, alive or dead.

Upon their return to the station at Lochgilphead, Calvert and Sergeant O'Brien found Crossman and Davidson at their desks, exactly where they had been some three hours ago.

'Any updates to share?'

Crossman started, 'the missing persons index hasn't provided any info, guv, certainly not within the parameters of a two-year time period and a fifty-miles radius.'

'Okay, thanks. I don't think that it is worth widening those parameters for now. There's only one pattern that is opening up.'

The team looked expectantly for Calvert to conclude. He didn't, although each of them knew where he was going with his incomplete statement.

'Social services?'

'Yes, guv. Neither of the parents are known to social services, and Florence isn't on the at-risk register. In fact, the only time that either Callum or Aileen appear on anyone's radar is the disappearance of their other daughter, Hayley.'

'Yes, hold that thought, I want to come back to that. And the PNMPB?'

'Report filed, guv. They promised to review and report back with any kind of profile and potential scenarios within forty-eight hours.'

'Forty-eight hours? Too bloody late. Get back onto them and tell them that we want something tomorrow.'

'Yes, guv.'

'And finally, guv, we've extended the awareness all across Scotland through the usual channels. Didn't think it would do any harm.'

'Agreed, well done. Right, let's refresh our coffees then let's get into the detail on the Findlays' other daughter. A story that I found out about last night actually, from some of the villagers in Kelvedie.'

'So, I have to admit that what I know about Hayley Findlay is limited to twenty minutes of conversation in the pub last night. Some of the villagers that were in last night had fairly strong opinions, whereas others were simply bewildered that one family could be beset by so much tragedy.'

'I was a constable at the time, guv,' said Sergeant O'Brien, 'but I remember the case quite well. We don't get many juvenile disappearances around here, and as Hayley is still missing, this case is one that still haunts some of us.'

'I understand. Take me back to the very beginning and talk me through the timeline.'

'Sure. Well, it was back in 2011, May, if I recall correctly. Hayley Findlay aged nine, left her parents' house and went to play in the nearby park on Leslie Street. She left to walk there on her own, but it was only two minutes away and her mother said that she had allowed her to do so a few times before. She said that she had no concerns about her safety. Hindsight is a wonderful thing, but she believed that the village was safe, and that Hayley was old enough and responsible enough to walk to the park and back. Anyway, after a while, Mrs Findlay took a stroll to the park to check on Hayley, but when she arrived there was no sign of her. There were no witnesses that actually saw her in the park, but her mum did find a doll under the climbing frame, or something, that she had taken with her to the park. So, we were pretty sure that she had at least made it to the park.'

'She was on her own then?'

'Yes, all of her friends were interviewed and none of them met her in the park, or anywhere else in the village that day. Anyway, both parents searched the village, rang family and friends, and called on neighbours before calling the police.'

'That sounds familiar.'

'Doesn't it just?'

'So, give me the highlights from the investigation,' asked Calvert.

'Well, appropriate resources were mobilised. DCI Ken Glenratty was the SIO at the time.'

'Glenratty?'

'Yes, guv. He's retired now.'

'Okay.'

'To be honest, there was no discernible breakthrough, and leads were in short supply. Both parents were called in for questioning, and the dad, Callum, was pulled in several times,' he paused for a second and looked pensive 'if I remember correctly, Inspector Mason was closely involved in the investigation. She would have been a sergeant at the time, I guess. Anyway, there was much suspicion that one or both parents were involved in some way, but there was no evidence. No-one was arrested, let alone charged, and to this day it remains an open case.'

'And here we are ten years later, looking down the barrel of another missing person with an almost identical situation. Do you believe in co-incidence, sergeant?'

'Me? No, guv.'

'No, me neither.'

CHAPTER 12

Superintendent Talloch checked the time as the incoming call awakened her as yet dormant mobile phone. It was just before eight am, and the phone displayed a number that she didn't recognise.

'Morning, ma'am, it's DI Calvert, not too early I hope?'

'Of course not, I'm just on my way into the office. Is it a long one?'

'A long what?'

'Call. I'm driving, do I need to pull over?'

'Yes, ma'am, that's probably wise.' Calvert wanted to ensure that he had her full attention, and wasn't sure if she was driving, or being driven.

'I want to set up a press conference, and I'm sure that I need your approval to do so, correct?'

'Correct. Remind me again, how long since the disappearance?'

Calvert checked his watch, although he didn't need to. He was acutely aware of both the current time and the elapsed time since Florence went missing. He also wanted to ensure that Talloch was reminded that this was a little girl.

'Florence. Florence Findlay, and she has been missing for sixty-three hours.'

'Florence, yes. Where are we with the investigation? Any leads?'

'To be honest, ma'am, we have nothing positive at present.'

'You do know that most…' She was cut short by Calvert.

'Yes, ma'am.' Calvert wanted to remind her that this wasn't his first rodeo, but chose a more restrained response. 'I am all too aware that there is a high probability that one or more parents, or other close family members, might be involved in the disappearance of a minor. This is to become our main line of enquiry moving forward, but I wanted to ensure that we cover all bases, and that we don't miss the opportunity to raise awareness with the wider public too. You know, in case Florence is still alive and was abducted by someone outside of the family circle.'

'Are you proposing a police-only press conference, or one with the parents included?'

'One with the parents I think, ma'am. We have nothing

at present to suggest or suspect any foul play so it's probably right that they are involved for this.'

'I agree. How do you think they will hold up?'

'Well, I haven't spent a lot of time with them, but I've spoken at length with the family liaison officer, and she is confident that they will be fine. Do you have a press liaison officer that can help put this together with me?'

'Indeed, we do, her name is Siobhan Campbell and I'll get her to come and see you this morning.'

'Thanks, ma'am.'

'Will you be at Lochgilphead?'

'Yes, ma'am.' Calvert hadn't said *ma'am* this many times for as long as he could remember, let alone in five minutes.

'Okay, Siobhan will keep me up to date with the details. I assume that you'll be needing me to attend?'

'Yes, ma'am, seems appropriate, don't you think? I'm happy to lead as I am SIO, or just as happy for you to lead.'

'I'll open up with some introductions and headlines, then pass over to you, if that suits?'

'That's fine, ma'am. Right, I'll let you go, and I'll look out for Siobhan later this morning. Bye.'

'Lisa, hi, how are you?'

'Hi, Dad, is this a good time?'

'Sure, I've just sat down with a coffee.'

'I haven't caught you at breakfast, have I?'

'Breakfast? No, I was up and about early this morning.

I'm at the station now.'

'The station?'

'Yes…' he paused for the briefest of seconds, 'I guess I need to update you since our last chat on Friday.'

'I guess you do. What have you got yourself into?'

'Well, the short version is that I'm working for Police Scotland for a few days.'

'Bloody hell, Dad,' said Lisa with more than a hint of exasperation in her voice, 'you went there to relax for a week. You know, lazy lie-ins, long walks in the countryside, and knowing you, one or two glasses of whisky. What's the long version then?'

'Well, on Friday late afternoon or early evening, a young girl went missing in the village where I'm staying, and on Saturday morning I joined a group of volunteers looking for her.'

'How awful. Any luck?'

'No, I'm afraid not, she is still missing.'

'So, you are still helping the local police then, in what capacity?'

'As senior investigating officer.'

'SIO.' Lisa was familiar with most police acronyms having heard her father's parlance first hand over the years. 'How and why are questions that spring to mind, Dad?'

'Well, the how and why are pretty much the same to be honest. After I volunteered to support the search on Saturday morning, I ended up meeting the superintendent.'

'And…'

'And it was a case of right place, right time due to a set of unfortunate circumstances.'

'You mean wrong place, wrong time?'

'Possibly. Both of her senior DCIs are away on leave, and the local inspector was injured during the search on Saturday.'

'Injured?'

'Yes, nothing major, well…she fell and broke something, an ankle, a leg, I can't remember. Anyway, she will be off work for a few weeks too. I was asked if I would step in for two or three days to ensure the investigation continues with some momentum, and I said yes. So here I am.'

'Isn't there anyone else that can do it, Dad? Scotland must have thousands of police officers, and you're on leave, remember.'

'It's just for a few days. This is my second day, and I've been told that one of the DCIs will be back from his leave tomorrow, or the day after latest.'

'Yes, well make sure it is your last day, and do not,' she stressed, 'offer to remain as a consultant or some other advisory role. Promise me.'

'God, you sound like your mother. I promise, Lisa, I promise.'

'Right. Good. Anyway, what about this poor young girl?'

'Well, she's just nine years old, and went missing late on Friday afternoon. To be honest, we're struggling for any meaningful leads at present, but we have a press conference to arrange soon, and we remain optimistic. You know me.'

'Indeed, I do. Right, I've got to go. I'll check in with you again tomorrow.'

'Looking forward to it already, Lisa.'

'Sarcastic git. Love you. Bye.'

Siobhan Campbell, the press liaison officer, arrived promptly just after midday. She had called Calvert shortly after his call with Superintendent Talloch and had arranged a mutually convenient time to meet. Calvert had noted that she sounded very young on the phone, and that her well-spoken Scottish accent was soft and rounded, and no doubt hailed from more on the east side of the country. Either way, she sounded quite sexy. A thought that Calvert did not share with her at the time.

Siobhan was shown into the room where a waiting Calvert rose to greet her. She was indeed quite young, perhaps in her late twenties he thought. Her smart navy suit, comprising of a pencil skirt and tailored jacket, complemented by a crisp white blouse and those all-important killer heels, marked her out as a high-flying advertising or public relations executive. Certainly not acting as a go-between for the police and local media, although Calvert was sure that she, if asked, would define her role as somewhat more valuable and influential amongst both sides of the table.

'DI Calvert?' She held out her hand, which was taken.
'Correct.'

'Siobhan Campbell, nice to meet you.'

'Likewise.'

'So, Superintendent Talloch informed me that you are wanting to arrange a press conference in relation to a missing person investigation.'

'That's right, yes. A young girl from a local village, Kelvedie, do you know it?'

'No, sorry, I can't say that I do. I hail from Prestonpans, a relatively small town east of Edinburgh. Can't say that I've spent a great deal of time in and around Argyll.'

'Ah, okay. Anyway…'

'When are you wanting to arrange this for?'

'Tomorrow, sometime tomorrow ideally.'

'Okay, that should be fine. Usually, we would issue a briefing pack for each attendee just as they arrive. Is that something that you can help pull together?'

'Yes of course.' Again thoughts of this not being his first rodeo were bubbling towards the forefront of his lips, but he suppressed any desire to gently propel this down her throat. 'What would you need in the pack?'

'Well, a photo of the missing person…'

'Florence. Her name is Florence.'

'Yes of course, sorry. A photo of Florence, and a one-page statement with all the details that you wish to convey about the investigation. The stuff that I know you will go through verbally during the press conference anyway.'

From his seated position, Calvert reached over to the board and tugged at the colour photograph of Florence that was held by sticky tape. 'Here, let's use this. This is the most recent photo that we have, and the one that we have been using in the investigation. It was released to us by her parents, so there should be no problems using this across all media platforms.'

'Great, thank you. And the statement?'

'I'll get that written up later today and emailed across to you if that's okay?'

'That will be great, thank you. Will it just be yourself and Superintendent Talloch, or will Florence's parents be participating?'

'The plan is that both parents will be there. I need to speak to them first and make sure that they are comfortable with it, but yes, the plan would be for them to attend and make some kind of statement in front of the press.'

'Okay. If you need any support on scripting or pointers on what we might want them to say, just shout and I'll be glad to help.'

'Appreciate that, thank you, Siobhan. Fortunately, or unfortunately, whichever way you want to look at it, I'm an old hand at these things, having attended more than my fair share of press conferences.'

'Right, okay. I haven't seen you before, and I support most police units across Western Scotland.'

'No, you won't have met me before, Siobhan, I'm a detective inspector with the Humberside Police Force, in Hull.'

'Right. Have you recently relocated to Scotland?'

Calvert couldn't help but smile broadly and briefly chuckle.

'Have I said something wrong?' continued Siobhan.

'No, no you haven't. If I told you that I am still a serving police officer in England, and I arrived in Scotland, Kelvedie to be specific, five days ago on a week's holiday, would you believe me?'

'What? And now you're SIO on a missing persons investigation? I would say that there is probably far more to the story than you have conveyed so far.'

'Well, not much more, to be honest with you.'

Calvert spent the next ten to fifteen minutes walking Siobhan through the timeline and key activities over the last five days, eventually ending up right at the present day.

'Bloody hell. Now that's dedication.'

'Well…perhaps right place, right time.'

'Or wrong place, wrong time.'

Calvert chuckled again.

'I spoke to my daughter earlier this morning, just after I had spoken to Superintendent Talloch, and she said exactly the same thing; wrong place, wrong time.'

'How long has she been missing, Florence?'

Calvert took a quick look at his wristwatch; he didn't need long for the calculations as every hour that passed was indelibly engrained in his mind as an hour further away from finding Florence safe and well.

'Sixty-eight hours.'

CHAPTER 13

Calvert had made a phone call to the Findlays late the previous afternoon to advise them of his intention to hold a press conference. Their initial reluctance to appear in front of a room full of journalists, and ultimately on television, baring their emotions, was completely understandable, Calvert had advised. And whilst he would not force them into appearing, he did ask them both to think about it overnight, and that they would talk again in the morning.

Superintendent Talloch had suggested to Calvert that he might move to a hotel nearer the police station, and with all expenses paid, but he was happy to remain at Shallowbrook Lodge in Kelvedie. As such, his travelling time this morning from there to the Findlay residence was to be less than five minutes. He had advised Callum and

Aileen that he would be with them just after nine am, and that he would arrange for the family liaison officer to accompany him too.

The FLO, Jackie Macallan, had been asked to meet Calvert at the B&B prior to the attending the Findlay house, and she arrived promptly at eight am as requested. After having been greeted by Brian, she was taken through to the dining room where Calvert was to be found tucking into a full Scottish breakfast.

'Sorry, sir, I didn't realise that you would be having breakfast, I'll wait near reception.'

'Nonsense, sit yourself down,' Calvert gestured towards the chair opposite, 'can we get you a breakfast?'

'No, thank you, sir.'

'Are you sure? The black pudding is fantastic.'

'No, thank you.'

'Well, some coffee then?

'Coffee would be great, thank you.'

He looked up towards Brian. 'Brian, some more coffee please, and a few rounds of toast for my guest please.'

'Coming right up, Paul.'

Without lifting his eyes from his plate, and still whilst slicing a rasher of bacon, he asked, 'how long have you been a FLO, Jackie? Is it okay if I call you Jackie?'

'Yes, of course. I've been a police officer for twenty years, and a FLO for eighteen of those.'

'You must enjoy the work?'

'It has its ups and downs, as I'm sure you are all too

aware, but in the main it is very rewarding, yes. It certainly plays to my strengths, both as a police officer and as a person.'

'Good for you. I envy you.'

'Me?' she said, somewhat startled, 'what on earth for?'

'It's not a job that I could do. I've been a police officer for twenty-five years through various roles, and if I've learned anything during that time, it's that I don't have a natural sensitive and compassionate manner.'

'Not everyone does. I guess that's also why most FLOs are female.'

'Yeah, probably.'

Brian arrived with more coffee and enough toast to sink a battleship.

'Tuck in,' advised Calvert, 'the toast is for you.'

In between mouthfuls of buttered toast and piping hot coffee, Calvert spent the next fifteen to twenty minutes talking to Jackie about the press conference later that afternoon, and how he was looking for her support to convince Callum and Aileen to participate, should they still remain a little disinclined.

Jackie agreed, and advised Calvert that in her opinion they would agree.

Despite the Findlay house being a five-minute walk from the B&B, Calvert drove, and Jackie Macallan followed in her car. Calvert thought that they would, hopefully, leave directly for the venue of the press conference and wanted to ensure that his car was parked outside.

They were both shown through to the lounge and provided with coffee, but not before Calvert had managed to quietly remark to Macallan that he thought Aileen was looking particularly frazzled. Macallan was a little unsure that his choice of adjective was appropriate, but she too had noticed that Aileen looked as though she had little or no sleep last night.

'How are you both doing this morning?' asked Macallan. There was a look of despondency about the pair, and neither managed to formulate any kind of response.

'Did you get any sleep last night?'

'Some. Yes, a little.'

Her attention moved to Callum. 'And you?'

Macallan had seen a noticeable change in Callum over the last forty-eight hours. Initially he was angry, angry but focussed, focussed on practical matters that would help to find his daughter. He had quite probably scoured every inch of ground across Western Scotland in the first couple of days looking for Florence, or any sign of her, and he had proactively marshalled help and support from almost everyone in the village. But so far to no avail. Perhaps he was resigning himself to the fact that he would never see his daughter again, never read her a bedtime story, and that she would never come running to Daddy for comfort after falling down and grazing her knee. The fire in his belly was slowly being extinguished and, this morning at least, he looked like a captive male lion in a zoo, one that had been caught during its adolescence and had known the wilds of Africa, before being forced to live out its days in a two-acre field in some British countryside wildlife park, its natural predatory hunting instincts slowly dissipating with every day.

'Yes, some,' he finally confirmed.

'Callum, Aileen, have you had any further thoughts about the press conference later today?' asked Calvert.

'A little. We think that it's probably the right thing to do,' confirmed Callum, 'but we don't really know what we should be saying.'

'That's fine, Callum, we can help with that. We can either give you some pointers, some things to remember when you provide your statement, or we can script it for you completely and you can either rehearse it in advance, or simply read it out. Either is good, and it really doesn't matter.'

'What else do we need to know? Who will be there?'

'Well, firstly, don't worry too much about all the details, we've got everything covered. Just try to relax about it all. In terms of who will be there, sitting at the table facing the press, aside from yourself, there will be myself and Superintendent Talloch. You'll meet her beforehand, she's really nice. Jackie…' he looked towards her '…will be there too, as will our media liaison officer. In terms of the press, to be honest I'm not sure on numbers, but it will be just a few journalists. They will mainly be seated in front of us, and will represent both newspapers and television networks, so expect both flash cameras and television cameras. All small-scale stuff, it won't be set up like a television studio. It should be all fairly informal in a meeting room.'

'How long will we be there?'

'Well, we'll leave within the next hour, there's no rush, and aim to get there just after midday. I'll introduce you to Superintendent Talloch, and if you like we can have a look at the room before anyone arrives. Just a thought, it's up to you. The press briefing itself won't last more than fifteen or twenty minutes, even allowing for a limited number of questions; and I anticipate that your part will be no longer than a couple of minutes.'

'Questions?' Aileen looked worried.

'Don't worry, Aileen,' advised Macallan, 'we will only allow questions to be presented to the officers in attendance; isn't that right, sir?'

'It is, yes. The press will ask several questions, all of which we will either provide a response to, or we will deflect away. I would ask that you don't try to join any conversations or jump in with any responses. Best leave that to us, eh?'

'Yes, yes, of course.'

'Okay.'

'Does it matter what we wear?'

'No, Aileen, it doesn't,' advised Macallan, 'I suggest that you both wear something that you feel comfortable in. As the inspector said, it will only be twenty minutes or so.'

'Okay.' Aileen looked very nervous and Macallan

moved to sit beside her and took her hand.

'You don't need to do this, Aileen, if you don't want to, but we are all here for you, for you and Callum.'

'Would you do it, Jackie?'

'Honestly?' she started before pausing. Calvert held his breath.

'Yes, I would. Florence is still missing, and this is an opportunity to leverage the power of the media to help find her. I firmly believe that someone knows where Florence is, that someone may have seen her since her disappearance. We need to bring the awareness of Florence's disappearance to the wider public, ask for their help and support. It's a positive move, Aileen.'

She squeezed her hand tightly, reassuringly. Aileen looked at her husband and they shared a smile.

The tender emotional moment was broken by Calvert. 'Right, I'll wait in the car whilst you get yourselves ready.'

The ninety-minute drive to Greenock station was fairly uneventful, and for the most part made in silence. Callum and Aileen travelled with Calvert, and Macallan followed behind. Calvert had tried to stimulate conversation on a few occasions, staying away from all things Florence related, and chatting about subjects ranging from the local pub, The Plough, the eccentricities and relationship between the B&B owners Brian and Antonio, and things to pass the time in nearby Tarbert. He surmised that both Callum and Aileen were lost in their own world, flitting no doubt between the constant agony of not knowing where their daughter was, mixed with the understandable nerves and trepidation about the press conference.

He did, however, discover that The Waggon and Horses pub in nearby Tarbert did a cracking Sunday lunch should he want to venture there this coming weekend, although he was advised that he would need to ring and reserve to be guaranteed a table. Calvert stored it in the back of his mind in case, for any bizarre reason, he found himself still here in five days' time.

'Ma'am, this is Callum and Aileen Findlay.' Both were shown into the room as Calvert and Macallan followed and closed the door behind them. Talloch rose from her chair and approached to greet them.

'Hello, nice to meet you, I'm sorry it is under these circumstances. Take a seat, please.'

'Thank you.'

'Thank you for agreeing to do this, first of all. I know it's probably quite daunting, but I also know as a mother myself that you will do just about anything to see the safe return of Florence. And whilst there are no guarantees, clearly this will help. Getting the media on our side, and more importantly expanding the awareness through the general public, will mean that we have a much greater chance of finding Florence.'

'Alive or dead?' asked a sombre Callum.

'We are very much still hopeful, Callum. Try and stay

positive. DI Calvert and his team are doing all that is humanly possible to locate Florence.'

'I know. Sorry.'

'There's nothing to apologise for. Have we talked you through what to expect during the press conference?'

'Yes, we chatted about it earlier, before we set off.'

'Okay, that's good. You're in capable hands. Try not to worry, it will be done before you know.'

After a little more small talk, the meeting ended shortly after ten minutes, with Superintendent Talloch stating that everyone, the Findlays included, needed to prepare for the press conference.

The small group settled for a while in a room adjacent to where everyone would be gathering over the course of the next hour. With a pot of coffee and couple of Danish pastries, Macallan was doing her best to calm and reassure the Findlays whilst Calvert was off looking for the media liaison officer. He duly returned after ten minutes.

'Callum, Aileen, this is Siobhan Campbell, our media relations officer.'

'Hello.'

'Hello, Callum, hello, Aileen, how are you?' Her question was taken as rhetorical and didn't elicit any response.

'DI Calvert tells me that you wanted a little support with what you want to say.' Campbell took out a single piece of paper from a file she had been carrying. 'Have you decided which one of you is to speak?'

'Me,' said Callum.

Campbell passed Callum the piece of paper. 'We've scripted this brief statement for you as you requested, take a few moments to read it through. You can either read it out verbatim, or simply chose your own words and draw on some of the points raised. It can be very emotional, and if there is a key message to get across, it's best probably to read it so you don't miss anything. It's up to you of course.'

Campbell spent the next fifteen minutes talking the Findlays, and Calvert to some extent, through what they could expect to see and what the running order would be. Then she disappeared to greet and settle the journalists.

The group entered the room to the sound of camera flashes and lingering chatter between the journalists. Talloch entered first, followed by Callum, Aileen, Calvert and finally Siobhan Campbell, with the latter remaining standing and staying away from the gaze of any cameras, still or moving picture. The time was a little after two pm, and the remaining chatter died down as they took their seats at a table facing the assembled crowd.

Aileen looked ahead towards the faces staring at her. The room was packed, all the seats had been taken and there were a number of people standing towards the rear and sides of the seating area. She was nervous now, very nervous.

Superintendent Talloch cleared her throat. 'Thank you for attending this afternoon, I am Superintendent Talloch, to my left is Detective Inspector Calvert and Callum and Aileen Findlay. We will take some questions towards the end of the briefing, but for now we have a statement to make, and ultimately a plea for public support. Last Friday the fifteenth of July, late afternoon, around five pm, Florence Findlay went missing from near her home in Kelvedie, and has not been seen since. Florence is nine years old, and naturally the police and her parents, Callum and Aileen, are concerned for her safety. DI Calvert.'

Calvert took over the reins. 'The picture that you can see on the screen behind me is Florence Findlay.'

Calvert briefly looked over his shoulder towards the large flat-screen television that was mounted on the wall behind where they were seated.

'It was taken a few months ago and shows her in a school uniform. Florence went missing shortly after returning home from school on Friday afternoon. The clothes that she was wearing at the time are the same as you can see in the photograph: white blouse and a navy school cardigan with the school logo, Tarbert Comprehensive, embroidered on the left-hand side, grey pleated knee-length skirt, white socks and black shoes. Naturally her parents, Callum and Aileen, are very worried and are wanting the safe return of their daughter.'

Calvert looked across to the parents. 'Florence's father would like to make a brief statement. Callum.'

Callum picked up the single piece of paper that he had carefully laid in front of him when he had sat down. After a moment's pause, he placed it back down again and looked straight ahead towards the throng of journalists.

'We have both been humbled and heartened by the support that we have received so far, many members of the public have helped in so many ways. Our adorable princess, Florence, is still missing and we ask anyone who knows where she is, where she might be, or who may have seen her in the last few days, to come forward with that information to the police. Florence is a wonderful, outgoing, and lively girl who gives joy and brings a smile to anyone she meets. She is missed by her mum and me, and we just want her back home with us. Please, if you know anything, however small, please come forward with the information.'

Calvert was inwardly impressed. Callum had managed to remember almost all the script, and the key points to mention, without reading directly from the paper. It would certainly draw more empathy from the public, and as important as it sadly was, from the reporting journalists too as they scribbled away in their notebooks.

Despite his statement lasting less than a minute, Callum had started to choke towards the end, and the emotion had broken through in his voice. The journalists were quick to capitalise on this.

Their thirst to replay the story of *grieving parents' breakdown at press conference for missing daughter* was further fuelled when Aileen broke down and Callum placed his arm around her shoulder.

'Thank you, Callum. Just to repeat, if anyone has seen Florence in the past four days, specifically since five pm last Friday the fifteenth of July, or anyone that knows where she is, please come forward and speak to the police. You can call the incident desk number on 0845 4564561, your calls will be treated in the strictest confidence, and you don't need to provide us with your name or any personal information. The objective here is quite clear; to locate and facilitate the safe return of Florence Findlay.'

Calvert glanced briefly at his watch. 'It's now just after fourteen-twenty on Tuesday the nineteenth, and Florence has been missing for ninety-three hours. Someone out there knows where she is, someone out there, many people perhaps, may have seen her. We would urge you to come forward with information.'

Calvert discreetly nodded towards Superintendent Talloch, signalling the end of his contribution.

'Thank you. Now, I would like to invite any questions,' said Talloch.

Several hands were raised, and Talloch pointed to one.

'Superintendent, do you believe that the girl is still alive?'

Bang! There it was, the question she was expecting of course, but acknowledging that Callum and Aileen were still sitting in the room and adjacent to her, there could not have been a more insensitive question posed.

'Florence,' she started, reminding the journalists that *the girl* had a name, 'yes, at this point in time we still remain hopeful that Florence will be found safe and well, and our lines of enquiry are based on this presumption.'

'Do you believe that she has run away from home, or

was she taken?' asked another.

'We remain open-minded to all possibilities at the present time, and whilst it is possible that Florence left home and remains away of her own free will, we are becoming increasing concerned for her safety.' Talloch purposely stopped short of saying that she might have been abducted, but this wasn't lost on anyone present.

'How are the budget cuts, recently announced by the Scottish Parliament, impacting on the investigation? Surely the reduction in police officers means that you have less resource available?'

'I'm not entirely sure that this is the right time and place for what is clearly a question more tainted towards politics, as opposed to the disappearance of a nine-year-old girl.'

'Nevertheless, the question is valid and still stands,' came the quick retort.

The exasperation in Talloch's voice was clear, and targeted right back to the journalist. 'The answer to your question, however, is that we have all the resources that we need. Kelvedie and the surrounding area is relatively rural as you may know, and we have many officers assigned to this investigation, add to which there are a further number that have been seconded from Greenock.'

Talloch paused for a second. 'Right, one final question, anyone?'

After a brief moment of silence, possibly as one journalist in particular wondered if he should ask his question or not, especially after the scolding his colleague had received a few moments ago, a voice from the second row announced, 'I have a question for Detective Inspector Calvert…a source tells me that you are not a serving police officer, so the public would no doubt be questioning if you should be leading this investigation, or perhaps why you're involved.'

Before Calvert could respond, Talloch jumped in, 'do you not have any better or more appropriate questions to ask? DI Calvert is, of course, a serving police officer. We don't conduct investigations like Miss Marple or The Red Hang Gang.'

Her retort drew some laughter from the assembled crowd; even Calvert struggled to hold back his smile, which, of course, was inappropriate at best.

'Allow me to rephrase,' said the journalist.

'Please do.'

'I understand that Inspector Calvert is not a serving officer with Police Scotland.'

Calvert managed to get in before Talloch this time. 'Correct. I'm a serving officer with Humberside police force and have been so for twenty-five years. I have been temporarily seconded to Police Scotland to lead this investigation. It's a temporary appointment and a senior member of the Police Scotland CID will be taking over the investigation in due course.'

'Superintendent Talloch, is this absence of local senior management hindering the investigation?'

This time Callum Findlay interjected, much to the surprise of both Talloch and Calvert. 'Please! please…can we remember that we came here to tell you about our nine-year-old daughter Florence, who is missing. Can we all focus on what is important here, finding her.'

'Thank you, Callum,' noted Talloch, 'a sensible message to end on, I think.'

As Jackie Macallan had offered to take Callum and Aileen Findlay back home, Calvert decided he would head straight out to see Ken Glenratty.

Retired Detective Chief Inspector Glenratty was the senior investigating officer in the disappearance of Hayley Findlay ten years ago, and Calvert had called him earlier that morning to say that he would be dropping by sometime in the next couple of days. Glenratty had left Greenock, a town where he had lived and worked for the best part of thirty years, and retired to a bungalow in Inchinnan, a small village in Renfrewshire, and Calvert had initially winced at the satnav when it informed him that the ninety-five-mile journey would take him two hours and fifteen minutes.

After a rather uneventful journey that saw the scenery morph from beautiful countryside into major highways and industry and on to leafy suburbia, Calvert's satnav guided him within a few metres of his desired destination. He had taken the opportunity to finish listening to the audiobook, *Cilka's Journey*, that he had started during his journey to Kelvedie six days earlier. He was slightly frustrated that he had ten minutes of audio remaining as he parked his car. The story would leave him hanging for now, until the start of his return journey at least.

You have reached your destination the computer-generated but yet slightly sultry and alluring voice informed him.

27 Buchannan Avenue was not unlike the other twenty-six that Calvert driven past, a large five-bedroom bungalow with neatly manicured lawns and a row of bright colourful shrubs underneath a large bay window that faced out towards the road. In the driveway there was a new gold-coloured Citroen DS7 Crossback. As Calvert parked and stepped out of the car into the late afternoon sunshine, he paused for a second to take in his surroundings; *if this is what retirement is like*, he thought, *I'll take some of this.*

'Mr Glenratty?'

'Ken, please, call me Ken. Come in, inspector.'

'Thank you.'

Ken Glenratty was sixty-one years old, six feet tall, and looked to be in good physical shape. His broad shoulders and left-sided perichondrial hematoma, known more colloquially as cauliflower ear, immediately highlighted that he probably had a long amateur career in rugby. His jaw was covered with a grey-white thickset goatee beard, and he had more than a passing resemblance to the Scottish actor James Cosmo; he who played key roles in movies such as *Braveheart*, *Troy* and *Highlander*.

After settling back into an armchair, Calvert asked,

'how long have you been retired, Ken?'

'Almost five years come September. I joined the, as then, Strathclyde Police back in 1984 and stayed for thirty years. I left just after the amalgamation of the regional police forces under the new banner of Police Scotland.'

After a brief pause, he asked, 'you look a little long in the tooth yourself, inspector, how long have you been in?'

'Me? Twenty-five years. I'll do another five and then call it a day, although I'm not sure how I'll fill my days when I'm retired. How have you been occupying yourself?'

'Well, the wife and I go on two or three cruises each year, and we try to travel fairly extensively within the UK too. I did get restless fairly quickly after retiring.'

'Golf?'

'Nah, not me, I never took to it, I never saw the point of hitting a rubber ball with a length of metal piping and chasing after it for five miles.'

Calvert laughed. That had been his exact sentiment throughout his entire adult life too.

'Golf is a game whose aim is to hit a very small ball into an even smaller hole, with weapons singularly ill-designed for the purpose,' said Calvert.

'Churchill, wasn't it?'

'Correct. Winston Churchill.'

'Did he ever play?'

'God knows, Ken, although based on that witty observation, I wouldn't have thought so.'

'No…so no golf, but I have got a part-time job though.

I've been working at B&Q for the past fifteen months as a general store assistant.'

'Okay. That's quite a departure from the force.'

'It is, and that's the point probably. B&Q has a long-standing policy of employing staff past the usual retirement age. It's not too physically or mentally taxing, but gets me out of the house, a little exercise and does keep that grey matter ticking along.'

'Sounds good, I'll bear that in mind, although not for a few years yet.'

They both refreshed their palates with a gulp of coffee.

'You haven't come all this way to gain an insight into my retirement activities, inspector, how can I help you?'

'No, I haven't. Well as I briefly mentioned in our phone call, I understand that you were the SIO on the investigation into the disappearance of Hayley Findlay back in 2011?'

'That's correct.'

'Well, I'm the SIO on the misper of Florence Findlay, her sister.'

'Her sister?'

'Yes, Florence is nine, she was born after Hayley went missing.'

'Yes, I think I remember the mum being pregnant again on one of the last times that I saw her. Well, isn't that just an awful stroke of bad luck…or not.'

'Yes, exactly. I wondered what you might recall from the investigation back in the day. I've read the case files but wanted to get your thoughts and take on it.'

'Okay. So, back in 2011, May, I think it was, Hayley Findlay left her parents' home to go and play in the park. The park wasn't too far away, and this was by all accounts fairly usual. She would walk to the park and play with friends, then walk back. Her parents trusted her to do just that, and there had never been any previous issues or incidents that would cause them to curtail this. Quite simply, she disappeared. We know that she reached the park because her mum...' He struggled to recall her name.

'Aileen,' offered Calvert.

'Yes, that's it, Aileen. Aileen found the doll that she had taken with her. It was lying on the ground underneath the swings or slides. Shortly after which she called the police, and we attended the scene and opened a misper investigation.'

'Anything of interest at the park?'

'No, nothing. We took fingerprints from all of the apparatus in the play park and gathered dozens of different prints, none of which we were able to match against the database.'

'I guess it's a high-traffic area, but mainly with children.'

'Exactly. The forensics team were able to establish that almost all of the prints lifted were from children; there were half a dozen adult prints, but as I say we didn't have any database matches, and over a short period of time we matched those to several parents of local children, none of whom we suspected nor had any evidence to suggest they were involved either.'

'Okay.'

'Over the next few day, weeks, and indeed months, we allocated a growing number of resources to the investigation. We had several reported sightings from as far away as Edinburgh, none of which panned out.'

'What about the parents, Callum and Aileen? Was there any indication that they might have been involved in Hayley's disappearance?'

'Possibly, or probably, one or both of them, but we had no evidence. We pulled them both in for questioning, in fact if I recall correctly, we had Callum in three times. Their respective alibi was each other and neither wavered under questioning; they couldn't be broken, either of them, but as you will know yourself, no doubt, so many of these types of cases involve immediate members of the family.'

'Yes, I know all too well, unfortunately. There truly are some very sick people out there, family members and close friends that you would expect to love and protect young children.'

'Indeed.'

'Did you have any other suspects during the investigation?'

'No, not really. Hayley went missing in May of 2011 and by that time there were plenty of new faces and strangers in the village and surrounding area. The weather was getting better; that in itself was attracting the usual seasonal walkers, plus the market in Tarbert gets much busier from that point onwards too. It could, I suppose, have been an opportunist snatch, but my money is still on someone that she knew; family, friends…but, in the end we drew a blank. Sorry.'

'I guess anything is possible, but I'm not sure that I buy into a tourist, for want of a better word, taking an opportunistic snatch. It has to be someone close, someone local, someone known.'

'I agree. It remained an open case right up to the point where I retired from the force, and to be honest with you, it has always haunted me…the girl that we never found.'

'James Harvey.'

'Sorry.'

'James Harvey,' Calvert repeated, 'he is my Hayley. I've been SIO on thirty-five mispers, and we successfully recovered thirty-four of them, albeit four were deceased. But James Harvey, he was the one, the only one that we never found.'

'How old was he?'

'About the same age as the young girls in question here, he was ten years old.'

They both sat in silence and pondered for a few seconds.

'Aye, they certainly stay with you, that's for sure.'

Glenratty refreshed their coffee as Calvert politely declined to partake in a *snifter or two of Glenlivet* and took the next fifteen minutes to appraise Glenratty of the current misper involving Florence Findlay.

By the end of the fifteen minutes, Glenratty added little of value other than confirming that the similarities were worrying at best, and actually quite disturbing. They both agreed that the focus had to be on the parents, they had to be involved in some way, either directly or through some kind of indirect negligence. Either way, Callum and Aileen Findlay were about to become front and centre in the unexplained disappearance of their daughter, once again.

CHAPTER 14

Calvert was woken by his mobile phone. He looked at the time. 6.57. His alarm was set for seven-thirty.

'Inspector, this is Superintendent Talloch, I didn't wake you, did I?'

Normally Calvert would have been wide awake and probably on his way down to breakfast at seven am, but today his first activity would be at the Findlay home, and that was literally a stone's throw down the road so he had planned on arriving there shortly after nine. That was to have been preceded by a bit of a lie-in. Never mind.

'No, ma'am, I'm awake, just getting ready for the day.'

'Good, okay. The reason for my call is that I wanted to give you an update on something, and to also ask for a favour.'

'Okay, I'm all ears.'

'Well, you will recall when we met four days ago, I noted that my two DCIs were out of action, both on vacation.'

'Yes, ma'am, and DCI Geary was to cut short his Jamaican holiday and was due back yesterday.'

'That's correct. Well, unfortunately I have received some news last night that DCI Geary's young son has been taken ill whilst in Jamaica. He's been hospitalised with some kind of virus.'

'Oh dear, I hope he's okay.'

'Yes, I believe he'll be fine, but it has meant that DCI Geary, obviously, will be remaining in Jamaica and not flying home early.'

'Understandable of course,' replied Calvert, 'and, yes, to your request by the way.' He had anticipated the obvious.

'That's much appreciated, thank you.'

'You're welcome.'

'How long were you originally planning to remain in Kelvedie, you know, for your vacation?'

'Seven days.'

'And you've been here, six?'

'Seven. Today will be my seventh.'

'Are you able to extend your accommodation where you currently are? Is it okay? Should we find you alternative lodgings for the balance of your time here?'

'That's kind of you, thank you, but I'll stay where I am, it's quite nice and I'm sure that I will be able to extend my stay, it's also, sadly and ironically, right in the middle of where I need to be.'

'Okay, well look, we will pick up your accommodation costs from this point onwards, just let me know when you've got the final invoice and we'll sort it out.'

'Thank you, but there's really no need to do that.'

'No, I insist.'

'Okay, I appreciate that. Thank you.'

'And thanks once again for agreeing to what might, hopefully, be a couple of extra days.'

'It's fine. Hoping to have it all wrapped up within that time, ma'am.'

'Loving the optimism, Paul. Thanks again.'

Calvert made his way downstairs and into the dining room.

'Good morning, Paul, how are we this fine morning?' Brian was his usual chirpy self.

'Morning, Brian. Yes, very well, thanks. You?'

'Aye, fair to middling as they say.'

Calvert was familiar with the phrase, but unsure who actually said that.

'Brian, I need a word about extending my stay here, do you think that would be possible?'

'Yes, of course.'

'Great, thank you.'

'I took a look at the bookings earlier this morning as I expected that you would ask me that. I've got another couple arriving tomorrow, but that's all. You can remain in your current room.'

'Thank you. Well, that was easy.'

'How long do you think that you will be staying for?'

'Not sure, if I'm honest. The DCI, the local DCI, that was supposed to be relieving me is stuck in Jamaica, so, can we say another five days for now, then we'll review?'

'Works for me,' Brian confirmed, 'stuck in Jamaica, eh, well I can think of worse places to be stuck.'

'Me too.'

'Look, as you're obviously working to help locate little Florence, and not really getting much vacation time, let me charge you half price for the room and I'll throw in a free evening meal. How does that sound?'

'That sounds great, that's very nice of you. The police force will be picking up the tab for the accommodation, so keep it at the full price, but that evening meal sounds nice, thank you.'

'Good, all done and agreed then. Let me go and get your breakfast.'

Calvert had asked the police contingent to meet him at the B&B, and they would travel together to the Findlay home. Right on time, just before eight forty-five, Sergeant O'Brien, FLO Macallan and Constables Crossman and Davidson arrived. Calvert took a seat in the rear of O'Brien's car, and they set off for the Findlays', which would be little more than five minutes away.

With Davidson and Crossman waiting in their vehicle, Calvert opened the little picket gate and walked towards the house, accompanied by O'Brien and Macallan.

Aileen, used to knocks at the door at all hours over the past few days, was a little shocked to see three police officers at her door at nine am, and immediately feared the worst.

'Have you…'

'No, Aileen,' reassured Jackie Macallan, 'no, there is no fresh update with Florence.'

'May we come in please, Mrs Findlay?' Calvert asked as he stepped forward.

After walking through to the kitchen at the rear, Calvert was about to ask if Callum was at home, when he walked down the stairs and into the kitchen.

'Mr Findlay, Mrs Findlay, I would like you both to accompany us to the police station please, where you will both be interviewed under caution.'

'Interviewed, why? What for?' asked Callum, 'are we under arrest?'

'No, neither of you are under arrest at this time, we have a number of questions, and we would like to undertake the interviews at the police station.'

'Why can't you ask your questions here?'

'It's fine, Callum, leave it,' replied Aileen.

'No, it's not fine. You're treating us like suspects. Suspects!'

To that, he received no response from the police officers.

'What if I don't want to come with you? What if I refuse?'

'Well, if necessary we will arrest you, but I don't want it to come to that. There is no requirement for us to arrest you. I would hope that you would both come voluntarily.'

'We will,' Aileen said, 'how long will it take? We need to be here if Florence returns, or someone makes contact with us.'

'I can't say exactly how long you will be away. Sorry. Don't worry about not being here, with your permission your FLO, Jackie, will remain here. Is that okay?'

'Yes.'

'There is something else that I need to advise you of. Whilst you are en route to the police station, we will be undertaking a search of your house.'

'But you've already looked in Florence's bedroom on two occasions,' Aileen commented.

'Yes, but this will be a wider search of your entire home. Do we have your permission?'

'Suspects! I fucking told you,' Callum looked at his wife, 'they're treating us like fucking suspects. No. No you don't have my permission to search the house.'

Calvert reached inside his jacket pocket. 'Okay, it's just as well that I have this search warrant then.'

He handed it to Callum, who snatched it from his hand. 'You can read it in the car on the way to the station.'

Callum and Aileen Findlay were escorted to the waiting police car. Sergeant O'Brien got in and Constable

Crossman got out.

'I'll be back at the station in a couple of hours,' confirmed Calvert. O'Brien nodded and they set off towards Lochgilphead station.

'You start downstairs,' Calvert said to Crossman, 'and I'll start upstairs.'

'Okay. What are we looking for, you know, exactly?' asked Crossman, clearly showing his inexperience.

Calvert was fine with this, he would rather that his team ask questions and fully understand what was expected of them, as opposed to winging it and missing something vital. After he'd provided a number of tips, or pointers, they both set about a thorough search of each room.

After ninety minutes of looking through three bedrooms, bathroom, lounge and kitchen, they moved outside to look through the garage and the back garden shed. Nothing, or at least nothing that would help them in the questioning of Callum and Aileen, or in the wider lines of enquiry within the investigation.

The search had not recovered any more electronics, laptop, tablet, phone, that had been missed from the last search. There were no signs of disturbance that might have suggested some kind of struggle. All Florence's clothes, to the best guess that Calvert could make, were still hanging in her wardrobe or neatly folded within the drawers.

Calvert had found three passports in a drawer in Callum and Aileen's bedroom. The ones for Callum and Florence had expired six and eighteen months ago respectively, so there was obviously little need to formalise any lines of enquiry about Florence leaving the country. Well, not through official routes anyway.

No, nothing was out of the ordinary. The search had drawn a blank.

CHAPTER 15

Calvert met Sergeant O'Brien in the police station's small kitchen area, where he was offered a brew and accepted.

'Thanks. Did you receive any further grief from Callum on your way here?'

'No, not really, he calmed down and didn't say a lot.'

'Where have you got them now?'

'Aileen is in interview room one, and Callum is in interview room two.'

'Okay, we've probably kept them waiting long enough.'

'Any joy with the house search by the way?'

'No, nothing. Let's focus on the day that Florence disappeared, but I also want to tap into the memory banks about Hayley's disappearance ten years ago too. Okay?'

'Sure.'

'Hello, Mr Findlay.' DI Calvert and PC Davidson took a seat across from Callum.

'Just a reminder that you are not under arrest and that you are free to leave at any time.'

'That's laughable considering your insistence that we come with you to the station,' Callum replied.

'Nevertheless, you are not under arrest, and as such are free to leave. Despite that, we do need to ask you a few questions, which is why you are here.'

No response.

'My colleague has asked if you want a solicitor present, and you have declined. Is that correct?'

'I've got nothing to hide.'

'Okay, good.'

'Where is my wife? Where is Aileen?'

'Your wife is being interviewed simultaneously in a separate interview room by my colleagues. Right, let's get started.'

Calvert pressed the button on the recording device and after the three-second beep, he said, 'interview of Callum Findlay at Lochgilphead police station, the date is the twentieth of July 2021 and the time is 12.13 pm. Present in the room are Callum Findlay, Detective Inspector Calvert and Constable Davidson. This is a voluntary interview and Mr Findlay has declined any legal representation.'

Calvert paused for a second before looking up towards Callum.

'Tell me about the day that Florence went missing,

where were you?'

'You know exactly where I was, I was at work in the garage in Tarbert. I received a call from Aileen to say that she couldn't find Florence.'

'And what time was that?'

'Five forty-five, I think.'

'And you arrived home…?'

'Around six o'clock.'

'And then what did you do?'

'Well, after I had tried to calm Aileen down, I asked, obviously, where she had looked for her, then we started to look again. We checked our house and garden, our next-door neighbours, the field at the back of our house, then we started into the village. By this time a few of our neighbours had joined us and we searched everywhere we could think of.'

'And Aileen eventually called the police?'

'Yes, about nine pm, I think.'

Sergeant O'Brien and Constable Crossman had reached roughly the same point in their interview with Aileen Findlay.

'You say that Florence came back into the kitchen?'

'Yes, I heard her say *thanks, Mum* after I had left a glass of lemonade on the kitchen table, then I assume she left out of the back door to go to play again.'

'And this was what time?'

'Just before five, I guess.'

'You guess, or you know?'

'Well, I didn't look at my watch, but if I think back from when Callum got back home at six, then, yes, about five o'clock.'

'Does she often go out to play, and you are unaware where she is?'

'She is always close by. The house, back garden, next-door neighbour, the park.'

'And you always know where she is, do you?'

'Aye.'

'Well, it doesn't appear so, does it?'

That was a bit below the belt and Aileen was starting to seethe at the implication.

'How many times has she gone missing before? You know, turning up later.'

'Never. I always know where she is. She is a good, sensible girl.'

'What kind of relationship do you have with your daughter, Mr Findlay?' It was a searching question from Calvert, and one that had sneaked past Callum's guard.

'We have a great relationship.'

'Do you ever fall out? Ever argue? Ever tell her off?'

'Occasionally, why?'

'Had you had an argument with Florence on the morning of fifteenth?'

'No.'

'If I was to ask Aileen about your relationship with

Florence, what do you think she would say?'

'What would she say? She would say that it's good, and that we get on fine.'

'Fine. Just fine?'

'Now you're just picking at my words. My relationship with Florence is great, and no, we didn't have any kind or argument or falling out that morning.'

'It's much more than a coincidence isn't it, Mrs Findlay,' O'Brien started, 'that Hayley, your other daughter, should go missing in pretty much similar circumstances?'

No response.

'Ten years ago, wasn't it?'

No response.

Calvert was to be somewhat more blunt on the same topic.

'Mr Findlay, let me take you back ten years when your other daughter, Hayley, went missing. She was playing outside and hasn't been seen since. Now, fast forward ten years and Florence has disappeared in virtually the same circumstances. What does that tell us?'

No response.

'No? Okay, well, it tells me that there is a common denominator with the disappearances. You. Well, specifically you and your wife Aileen.'

'We had nothing to do with the disappearance of Hayley, and we have nothing to do with Florence's disappearance.'

'Well, I beg to differ,' replied a purposely antagonistic Calvert.

'Why don't you spend your time looking for my daughter instead of wasting it in here asking me stupid questions, and accusing me and my wife of something that we didn't do, something that we could never do?'

'Do you know how many abductees are taken by someone they don't know?'

No response. Calvert waited a while and let the question hang.

'No? Okay, let me tell you. It varies based on a few factors, but the headline figure is thirty percent.'

Again, he let that hang for a few seconds.

'Thirty percent of all child abductions are what we call stranger abductions, so conversely this means that seventy percent of abductions are carried out by people that are known to the abductee.'

The facts and figures still didn't elicit a response from Callum.

'Now, you see where I'm going with this, Callum. There is a seventy percent probability that Florence knew her abductor, then factor in the fact that ten years ago Hayley disappeared and there was a seventy percent chance that she knew her abductor. Then overlay that with the common denominator across both disappearances, who would they both know?'

'Fuck off.'

Callum's response, whilst less than eloquent, reassured Calvert that his narrative was starting to penetrate.

'Perhaps it wasn't you, Callum, perhaps you weren't involved. As you say, you were at work, probably, when Florence went missing. Perhaps we need to be focussing our attention on Aileen. What do you think? Do you think that your wife has the capability or propensity to have been involved in the disappearance of Florence, and Hayley?'

'Fuck off, fuck off, fuck off.'

Callum had reached, and breached, his tolerance levels and he threw back his chair as he stood and shouted at the two police officers.

Davidson stood too, with one arm slightly extended in a defensive posture, waiting for Findlay to make a further aggressive gesture, perhaps an assault. He didn't. Calvert remained relaxed and seated.

'Do you know what, Aileen…' O'Brien said, taking a calmer tone and using her first name, 'I'm not sure that you were involved in the disappearance of either Florence or Hayley.'

He remained silent for a few seconds.

'No, but we do believe that Florence was taken by someone she knew. If you take that same logic back to Hayley's disappearance, then, well, you see where we are going?'

'There are literally dozens of people in the village that knew both Hayley and Florence. It's a small, tight-knit, community and everyone knows each other, but what you're proposing is preposterous.'

'Agreed, with regards the village. It's possible that it was Morag ABC or Shona XYZ, but unlikely. No, we are looking closer to home, Aileen. If it isn't you, then it has to be your husband, doesn't it?'

Aileen Findlay shook her head.

'Your husband Callum, is he a violent man? Has he ever been violent towards you or either of your daughters?'

'No, no, he's never laid a finger on either of us. He's…'

'He's what, Aileen, what has he done?'

'Well, he's smacked the children, you know, when they've been naughty, but only occasionally, but everyone does that, don't they?'

Sergeant O'Brien didn't respond, intelligently using his silence to suggest his disappointment, and perhaps his confirmation that *no, parents do not smack their children.*

'On the day that Florence went missing, you said that you called your husband.'

'Yes.'

'Was he at work?'

'Yes.'

'How do you know? Did you call the garage number, or did you call his mobile?'

'I called his mobile.'

'So, how do you know he was at work?'

'Well, because of the time. He wasn't due to finish work. I called him about five forty-five I think, and he finishes work at six o'clock.'

'Do you think that he could have been closer to home when you called him?'

'No. Why?

O'Brien thought that he had been fairly direct with his questioning and leading of the conversation, but it wasn't until just now that the seed he had planted was realised in full by Aileen.

'Callum was at work when Florence went missing, he was. He is not involved. He is not responsible. He is a loving husband and father and would never harm a hair on her body.'

Aileen was waiting outside the station, having been told that Callum would be released at the same time. He would be with her within five or ten minutes.

They had been offered a lift back home, but the last couple of hours had left a bad taste and an unforeseen resentment of the police. They politely declined and contacted a friend from the village to come and collect them.

'Inspector Frost, this is DI Calvert, I'm heading up the Florence Findlay misper investigation.'

'Ah yes, nice to meet you, virtually. Superintendent

Talloch mentioned that you would most likely be in touch soon.'

Talloch had, in a very short space of time, facilitated the set-up of a reasonable sized helpline within Greenock police station. There was little, if any, resource available locally to Calvert to field any incoming calls from the public as a result of the press conference, and Talloch's quickly assembled team under the supervision of Inspector Frost, were able to take thirty calls per hour should they arrive in a linear way, which of course calls never did.

'I was just ringing to see what kind of response, if any, we have had to yesterday's press conference.'

'Indeed. Well, a fairly positive and busy start, as expected. To date we have received about forty calls, of which I would say that around ten to fifteen are potentially credible.'

'Ten to fifteen out of forty.'

'Yes, when you weed out the crackpots and those callers that really don't have anything substantive to provide.'

'Right, okay.'

'We've started to send details over to Lochgilphead for your team to work through. We've received reports of a number of sightings, some as far away as Glasgow.'

'Glasgow?' Calvert wasn't sure of the actual distance, not being local.

'Yes, that's about one hundred miles from Kelvedie. We've received reports of sightings from much further afield too, a couple from Edinburgh and one from Stirling.

Those I've already passed to the local teams to investigate, and I've provided your contact details for them to report back, is that okay?'

'Of course, yes, thank you.'

'All told, at the minute, you've probably got eight or nine possible sightings to follow up.'

'Okay, thank you, I'll pick up with the team back in Lochgilphead. How long will you continue to man the helpline?'

'Superintendent Talloch said seven days initially, then we'll review from there.'

'Sounds good to me. Keep me in the loop, yes?'

'Yes, of course.'

'Great, thanks.'

'Okay, speak again soon. Bye.'

Having just finished his dinner of grilled Scottish salmon, dauphinoise potatoes and fresh vegetables at Shallowbrook Lodge, Calvert had moved into the snug and settled into one of the armchairs in front of the roaring log fire. Despite it being the middle of July, Brian always insisted on having the fire lit when they had guests staying. For some over the years, it had proved a touch too much at this time of the year, but in the main it was warmly welcomed even if that meant sitting in the snug in shorts and a t-shirt. It had been a while since Calvert's lower legs had seen anything but the inside of his trousers, and this evening wouldn't be any exception.

He had observed another guest when he entered the snug, a woman, who was seated in another of the armchairs. He hadn't seen her before and assumed that she was a new guest.

'Hello.'

She looked up from her book. 'Hello,' she replied with a warm smile.

'Are you settling in okay?'

Again, she lowered her book, only slightly. 'Yes, thank you.'

'Good. Have you been here long? Sorry, I haven't seen you before.'

Have you been here long? She thought *that's almost as bad as do you come here often.* She knew that her time with the book had come to a temporary and abrupt halt, so she placed the bookmark inside, closed the book and placed it down onto the table next to her chair.

'I've been here two days, well, today is my second day. I haven't spent a lot of time here at the B&B, so you probably won't have seen me.'

'Yes, likewise,' Calvert replied, 'I've been overly busy too. I'm Paul, by the way.'

'Sarah. Hi.'

They both leant forward and shook hands.

'Do I detect a Yorkshire accent there?' asked Calvert.

'Yes. Leeds.'

'Ah, I thought so.'

'And you?' asked Sarah, 'I would place you somewhere close too.'

'Yes, a little over the M62 in Hull.'

'There's no mistaking a Yorkshire accent, Paul.'

'Isn't that the truth.'

'Are you here for the walking? I hear that it's a great place to strap on your walking boots and get out to explore.'

'Yes, and no. Well, that was the plan initially. I arrived seven days ago with the intention of doing that very thing, a week of walking, relaxing, some good pub grub and few snifters of the local alcoholic beverages, but things kind of moved on and my time here to date has taken a different path. A very different path.'

Sarah didn't want to pry, so simply smiled back at him.

'And you…' he asked, 'leisure or business?'

'Definitely leisure. I'm visiting some old friends in a place called Tarbert.'

'Yes, I've heard of it. A few miles down the road.'

'That's right.'

'I haven't had time to visit yet, but I hear that it's very nice, very picturesque.'

'It is, well, like you I haven't see much of it, but what I have seen so far, is, yes, as you say very picturesque.'

'Was there no room at the inn?' Calvert asked.

'Sorry?'

'Was there no room to stay with your friends? Did they make you stay here?'

Sarah looked around the snug, although she had no

idea why she had done so. 'Why, it's nice here.'

'Yes, it's very nice.'

'I could have stayed with them as they do have a guest room.'

'But…'

'But…they have two children, both under five years old, and to be honest I think it would have driven me mad over the course of the week. I thought it best to limit my exposure.'

'Hear, hear. Completely on the same page with you there. How long are you staying?'

'Just another two days,' Sarah confirmed, 'and you?'

'Well, I'm not sure to be honest. I've yet to achieve the rest and relaxation that brought me here in the first place.'

Now she was intrigued, and now she would pry. Just a little. But before she could ask her question, his mobile phone rang.

'Sorry, let me take this, and when I come back, I'll bring a fresh round of drinks, and I'll fill you in.'

'Sounds great.'

'Ma'am.' Calvert answered the phone like most senior detectives, short on words, brisk and to the point.

'Good evening, DI Calvert, I hope this isn't a bad time?'

Calvert checked his watch, eight pm, and looked back into the snug to see that Sarah had returned to her book. 'No, it's fine.'

'Great.'

'I've just seen you on the local evening news,' said Calvert, 'STV Glasgow and West, I think it was, perhaps about seven o'clock.'

'Yes, I was leaving the office just after six and I was doorstepped by an eager journalist.'

'It looked like you weren't expecting to be interviewed. I would have thought that you would have given her a short shrift.'

'Normally I would, but I know this young journalist, well sort of, she's trying to break through and occasionally I try and ensure that she gets some official comments from my office, you know, ahead of the old male hacks that would stamp all over her to get to the story first.'

'Yes, we all know our fair share of those, there's plenty back in Yorkshire.'

'Anyway, as you probably saw, I gave her a bit of an update, although there's not a great deal to share at present, is there? Anyway, that's the reason for my call, I'm just looking for a current status and thoughts on next steps, timelines etc.'

'Sure. Well, today we interviewed the parents, Callum and Aileen. To be honest it was always going to be a bit of a long shot at this stage. We've got no evidence on either of them and we were unable to break them down, either of them. They both seem quite genuine... but for one nagging point.'

'Hayley?'

'Correct. The fact that their other daughter, Hayley, went missing in pretty much similar circumstances is too much of a coincidence to overlook. Hundreds of parents over the years have suffered the tragic loss of a child, most recovered, some not, but I'm struggling to recall many other incidents where parents have lost two children, years apart, both in unexplained circumstances, and both where the child remains missing for a long period of time.'

'I agree, for me they have to remain our primary suspects, unless we open up any other lines of enquiry.'

'Agreed.'

'Inspector Frost tells me that we have had a half-decent response to the press conference, quite a few sightings to follow up?'

'Yes, ma'am. After the crackpots have been weeded out there are perhaps ten or so half-credible calls. We have sightings as far as Edinburgh and Stirling, which whilst possible, are both fairly unlikely in my opinion. We've got eight or nine possible sightings closer to home, so I've got the team following through on those. As soon as we have any update, one way or the other, I'll let you know.'

'Okay, thank you.'

'Night, ma'am.'

Calvert returned to the snug.

'Sorry about that.'

Sarah placed her book down on the arm of the chair

once again. 'That's okay. Work?'

'Yes.'

Again, she chose not to pry.

'Why don't I refresh those drinks as I promised. White wine, is it?'

Calvert stood and picked up both empty glasses before sauntering off towards the bar.

CHAPTER 16

As Calvert entered the makeshift incident room at Lochgilphead station just before nine o'clock, his swiftly created temporary team were already assembled.

'Morning, all.'

There were several replies, all in the same vein.

Having dropped his bag and draped his coat over a nearby chair, Calvert perused the room. Sergeant O'Brien, Constable Davidson, Constable Crossman, DC Taylor and DC Waller. PCSOs Hayter and Greaves were both out, in Tarbert and Kelvedie respectively. Calvert didn't see any need to call them in.

'DC Taylor, DC Waller, glad that you could both join our merry band.'

'Guv.'

'Guv.'

'Right, let's get ourselves up to speed on any recent events,' Calvert said, 'talk to me about the output from the press conference, and the follow-up on the various potential sightings of Florence.'

'Guv, so, starting with the furthest afield, we've had feedback from the teams in both Stirling and Edinburgh. They've taken statements from those that made the call into the incident desk, but to be honest, nothing really tangible in either city. Both were relatively short glimpses, neither of them involved any actual engagement with the young girl, and with the sighting in Stirling, the girl was apparently holding hands with a woman.'

'Her mother?'

'Yes, quite probably, guv.'

'CCTV?'

'Yes, guv. They looked at the date and time suggested by the caller but couldn't see anything.'

'Okay.'

'The teams in both areas are still vigilant, and despite the distance between here and there, they assure us that all of their officers are suitably briefed and aware of Florence's description.'

'Yes, I'm pretty sure that they'll be on top of it,' replied Calvert, 'what about the other sightings, the ones closer to Kelvedie?'

'Not much better to be honest, guv. Multiple sightings reported but, like Stirling and Edinburgh, no-one actually engaged the young girl or spoke to her. No names were provided in relation to people she was seen with, or people that we should check out.'

'So, we've drawn a blank then?'

'Yes, guv, sorry.'

'No need to be sorry, it happens. Press conferences are sometimes useful, especially when the victim was abducted by a stranger. In those cases, generally, someone has always seen something. But I still think that Florence was taken by someone she knew, and I still believe that she is still local, dead or alive.'

'We've not given up on finding her alive yet, have we, guv?'

There was a slight pause before Calvert responded, 'not yet, no. We'll keep working until we find her. Did we contact the Police National Missing Persons Bureau?'

'Yes, guv. We received a brief report from them. I'm not sure how useful it is…well, what I mean is that it pretty much supports your theory that Florence was taken by someone she knows, and that there is a high probability that it may be a family member. I've got the report if you want it, guv?'

'Thanks, I'll have a look through later, but yes, I'm not surprised at the content and the direction at which they are pointing us. We've had both Callum and Aileen in for questioning and been unable to break either of them.'

'What now, guv?'

'Well, we need to undertake another search for

Florence. I'm adamant that she is still local, hopefully alive, but even if dead, we need to find and recover her body.'

Calvert thought for a minute. 'Do you have an Enhanced Search Team up here? You know, a team that specialises in managing and delivering searches of this nature. You might call them something else in Scotland.'

'Aye, we have one of those, guv, and we call them the Enhanced Search Team too.'

'Ah, good. Where are they based?'

'Glasgow.'

'Sergeant, can you contact them please and see how long it will take for them to muster their resources for a search in and around Kelvedie. I'm sure that they will be aware of Florence's disappearance, but if not, feel free to bring them up to speed.'

'Yes, guv.'

'Oh, and by the way, if their answer is anything other than *fairly immediately* remind them that we have a nine-year-old girl missing.'

'Yes, guv, will do.'

'If you still don't get the response that we need, come back to me and I'll ask Talloch to intervene.'

Aileen had been awake since five am. She had been downstairs five minutes later and had done three baskets of washing in the following four hours. Having hung the clothes over several radiators and two clothes horses, she sat down with her third cup of coffee. Callum, by contrast, was still in bed. He had drunk himself into a stupor last night, finishing three-quarters of a bottle of Jack Daniels, and finally collapsing on the sofa around two am. Aileen had not joined him, and in fact she had remained teetotal since Florence disappeared six days ago. She had wanted to retain a clear head, although the urge to join her husband in excessive drinking to block out the pain and constant anguish was tempting to say the least.

Today's five am rising was becoming common, and had turned into a pattern of early mornings where Aileen had woken, if she had slept at all, well before the light had started to break through and herald a new dawn. But was it to herald a dawn of hope, anticipation and joy, or one of despair, worry and sorrow? Yesterday, shortly after four-thirty, she found herself in Florence's bedroom, lying on her bed with one of her cardigans clutched close to her chest, trying desperately to inhale her scent, hoping to feel closer to her. A moment of solace embodied the emotional bond between them, one that transcended distance and time. It was a bittersweet moment.

Aileen would do anything to have Florence back home. She would gladly trade her own life in an instant, in a heartbeat, just to have her daughter home safe and sound.

She stood and walked towards the lounge window, a large bay window that looked out towards the front of the house. The curtains were closed. They had been closed for several days and for various reasons, not least of all to try to block out the view of the group of journalists at the bottom of their garden.

Aileen took hold of the curtains and ever so slightly pulled them open, just an inch or two so she could see through. One, two, three, six, seven, eight.

A semi-permanent group of journalists had gathered at the bottom of their garden path. Respectful of their boundaries, they remained on the other side of the garden wall and rarely ventured up the path towards the house. The only time when any or all of them marched on the house was when they believed there was an update, some progress, a development, and that was sufficient reason and justification to knock on the door and request a statement or soundbite from either Callum or Aileen. In the absence of any such development, they waited patiently at the foot of the garden, waiting to ambush anyone either entering or leaving the house.

Their numbers had varied between three and ten over the last four days, and consisted of television, radio and newspaper reporters. Aileen got the impression that they would remain at the bottom of her garden until Florence had been found, hopefully alive and well.

The Family Liaison Officer, Jackie, had been out on a couple of occasions to fetch groceries for Aileen. The first time she exited the house, unknown to the journalists, she was confronted and hounded by numerous questions wanting to know who she was, how were Aileen and Callum holding up, did she have any information that she could share. Jackie Macallan flashed her warrant card in their general direction and told them, politely and diplomatically, to *fuck off*, and that wasn't to be used as an official police statement. Funnily enough they didn't bother Jackie again as she came and went.

'Do we have a list of the residents in Kelvedie?'

'Not to hand, guv, but I'm sure I can get one fairly quickly.'

'Yes, do it please. I want to run background checks on all the residents. Are they known to the police? If yes, what for?'

'What are you looking for, guv? You're not expecting to find someone fresh out of prison with a conviction for child abduction, are you?' asked Crossman.

Calvert smiled, 'no, I'm not that lucky. But I am convinced that she was taken by someone local, potentially someone from the village. Someone in this quiet, sleepy, little fishing village.'

'Very *Midsomer Murders*, guv,' commented Waller.

'Indeed. DCI Barnaby. You're familiar with him, and the television programme?'

'Yes, the missus watches it. I don't go for all that TV police show shit. Most of it is so far removed from the truth, they might as well be on Mars. Too much dramatic licence for me.'

'Interesting,' said Calvert, 'I would have thought that you guys would have been into *Rebus*, *Taggart* or perhaps *Hamish Macbeth*.'

'*Hamish Macbeth*, bloody hell, that's going back a few years.'

'1997, I think. Just after his *Trainspotting* phase.'

'Aye, what a contrast.'

'Anyway, we digress…'

CHAPTER 17

It was to be an early start for all but one of the police search teams this morning. The core team were travelling in from Glasgow, and others from Greenock and Lochgilphead. Many had left between five and six am.

Calvert on the other hand was staying at the Shallowbrook Lodge B&B, which was all of ten minutes' walk to their muster point at eight am. So, an alarm call at seven am was early enough. He might even manage breakfast if he was quick enough.

Calvert had mentioned to Gordon, that the muster point was to be outside his pub. He hadn't asked him directly, but was pleased to see that Gordon had heeded the implication and had set up a refreshments station on the tables outside of his pub.

'Morning, Gordon.'

'Good morning, Paul.'

'Listen, thanks for doing this, you didn't have to.'

'Yes, I did. A handful of tea, coffee and biscuits is just about the least I can do for you all. We've got plenty of hot drinks to go around before you set off, then I'll ensure that there's plenty available when you return.'

'Thanks, Gordon. There'll be a special place in heaven for you some day.'

'Not for a bloody long time I hope.' He laughed.

Many of the required number had already mustered as Calvert arrived just before seven forty-five. The head of the Enhanced Search Team was Inspector Finn Dalgleish, and Calvert wandered through the crowd to search him out.

'Inspector Dalgleish?' Calvert enquired as he stopped in front of an imposing man, all six feet seven of him.

'Aye, that's me. You must be DI Calvert?'

The pair shook hands. Calvert didn't confirm Dalgleish's assumptions, it wasn't necessary.

'Thanks for supporting this, I'm pleased that your team was available.'

'Aye, well, it's what we do, and we had no other party invitations for today.'

Calvert noted the slight humour in Dalgleish's response and allowed it to ride over him. He would be taking this situation, and his role here, seriously, wouldn't he?

Calvert agreed that he would address the team very briefly at the outset, then hand over to Dalgleish to own thereon in. Sergeant O'Brien had ensured that Dalgleish was sufficiently briefed in the preceding twenty-four hours.

Calvert stepped up onto one of the harbour walls and cleared his throat.

'Morning, everyone. For those of you that don't know me, and I appreciate that will be most of you, I am Detective Inspector Calvert. I am the temporary SIO of the investigation into the disappearance of Florence Findlay. Florence went missing around five pm on Friday the fifteenth from her family home here in Kelvedie, so that's almost seven days ago. Now, there was an initial search undertaken on the sixteenth using a small number of officers and a few willing members of the public, but Florence wasn't found, obviously, and neither was any trace of her, no clothing etcetera. Today we are looking to undertake a more comprehensive search of a slightly wider area, and the search will be led by Inspector Dalgleish of the Enhanced Search Team out of Glasgow. Inspector...'

Calvert took a sip of his coffee and stood down from the harbour wall.

Inspector Dalgleish spent the first five minutes elaborating a little on Calvert's brief opener and bringing everyone up to speed. They were an independent and specialist unit of twelve officers that travelled the length and breadth of Scotland supporting systematic searches for everything from bullets to missing persons, and doing so in a range of environments from relatively small buildings to open expanses of moorland, like today.

The thirty-seven officers would be split across four

teams. Teams A and B would commence at the south side of the village, and teams C and D would begin at the north. All teams would travel to their starting point, some six or seven miles from the village, using a series of minibuses and vans.

The objective would be to fan out at each commencement point and work towards meeting each other at a central point in a few hours. Dalgleish hoped that they would cover an area of approximately fifty square miles. It was going to be a comprehensive search, and a long day.

After being split into their respective four teams, each led by an experienced member of the EST, they departed in their vehicles towards their commencement point. It was eight-thirty.

Each of the four groups included three members of the EST, all of whom had radios, not that there appeared to be much interchange between the groups. It seemed there was no need, unless something was found.

Group A started three miles to the south-west; their route in was mainly open marshland, firm underfoot and they made good progress, probably the best of all four groups.

Group B started south of the village and made their way north-west. Their terrain was also mainly open moorland, but they did spend a disproportionate time within Killingbeck Woods, a natural obstacle in their path and an ideal place for someone to hide a body. There was no digging to be undertaken but each member of the team had been issued with a very sturdy four-foot wooden pole, which came in very handy when poking through the floor-covering brambles.

The third group, C, had commenced their search at the north-west of the village, and at the highest point. As they traversed their way towards the village, they ascended several hundreds of metres. The ground was tricky underfoot, especially when not taking the recognised footpaths, which was obviously all of the time; after all, what would be the point of walking single file over the footpaths.

The final group D came at the village from the north-east. Their passage was shaped primarily by Loch Fyne. The eastern side of the loch was to be their most westerly point as the group spread out over several hundreds of metres eastwards. Those walking on the loch shores made slow progress on the rocky shoreline and the advanced westerly side of the line had to pause and wait on a few occasions.

Calvert had called Gordon and advised him that they should expect all teams back at the harbour around five o'clock, and whilst it wasn't expected of course, noting that he had a pub to run, if he had an opportunity to lay on some hot drinks, the thirty-seven weary officers would probably be eternally grateful.

As the search teams started to return to the harbour,

Gordon and Angie were standing outside of The Plough with half a dozen stainless steel flasks and as many spare cups and mugs as they could find. Any shortage was made up with some of polystyrene cups that Gordon found in the cellar.

'Any joy, Paul?' asked Gordon as Calvert stepped forward to take a couple of biscuits and a hot cup of coffee.

'No, I'm afraid not,' he replied, 'but that's not necessarily bad news. It simply means that we haven't found a body. I still remain optimistic that Florence is alive and that she will be found. It might be by the police, it might be by someone else.'

Calvert sauntered off back towards the group of EST officers that had congregated.

'Thanks for your help today, it's much appreciated.'

'Aye, nae bother,' said one.

'Sorry we could'nae find the wee lassie,' replied another.

Finally, Inspector Dalgleish commented, 'it's good news, possibly, it raises the chances that she is still alive.'

'Agreed,' said Calvert, 'I've just said that very thing to someone else. Anyway, thanks for your support. Superintendent Talloch had asked to be kept updated, so I'll give her a call a little later. Thanks again.'

Having trekked twelve miles over undulating open moorland, regularly stooping down to look at something on the ground, a sore and weary Calvert walked through the door of Shallowbrook Lodge. His mood, however, was immediately lifted when he saw Sarah talking to Brian at the reception desk.

Their conversation finished and Brian peeled away. Sarah turned in the opposite direction and her eyes met Calvert's.

'Paul. Hi.'

'Hello, Sarah. How are you?

'Fine, thanks, and you?'

'A little tired and weary. I've been trudging over mountain and moorland today, and I'm feeling it a little in my calves now.'

'Ah, you managed to get some walking in then. Good for you,' she replied, not aware of the real reason that he had been out on the moor all day.

'It's your last night tonight, isn't it? You'll be heading back home tomorrow morning.'

'Yes, that's right. I'll probably check out tomorrow morning but nip over to Tarbert to see my friends before setting off back home to Yorkshire.'

She paused for a second. 'Are you for an early bath and bed tonight? You look like you've overdone it.'

'Me. No. Well, a nice soothing bath that's for sure, but I can't see me having an early night.'

Sarah was hoping that they might spend the evening together, and that he might ask her, but as the subsequent silence extended for a few seconds, she felt the opportunity was slipping away. She decided to take the initiative.

'Would you like to have dinner together this evening?' he beat her to it, 'and perhaps a drink or two?'

'Yes, that would be lovely, thank you.'

'I wondered if we might venture out to The Plough down the road for a bite, my treat, as long as we don't tell Brian.'

They smiled.

'That would be great,' Sarah confirmed.

Calvert looked at his watch, it was just after seven. 'Shall we say seven forty-five, is that doable?'

'It works for me, but does that give you enough time for your recovery soak?'

'It'll be more than enough time. You know men, we can get dressed in five minutes.'

'Take a little time longer. Have your soak in the bath and meet me down here in the snug when you're ready. I'll be here for seven forty-five, but I'll grab a drink and see you when you're ready. No rush.'

'I'll be down for then.'

'Okay, I'll see you at seven forty-five.'

It was a pleasant walk from Shallowbrook Lodge to The Plough as the warm summer's day had extended into the early evening. The sun lingered low in the sky clinging to the horizon, and cast a golden hue over everything. Despite the time nearing eight o'clock, both Paul and Sarah had opted for light clothing. For sure, the temperature would drop later, but it was a short walk back to the B&B.

As Calvert had expected on a Friday summer evening, the pub was fairly busy. The tables outside were taken by the relative youth of the village, but they managed to find a free table inside.

As Sarah picked up a menu from the table, Calvert asked if he could get her a drink.

'A white wine please, Paul. Pinot Grigio, if they have it.'

'A white wine it is. I'll be two minutes.'

'That's okay, take your time. I'll peruse the menu.'

After chatting to Gordon and Angie for longer than he really wanted, Calvert thought that he was neglecting Sarah, so made his excuses and returned to the table.

'Sorry about that, you know what landlords are like, they'll talk the hind legs off a donkey. Here you go.'

'Thank you.'

'Any good?'

'Sorry?' Sarah was a little confused, until Calvert pointed towards the menu.

'Is the menu any good? I have to be honest I haven't eaten here yet. I've only really eaten at the B&B, or perhaps in the station at Lochgilphead, and once at Greenock I think.'

'Yes, it's okay. As expected, it's traditional pub food. I'm sure that we'll find something to enjoy. I'm going to go with the salmon, I think.'

Calvert picked up the second menu from the table and took no time at all before declaring that he would have the steak and ale pie.

Having placed their order at the bar, Calvert returned to the table and advised Sarah that they should expect to wait no longer than twenty minutes. They both thought this was acceptable for a relatively busy Friday night, and clinked glasses.

'Cheers.'

'Cheers and thank you for the invite.'

'So, I discovered yesterday, purely accidentally, why you are here, or at least what you are doing whilst you are here.'

'Oh right. How did that come about then?'

'I overheard Brian at the B&B talking to someone about the disappearance of a young girl from the village. He also mentioned that you were the officer in charge of the investigation.'

'Yes, that's correct. Call it a busman's holiday if you will.'

Sarah laughed, 'oh my God. Busman's holiday, that brings back some memories. Do you remember that television programme from the late eighties, or perhaps early nineties?'

Calvert chuckled too, 'yes, I remember, and I think you're right, I think it was on for a few years across the eighties and nineties.'

'I always found it strange,' remarked Sarah, 'that teams competed to win a holiday where they had to work and learn how their jobs were performed in other countries. Honestly, I couldn't think of anything worse.'

'I know. Can you remember what the contestants were wearing?'

'Wearing? What do you mean? When they were on the show? No, I'm not sure I recall.'

'They all had to wear their day-to-day work clothes, you know, midwives, policemen, croupiers and the likes.'

'Do you know, I don't remember that part of the show,' Sarah replied, 'now I'm wondering if I actually watched it at all. Perhaps I just remember the myth and the legend that was *Busman's Holiday*.'

'Yes, perhaps.'

They both laughed and took the opportunity to take a drink.

'Anyway, before we digressed, yes I am heading up the investigation into the disappearance of a local girl, Florence Findlay, well I'm temporarily in charge anyway.'

'Assuming that you came here for some R&R, how on earth did you get yourself into that position? When I ask that by the way, I have already assumed that you are a police officer, although you didn't say so the other day when we were sitting in the snug at the B&B.'

'Did I not say? Ah, okay, sorry. Anyway, yes, I am a police officer, a detective inspector with the Humberside Police based in Hull. I told you that I was from Hull, right?'

'Yes, Paul, you did.'

'Ah good. So, yes, I booked a week at the B&B for some R&R as you say, but two days after arriving, the little girl went missing. Initially I joined a search party, as did most of the village to be honest, but we had no luck in finding her or any trace of her. It quickly became known that I was a police officer, a detective, and someone who is fairly experienced in mispers.'

'Mispers?'

'Sorry, missing persons. Police jargon. I guess all industries have their own jargon and ours has more than its fair share.'

'Misper. Missing person. Right, got it,' Sarah confirmed.

'Anyway, through luck, good or bad, and a terrible habit of being in the right place at the right time, or vice versa dependent on your view, the superintendent asked me to head up the investigation until one of her own senior officers was available.'

'I'm sure that you are very good at your job, Paul, but that being said, doesn't Scotland have any senior, experienced detectives of its own that could be seconded? Kelvedie really isn't too many miles away from civilisation.'

'Like I said, right place, right time.'

'Or wrong place, wrong time.'

'Correct. So, I've been working with some of the local police teams trying to generate some leads, following up on others and trying to locate young Florence. Hopefully alive.'

'That's the million-dollar question, I guess, is she still alive? Are you hopeful? Optimistic?'

Calvert paused for a second. 'Outwardly, yes, I'm still optimistic. We haven't found a body yet, and she could still be alive, and being held by someone she knows.'

'Inwardly? Your own personal thoughts are somewhat different then?'

Calvert looked around and lowered his voice a little, conscious of his environment. 'They are, Sarah, yes. As each and every day passes, I get less and less optimistic about finding her alive. We can only do what we can do. If the cards have already been played, then all we can do is be there to see what hand has been dealt.'

'I guess so. Well, I wish you the best of luck anyway. I'm sure that you'll find her alive and well.'

'Thank you. Anyway, let's change the mood shall we, and talk about something lighter, something more in keeping with the evening. So, today is your last day here, in Kelvedie?'

'Yes, that's right, I'll be driving back home tomorrow.'

'And who is waiting for you back home?'

In hindsight, Calvert thought it a little forward and perhaps somewhat intrusive, but it was too late, the words had passed his lips now.

'Back home, ah, that'll be Jack.' The very name brought a huge smile to her face.

Calvert couldn't deny that he was surprisingly a little despondent. Although he hid it well and gave her a broad smile in return.

'Jack. Okay. Is he your…'

'Cat. He's my cat.'

Calvert smiled again, this time quite probably more for

his pleasure than Sarah's.

'Yes, it's just me and Jack. I was divorced about ten years ago. The kids have long since grown up and flown the nest.'

'How old are they?' asked Calvert.

'Lilly is nineteen and Samuel is twenty-four.'

'I have two myself,' Calvert replied, 'Lisa is twenty-two and Carl is twenty-five.'

'Ah, not too dissimilar in age then. I see my daughter, Lilly, most weeks as she lives in Leeds.'

'And your son?'

'Sammy,' she smiled, clearly recalling an image of his face or of some other treasured family moment, 'he doesn't like me calling him Sammy. Well, he lives in Lympstone, Devon. He's in the Royal Marines, a corporal.'

'Wow, impressive.'

'Yes, apparently so. So he keeps telling me. He's currently at the commando training centre putting the new recruits through their training. He said it was tough and that I should be impressed that he made it as a Royal Marine.'

'You should. It's a very elite group of individuals.'

'Do you know much about the Marines, or the military, Paul?'

'Yes, I guess you could say that. I know a little about elite soldiers too. I'm ex-military. I served in the Parachute Regiment back in the day, many, many moons ago now, I might add.'

'Wow.'

Sarah tried her best to fake her understanding of elite military units, but it was clear that she wasn't as knowledgeable as she would have liked. Calvert noted her crumpled nose.

'You don't know who the Parachute Regiment are, do you?'

'Sorry. Is that bad?'

'Don't be daft, of course not. We are the silly buggers that jump out of a perfectly good aeroplane at ten thousand feet. Look, all you need to know is that I was ex-military too and I know a little about the ups and downs and the life that your son is leading, and you should be very proud of him.'

'I am.'

'Good.'

Having refreshed their drinks several times, Paul found that time marched on as good conversation flowed. The conversation swung from rugby union versus rugby league, to their thoughts on the best spa in Yorkshire, and finally ending up where it had started a few hours ago; Kelvedie, the investigation and Calvert's lost R&R.

Conversation never did turn to discussing Calvert's wife; it wasn't a subject that had been brought up by Sarah, much to his relief. He still wasn't comfortable talking to strangers about his wife and her death, six months and nineteen days ago, not that he was counting.

'Come on, you two, some of us have beds to get to.'

Calvert turned his head to see the landlord leaning over the bar. He looked over Sarah's shoulder and surveyed the room; they were the only ones remaining.

Calvert checked his watch; half past midnight.

'Oh, bloody hell, sorry, Gordon. I didn't realise it was so late. We'll gather our things and be on our way.'

'Nae bother, Paul. We closed at midnight, but I left you two chatting for a wee while. I've had plenty of stuff to tidy away in the meantime.'

Having thanked Gordon for his hospitality, a *scrumptious* traditional pub meal and plenty of fine drink, Paul and Sarah bade their farewells and started back towards the B&B.

Despite the hour, the air remained quite warm and neither of them felt the absence of a coat as they walked steadily back up towards Shallowbrook Lodge.

The conversation had continued from the pub, and they felt relaxed and completely at ease in each other's company.

As the rear entrance door was reached, handle tried, and confirmed locked as expected, Calvert withdrew the brass key from his pocket and showed it to Sarah. They immediately laughed together. It didn't need saying as it was obvious that they were both laughing at what wasn't there, what Calvert had detached; the six-inch wooden baton with the words 'Shallowbrook Lodge' burnt into the wood.

Having locked the door Calvert turned to find Sarah standing close to him; she leaned in and placed a tender kiss on his cheek.

'Thanks for tonight, Paul, I've really enjoyed it.'

'Me too.'

'Do you think that…' she paused for a second, unsure of herself or her next words at least '…that, we might meet up again, back in Yorkshire?'

Calvert's delayed response provided a non-verbal indicator, but unfortunately not the one that she was seeking. But then, he answered.

'I'd like that, yes. But it's not a great time for me at the minute, Sarah.'

He stopped short of expounding and mentioning that he was recently widowed. 'I mean, I have really enjoyed your company, you are wonderful, you really are… perhaps if we had met in twelve months' time, it might have been better for me, easier for me. I'm sorry.'

'There's really nothing to be sorry about, Paul, nothing at all. Let's just put this down to a lovely fleeting encounter. Goodnight…and goodbye.'

'Goodnight, Sarah. Take care.'

CHAPTER 18

Gordon had woken early this Saturday morning, earlier than usual and that despite the late hour at which his head finally touched the pillow. He would be lucky if he'd had five hours' sleep, but he didn't feel any the worse for it.

With two hours cleaning the tabletops in the bar, together with dragging a vacuum around the floor in each room, he sat down at the table nearest to the door, with a cup of coffee and a toasted bagel. The table in question sat within a huge bay window and afforded the occupiers a great view over the harbour and out towards the expansive Scottish countryside. On bright mornings like today, it was a sight to behold, and Gordon felt blessed that he found himself in beautiful Kelvedie each morning, and not in some city centre pub, looking out on polluted and grimy sprawling urbanisation and a distinct lack of flora and fauna.

Twenty minutes had passed, and Gordon was about to shake himself into action once again, having thought that he had just about reached the limit of how lazy he could be this morning, reminding himself that he had a pub to prepare for opening in a couple of hours' time.

As he stood, something caught his eye out of the window, and he placed the coffee cup on the table and leaned towards the large bay window. His eyes were not deceiving him, it was a young girl.

She was staggering from side to side, as though dazed or drunk, as she made her way around the harbour wall and paused just in front of the pub.

Gordon peered intently through the window and focussed on the young girl. It couldn't be, could it?

He made his way to the front door, turned the key and released the two security bolts before opening and standing in the doorway. Again, he regarded the girl. She was dishevelled, her tangled mess of hair looked as if it hadn't seen a brush in over a week, and her clothes were torn and dirty. It couldn't be, could it?

As he slowly approached her, she took one step back.

'It's okay,' he reassured her. He remained where he was standing.

'It's Florence, isn't it?'

No reply.

'You're safe,' he continued, 'I'm not going to hurt you,

but I would like to help you. Is that okay?'

It took three or four minutes until the girl walked, tentatively, towards Gordon.

'Here, sit down here, on this bench.'

He regarded her further. She looked as though she had been dragged through a hedge backwards, as was a phrase used by his mother many years ago.

'It is Florence, isn't it?' he repeated.

The young girl nodded but did not speak.

As luck would have it, Gordon was carrying his mobile phone in his back pocket, so he didn't need to leave her, even for a second. Not having Calvert's contact number, he called the main number for Shallowbrook Lodge.

'Good morning, Shallowbrook Lodge.'

'Brian, it's Gordon.'

'Aye, Gordon, to what do I owe the pleasure?'

'I need to speak to Paul, quite urgently.'

'Paul.'

'Aye.'

'Okay. We don't have telephones in the room so I can't put you through, Gordon, but I do have his mobile number.'

'Thanks, that'll be grand.'

'Better still, will I go up to his room and bring him to the telephone here, if it's urgent?'

'No, his mobile number will be fine, Brian.'

After what was a quite surreal conversation, Calvert confirmed that he would make his way from the B&B

down to The Plough with all haste.

'Will I call her parents, Callum and Aileen?' Gordon asked.

'No.' Calvert's answer was a little sharper and terser than he would have liked, in hindsight, 'no, thank you, Gordon, let the police do that. Thank you anyway.'

Despite it being Saturday, and Calvert having elected to take the day off, he was dressed, and it took less than ten minutes from ending the phone call to reaching to The Plough. As he rounded the corner towards the harbour he could see Gordon, who had now been joined by Angie; both were sitting on one of the wooden A-frame tables outside the front of the pub. The third person, the girl, was initially obscured as Angie had her back to Calvert. She was cuddling the young girl, holding her close.

Gordon rose to greet him. 'Ah, Paul, you're here.'

Angie, still seated, turned her head towards Calvert and said, 'and this young lady here is Florence.' She continued to hold her tight and gently stroke her hair.

Calvert regarded Florence. She was still wearing the clothes from eight days ago when she had been reported missing; white blouse covered by a navy cardigan, knee-length grey pleated skirt and white socks, albeit all were dirty and torn. In addition, both of her shoes were missing.

'Has she said anything, Gordon?'

'No, not a word. She's shaking and scared out of her

wits, poor lassie.'

Calvert walked over to Angie and Florence.

'Florence. Hello, Florence. My name is Paul, I'm a police officer.'

Calvert knew better than to try to ask lots of difficult questions at this time. Florence needed some hospital treatment, and reuniting with her parents, after which she would be interviewed by a specialist officer when the time was right.

As he turned away and extracted his mobile phone from his pocket, he heard the faintest of voices. He turned back to see Gordon and Angie looking back at him; they had puzzled faces and hadn't quite heard it clearly either.

'Hayley.'

Florence kept her head buried in Angie's chest, but she could be heard a little better this time.

'Hayley.'

'Hayley,' repeated Calvert, 'that was her sister, wasn't it?'

'Aye, that's right,' Gordon confirmed.

They all continued with their puzzled faces, now clearly aware of what Florence had said, but none the wiser as to why she would be uttering her sister's name.

'Are you…'

Angie anticipated his question. 'Aye, she's safe with me.'

Calvert made three calls; one to Sergeant O'Brien to appraise him of the situation, and the next to request an ambulance at his location, although he was at pains to point out that whilst it was urgent, he didn't want the ambulance to approach with lights and sirens. He wanted a quick and silent approach so as not scare Florence further.

His final call was to PC Jackie Macallan.

'Jackie, good morning.'

'Morning, guv. What can I do for you this Saturday morning?'

'You wouldn't happen to be with Callum and Aileen, would you?'

'No, not at the minute. In fact, I didn't have any plans to visit them today, guv. I was there yesterday evening for a couple of hours, and we said that we would probably leave them to themselves this weekend, unless there are any developments obviously. Are there…any developments?'

'Yes, you could say that. How long will it take you to get to Kelvedie, Jackie?'

'Probably about thirty minutes. Why? What's happened, guv?'

'We've found Florence.'

Jackie waited with bated breath, heart pounding, for the next few words.

'Alive. She's been found alive.'

'Oh, that's wonderful news. Is she okay?'

'Well, physically she appears to be, but I can't say for certain. There should be an ambulance here about the same time as you arrive. I'll be waiting outside The Plough at the harbour, can you meet me here?'

'Sure. I assume we are off to see Callum and Aileen?'

'We are, yes.'

Jackie Macallan pulled up just in time to see Florence being taken into the back of an ambulance, helped by two paramedics. Florence had walked into the ambulance and was seated with a blanket around her shoulders when Macallan approached.

She didn't speak, she didn't ask any questions of the paramedics, she simply regarded Florence. *Rough and shell-shocked* were an understatement she thought, but at least she was alive, and now she was safe.

'Sergeant O'Brien will meet the ambulance at the hospital,' said Calvert as he approached her.

'Oh, hi, guv. Is no-one travelling in the ambulance with her?'

'She'll be fine with the paramedic.'

'Okay, we're away to see the parents now?'

'Yes but let me just have a quick word over here first.' Calvert nodded in the direction of Gordon and Angie, still standing outside of the pub.

'Gordon, Angie. Hi.'

'Hello, Paul.'

'Listen, I just wanted to thank you for finding her and taking care of her until we arrived.'

'I'm not so sure I found her, to be honest I think you would say that she found me,' Gordon replied.

'Well, yes, indeed. Either way, thank you.'

'We're just happy that she's been found alive and appears to be okay.'

'Yes, me too, Angie, me too. See you both later.'

Calvert started to walk away but stopped and turned. 'Just one thing, a favour to ask.'

'Sure, if we can.'

'Keep this to yourself please, just for now. We're away to see Callum and Aileen now, and I'm sure that it will be all over the six o'clock news later today, but if you wouldn't mind just keeping the events of the last couple of hours to yourself, just for a while. Is that okay?'

'Of course, Paul. We won't mention it to a soul.'

'Thank you.'

'Any comment for the media, inspector?'

Calvert and Macallan brushed past the journalists and reporters standing at the bottom of the garden path; their numbers had dwindled now to just two, although it was Saturday morning and akin to most picket lines manned by striking workers, their numbers generally swelled later in the day. Calvert was equally impressed and surprised that the media had maintained a near constant presence outside for several days, looking to pick up any snippet of information or that all-important exclusive scoop.

He offered no response to the pair. He wasn't about to provide them with the news before doing so with Callum and Aileen.

'Morning, come on in,' Callum greeted them both at the door and left it ajar for them.

'Morning, Callum, is Aileen home too?'

'Aye, she is.'

'Would you ask her to join us please?'

Calvert followed Macallan through to the kitchen and they both took a seat at the kitchen table.

They waited a couple of minutes before Aileen came striding into the kitchen. 'Oh, hello.'

In her role as family liaison officer, Jackie Macallan was ever present within the Findlay home, and her presence wouldn't normally imply any update and change in circumstances. But DI Calvert, he wouldn't come unless there was an update.

'We have an update; we have some news to share with you both.'

Fearing the worst, Aileen's knees started to buckle, and she took hold of Callum's arm to steady herself. The cold hand of fear began to pulsate through her body.

Not wanting to drag it out, Calvert came out with it as quick and direct as was possible. 'We've found Florence, she is alive and well.'

Aileen was temporarily stunned, frozen, paralysed for a few seconds, unable to laugh, to smile, to cry, to scream, shout or talk.

'Where is she? Can we see her?' Callum asked.

'Yes, yes, of course. She is en route to hospital…'

Callum interrupted him, 'hospital!'

'Yes, don't worry, hopefully it's just a precaution, just to get checked out. So, she's on her way to hospital, and yes, of course, you can see her. I'll take you shortly.'

'Where was she found?'

'Well, here in Kelvedie, this morning.'

'Here?'

'Yes. Gordon, the landlord at the pub, saw her walking near the harbour wall earlier this morning.'

'This morning, when?'

'Around ten o'clock I think.'

Aileen checked the clock on the kitchen call; eleven thirty-five. Her baby had been found, safe and sound, over an hour ago.

'Is she okay…physically? Did you see her?'

'Yes, I saw her briefly before she was taken to hospital. As far as I could tell she was physically fine, although let's wait until she's been seen by the doctor. She looked…' he paused to choose his words carefully so as to not overly worry them, '…a little shaken, tired, and as expected, a little scared perhaps.'

'Did she say anything?' Callum asked, 'you know, where she had been? Who had taken her?'

'No, no, she didn't.'

There was a pause in the conversation for a few seconds, and again Calvert was reflecting on what to say and what to withhold at this point. After all, the news of Florence's safe recovery must be overwhelming in itself.

'She did say something,' Calvert said, 'she said just one word.'

'One word? What was that?'

'Hayley.'

'Hayley?'

'Yes. The one word she said was Hayley.'

'Our Hayley?'

'Well, I'm not sure. Obviously, I am aware of your other daughter, Hayley, and yes that would be the logical context, but I'm not sure, she didn't expand. It was just, Hayley, that's all she said.'

Aileen and Callum were as flummoxed as Calvert had been and could offer no immediate reason to him, as to why Florence would utter the name of her sister.

'Come on,' Macallan said, 'get your shoes and coats on, let's take you up to the hospital to see her, shall we?'

'Yes, let's get you there and get you reunited with Florence,' Calvert added.

CHAPTER 19

Florence had been taken by ambulance the fifteen miles to Mid Argyll Community Hospital. Sergeant O'Brien was waiting upon her arrival, as was a small team of medical staff.

Doctor Isla Sutherland, an A&E consultant, was to take charge of her care. She had received a call from O'Brien whilst the ambulance was en route and had been advised who the patient was. She was informed that the patient might not, indeed, have any physical injuries, but required a head-to-toe assessment...and probably a rape test, although the specific detail of the medical assessment would, of course, be left to Doctor Sutherland and her team.

Doctor Sutherland understood the sensitivity of the information conveyed and ensured that the immediate team within the A&E were also cognisant of who their next patient would be.

'Hello, my name is Doctor Sutherland,' she said with a softened tone, 'can you tell me your name?'

No reply.

'It's Florence, isn't it?'

No reply.

'Florence, you're in hospital and I'm a doctor. I and these other nurses…' she quickly looked to her left and right as she waved her hand from one side to the other '… are going to look after you, okay?'

No reply.

'Your mum and dad are on their way, okay? What I want to do in the meantime is a couple of basic checks just to make sure that you are okay. How does that sound?'

No reply.

'I know that you are scared, Florence, but you are safe here, and we are here to look after you.'

No reply, well no verbal reply, but Florence did squeeze Doctor Sutherland's hand briefly as the doctor had taken a gentle hold as soon as Florence entered the cubicle.

Doctor Sutherland began to issue instructions to the assembled team and within a few seconds they were all busying themselves with their allocated tasks.

'Where is she? Florence Findlay, where is she?' Aileen flew through the entrance doors, flanked by Callum and Jackie Macallan. Calvert had dropped them off directly outside the door and gone off to park his car.

Aileen and Callum were taken through the doors, beyond the reception area, and into the beating heart of the A&E department. Having been asked to take a seat for a minute, they were advised by the nurse that she would see if the doctor was free.

After a couple of minutes, a woman in her early thirties dressed in green surgical scrubs appeared and stood in front of Aileen and Callum. They rose to greet her.

'Hello, Mr and Mrs Findlay? I'm Doctor Sutherland, I'm the lead clinician here in the A&E department.'

Aileen regarded her intently. This was the person who was in charge of looking after Florence, her baby. It was a mixture of both her youthful looks and flaming red hair that made Aileen question her competence, although the old adage of not judging a book by its cover immediately came to mind and she quickly dismissed her initial thoughts.

'Yes, of course.'

'Is…she okay?' asked Callum with more than a degree of trepidation.

'Yes, she appears fine in the main. We are waiting on some blood results, and she'll be off to X-ray shortly.'

'X-ray?'

'Yes, hopefully just a precaution. I can't be one hundred percent sure, not without the X-ray, but there may be a minor fracture to her right arm. If it is fractured, it's nothing serious and will heal perfectly well over the next few weeks. But, as I say, we've yet to send her to X-ray, so we'll need to wait for definitive confirmation.'

'So, can we see her now?'

'Yes of course,' Doctor Sutherland said, 'just one thing though…'

'What's that?'

'I know that you will have lots of questions; obviously eager to know many things.' The doctor paused for a second, 'the police have made me aware of your daughter's circumstances.'

'Okay, and…'

'All I would ask at this point is, try not to overload her with dozens of questions. Take your time. All she wants is your love and reassurance.'

Doctor Sutherland led them both into a cubicle and closed the curtain around them. As expected, Aileen flew into Florence's open arms as she sat up to greet her. Both mother and daughter began to cry. Callum stood by for a second; it wasn't that he felt like a spare part, no, it wasn't the time for a family hug, he would have his turn soon, after all his daughter, his princess, was home, safe and sound.

'I'll leave you to it for a while. I'll be back soon,' Doctor Sutherland said as she exited through the curtain.

In the preceding minutes Calvert had arrived in the treatment area, made himself known to one of the nurses and was waiting as Doctor Sutherland appeared.

'Doctor,' Calvert extended his hand, 'I'm Detective Inspector Calvert.'

The doctor was a little hesitant to take his hand in

return. It wasn't that she was impolite or being disrespectful in anyway, but she and her team had lived through the nightmare that was COVID-19, working long hours dressed in multiple layers of PPE, and now, without any surgical gloves, this had left an understandable nervousness for close physical contact with strangers. Quite ironic when you considered her occupation. Either way, she finally took his hand.

'Hi, Doctor Sutherland, I'm the clinical lead here in the A&E.'

'Yes. Your colleague here was telling me.'

'How can I help you, inspector? I assume you are here about Florence Findlay?'

'Correct. I believe that my sergeant managed to brief you prior to her arrival?'

'He did, yes.'

'Okay, so, at the risk of recapping, Florence went missing eight days ago and we firmly believe that she did not disappear of her own volition, you know, run away. She was taken by a person or persons as yet unknown. It is our working hypothesis that she has been held captive for the past eight days. How she escaped and from where, well, God only knows.'

'I understand, inspector. That pretty much aligns to what I have seen, a very frightened young girl who looks like she has been held captive, shackled, for a period of time, possibly beaten, and somewhat malnourished.'

'Shackled?' Calvert repeated.

'Yes. I can't be sure, but there is bruising on her wrists

that is consistent with some kind of restraint, handcuffs or shackles.'

'Interesting. Any other early observations from your assessment of her?'

'Well, there are no other obvious signs of trauma. There is a potential fracture of her right arm, but we won't know for sure until she has had an X-ray.'

'When is that happening?'

'Hopefully within the next hour.'

'Okay.'

'Other than that, she looks to be, well, fairly okay to be honest. Well, you've seen her I assume?'

'I have, yes.'

'Well, aside from the fact that she simply looks like she has been locked up in a cold, dark cellar for a week, shackled to the wall, has had very little food or water and clearly not much sleep.'

'As I said, we are not sure of any details yet, but I wouldn't bet against what you have just said. Did you find any signs of sexual assault?'

'No, not as part of my initial assessment, but that assessment was not specifically targeted at that area.'

'Is that an examination that you plan to do?'

'Yes. Now that her parents are here, I will ask for their permission to undertake such an assessment and take the usual swabs.'

'Has she said anything whilst she has been here?' Calvert asked.

'Not a word. You can tell that she is scared and withdrawn into her own world. It might be quite a while before she opens up in any way. Hopefully her parents now being here with her might make the difference.'

'Yes, hopefully.'

'Unfortunately, inspector, in my job I can only treat what I can see.'

'Yes, yes, of course. We have specialist officers that are trained in this area. Far more caring, diplomatic, and patient than a middle-aged Yorkshireman like me.'

They shared a smile.

Florence had just returned from having the X-ray on her arm and had been settled back onto the bed in the cubicle.

Doctor Sutherland entered to see Aileen and Callum still sitting in two chairs at the side of her bed. She greeted them with a warm smile.

'Right, I have the results from the X-ray, and unfortunately there is a small fracture on the right forearm.' She turned to Florence.

'It's nothing to worry about, we'll add a cast for four to six weeks and after that it will be fully healed, back to normal again. We can even cover your cast in some funky colours these days, so it's not boring white anymore. How does that sound?'

Florence just about managed to raise an acknowledging smile, but nothing more.

Doctor Sutherland gestured for both parents to step away from the bedside for a moment. They duly followed her lead.

The doctor paused for a second, preparing herself for the gravity of the next discussion point. Deep inhalation. She returned her focus to Aileen and Callum.

'There is another point that I want to discuss with you.'

'Okay.'

'There is another assessment, another set of tests, that I would like to perform.'

'More tests? Why? What for?'

'It would be an examination of an intimate nature, taking swabs, checking for evidence of sexual assault.'

'Rape…you mean rape! Are you saying that Florence has been raped?'

'No, no, absolutely not. What I am saying is that we need to perform this examination to confirm one way or the other; hopefully to definitively rule it out. The police will need to know, one way or the other.'

Neither replied, but sat in a state of shock, as though they had actually been told that Florence had been raped.

'As Florence is under sixteen, we need your consent to undertake this assessment.'

Doctor Sutherland waited for a few moments, watching Aileen and Callum as they came to terms with what they were being asked, and more importantly what impact, physically and psychologically, this might have on their daughter.

'Yes, yes, you must,' replied Callum finally, 'it sounds like it is necessary and important.'

'It is. Thank you.'

'Can we go home after that?'

'I would rather that we kept her in hospital overnight for observation.'

'And I,' said Aileen, 'want my daughter back home with us. If it's just observation, then we can do this at home, can we not?'

'If it's just an arm fracture, then we should be able to take her home, shouldn't we, doctor?' Callum asked.

'Yes, I would have thought so. We need to add the cast and undertake the assessment as we've just discussed, but, yes okay, I don't see any reason to keep Florence in hospital beyond that.'

'Thank you.'

'The police are here and will want to speak to Florence at some point, but I will let them know that you should, hopefully, be back home in a couple of hours and suggest that they do so there, is that okay?'

'Sure.'

Their remaining time at the hospital was as Doctor Sutherland had outlined; a twenty-minute session with a nurse applying a cast on Florence's right arm, and a period of thirty minutes where Florence was taken to a private room for a more intimate assessment. Aileen accompanied her daughter, but Callum remained in the waiting area.

Before long all three were being whisked away and back home again. The offer of an ambulance transfer was hastily rejected by Calvert, expecting news to have spread about Florence's reappearance, and he wanted to ensure that they had an appropriate level of police support when they arrived back in Kelvedie. They travelled back in Calvert's car, with Sergeant O'Brien following.

Before the police left that evening, Callum and Aileen were reassured that Calvert would have a uniformed officer stationed outside of their front door all night. The request by Jackie Macallan to stay over, sleeping on the sofa, was rejected by Aileen, saying that the officer stationed outside was all the police presence that they needed.

Calvert waited until the young officer was standing at his station before bidding them all goodnight and leaving them to commence the long journey towards regaining some degree of normality and family life.

CHAPTER 20

Calvert checked the time before picking up the phone to Jackie Macallan. It was Sunday morning after all. He expected her to answer, and possibly to be in Kelvedie with the Findlays, as was the demands of her role. The family liaison officer role was generally all or nothing, feast or famine.

With Florence Findlay having been reunited, relatively safe and sound, with her parents yesterday, you would think that there might be less dependency on Jackie. The conduit of information with the investigating team appeared less important. Their daughter was home.

But, for the police, and to a certain degree the family, it didn't stop there. There was a requirement, an absolute necessity, to find out where Florence had been for the last eight days.

Nine forty-five, that'll be fine, Calvert assured himself. He had just finished what might be his penultimate Scottish breakfast at Shallowbrook Lodge and had chatted briefly to Brian before making his way to the snug with a cup of coffee.

'Hi, Jackie, it's DI Calvert.'

'Oh, hi, guv.'

'Not too early, I hope. Sunday morning and all that?'

'No, guv, not at all.'

'Are you in Kelvedie? With the Findlays perhaps?'

'I'm not, no. I stayed for an hour or so yesterday after we all got back from the hospital. I offered to stay over last night but they declined, said they'd be fine.'

'How are they all bearing up?'

'Yes, okay, I think. I think Callum and Aileen want to try and return to some normality.'

'Understandable,' Calvert replied, 'but highly unlikely in the short term. Not only will they have the ongoing police investigation, but I dare say that the ranks of journalists and media hacks will have swelled in the last few hours, all wanting to gain that exclusive interview. Yes, it's not likely that normality will return for quite some time.'

'I am due to visit them later this morning, well noon actually.'

'Okay. Whilst you're there can you test the temperature for us to come and talk to Florence? Make sure that you stress that the interview will be relaxed and informal, and will be led by a specialist officer.'

'Yes, of course, guv.'

'Look, I'll put the resources on standby for, say, four o'clock, unless you call and say otherwise. I don't mind delaying the interview with Florence for a couple of days, but we really do need to try and speak to her as soon as possible.'

'Yes, guv, understood. I'll do my best.'

'Great, thanks, Jackie.'

Punctuality was a virtue and one that Jackie Macallan thought was being lost by a younger generation. The Iberian approach to timekeeping of *mañana, mañana,* seemed to be the norm creeping into today's society. Jackie didn't like it. *Be on time, or don't bother turning up at all,* was her mantra. As such, she made her way up the garden path of the Findlay home five minutes before noon.

If you're on time, you're late, was another maxim she tried to lead her life by. This kind of contradicted the first mantra, after all, should she be on time, or should she be early? Either way, she would never be late.

Neither Aileen nor Callum wanted to be filmed or photographed answering the front door, and Calvert had guessed correctly, the horde of journalists had swelled in numbers over the last few hours as news had leaked that Florence had been found and was back at home with her parents. Jackie had an agreement with Aileen that she would knock and walk in.

'Hi, Callum, how are you?' Jackie asked upon entering the kitchen and seeing him.'

'Aye, no bad, thanks, Jackie.'

'Good. Good. And how are things?' A ridiculous question perhaps when viewed in hindsight, but an obvious one, and one that should be asked.

'You know…'

'Aye.'

'Aileen is through there, in the lounge, if you're after her.'

'Well, I came to see you all, but I'll pop through. Thanks, Callum.'

'Aye, nae bother. Will you have a brew?'

'Aye, usual please. Thanks.'

Jackie walked through into the lounge to see Aileen cuddled up on the sofa with Florence. She checked to see if Florence was asleep before she spoke. She wasn't, and Florence raised her head to see who the visitor was.

'Hello, Aileen, hello, Florence.'

'Hello, Jackie, take a seat.'

'Thank you. How are you both?'

Aileen kissed her daughter on the forehead. 'We're okay, aren't we, princess?'

'Good.'

'I didn't think that we would be seeing much of you moving forward,' said Aileen.

'Yes, that's true. In fact, this might be my last visit. My role as family liaison officer has naturally come to an end.'

'I sense a but…'

'Yes, well, whilst I will take a step back, there will still be some police involvement as my colleagues continue with the active investigation.'

'Florence, sweetheart,' Aileen said, 'just go and see what your dad is doing in the kitchen. I don't know where he's gone to brew that tea.'

Jackie waited until Florence had left the room before she continued, 'we're overjoyed that Florence is back home safe and sound, we truly are, but the police investigation will continue until we have some answers around both her disappearance and where she has been for eight days.'

'We understand, we want answers too.'

'Has Florence opened up to you any further since she came home?'

'Well, she has started to communicate more, certainly this morning. We've had a few words from her.'

'Good, that's good. Look, Aileen, it's going to take time, isn't it? You just need to be patient.'

'Yes, but will your lot be equally patient?'

Jackie picked up on what Aileen had implied. 'Yes, they will. We have specially trained officers who will speak to Florence in a calm, patient and understanding manner. There won't be any pressure applied.'

Aileen didn't respond.

'But we do need to speak to Florence sooner rather than later, and preferably today.'

'Would we need to go to a police station?'

'No, I wouldn't have thought so. I'll check with my guv, but I'm sure that we could do it here if that's okay?'

'It would be better here. I'm sure Florence would feel more comfortable. I would feel more comfortable.'

'Yes, understood. I fully agree.'

'Would I be able to sit in, you know, whilst she is being interviewed?'

'Don't think of it as an interview, Aileen, there is nothing formal about it. The officers will try and make it as informal as possible. And yes, due to Florence's age, as long as there are no objections, you can sit with her.'

'Okay. When?'

'Well, today if possible. I'd like to inform my guv that we could set it up for later this afternoon. Do you need to speak to Callum?'

'I should really, yes, but go ahead and set it up anyway.'

'Hiya, Jackie, how are things there?'

'Aye, all good, considering. Listen, I've spoken to Aileen and we're on for four o'clock today if that's still okay?'

'Perfect, well done. I'll get it all lined up my side. Do they know what do expect?'

'I'm not sure. I've tried to play down the whole interview thing, and told them to expect a more informal chat, you know, something to put Florence at ease.'

'Good. Hopefully she will start to open up because we desperately need some kind of lead from her. We've got nothing from our other lines of enquiry. What Florence can remember, and what she can tell us, will be pretty much all we have.'

'Well, fingers crossed then.'

'Has Florence said anything more to Aileen or Callum?'

'Nothing of any note, no. She has said a few words, you know, in response to questions, but that's more just general family conversation; she certainly hasn't mentioned anything about the last few days.'

'Okay. Well, she might with the right approach and structured questions.'

'Yes, or she might bottle it up and suppress it for days, weeks or even months.'

'Yes, I guess. There is also the remote chance that, for whatever reason, she can't remember anything. She might have been drugged, sedated, and know very little about her whereabouts.'

'Well, I guess time will tell, guv. Right, I'm off. I'll be here when you lot arrive.'

'Okay, Jackie. By the way, what's the media circus like outside of the house?'

'There's one or two, that's for sure. Their numbers have certainly swelled in the last few hours, so it would be fair to say that word has got out. So far, they are respecting boundaries and remaining at the bottom of the path, outside of the gate. Just push your way through as I'm sure you would anyway.'

'You're getting to know me, Jackie, it's that Yorkshire diplomacy.'

'Aye, or lack of diplomacy. Right, see you anon.'

'Bye.'

Callum answered the knock at the door; it was three forty-five. Jackie had advised them that her colleagues would arrive around four o'clock.

Standing outside were DI Calvert and a young female officer dressed casually but smartly in a knee-length pencil skirt and navy blouse.

'Hi, Callum, can we come in? Hopefully you are expecting us.'

'Yes, yes, of course.' Callum left the door open and invited them to enter and follow him through to the kitchen whereupon they found Jackie sitting at the table.

'Oh, hi, Jackie.'

'Hi.'

'Can I get you both a drink?' asked Callum.

They both replied that a coffee would be welcomed.

'Aileen is upstairs with Florence; she'll be down in five or ten minutes, I guess.'

'That's okay, there's no rush,' Calvert confirmed. 'Callum, this is Constable Gillespie.'

'Mackenzie, although my friends just call me Kenzie. Nice to meet you, Callum.'

'Yes, you too, Kenzie. So, you're here to interview Florence?'

'Kind of. I'm certainly going to sit down with Florence and have a conversation with her. Perhaps try and help her remember some of the events over the last few days. Don't worry, it will be relaxed and informal.'

'Okay,' he said as he passed them their coffee, 'do you want to make your way through there to the lounge and I'll see where they are.'

After waiting ten minutes or so, Aileen and Florence entered the lounge and took a seat on the large sofa. Aileen had been introduced to Kenzie and they were ready to start.

'Hi, Florence, my name is Paul and I'm a police officer. I don't know if you remember me from yesterday?' It was asked more rhetorically but he let it hang for a couple of seconds in case she replied. She didn't.

'This is Kenzie. Kenzie is a police officer too.'

'Hi, Florence.'

'Florence, Kenzie has come to have a chat with you, okay, and I'm going to leave you to it. I'll have a chat with your dad in the kitchen.'

Calvert smiled at Constable Gillespie as he stood and made his way back to the kitchen.

Gillespie waited for the door to be closed, then she turned back to Florence and Aileen.

'Right, it's just us girls now. Florence, as my colleague said, I'm a police officer. You've got your mum here, and your mum can stay with you all of the time. I'm going to ask you some questions, okay, if you want to stop at any time, just say so. Is that okay?'

Florence nodded.

'Do you remember the last time you came home from school?'

Florence nodded.

'Do you remember what you did when you got home?'

She shrugged her shoulders this time.

'You dropped your school bag and ran into the back garden to play.'

Again, Florence nodded.

Constable Gillespie guessed, even at this early stage, that it might be challenging to get Florence to open up a little more, but she was trained for exactly this kind of engagement with a minor. She had lots of experience interviewing pre-teens following traumatic events. Slow and steady wins the race.

'You played for a while, then came back into the kitchen for some lemonade. Is that right?'

Florence, cuddled up next to her mum, looked up at her. Aileen smiled warmly back. Florence nodded.

'Can you tell me what happened then, Florence?'

Gillespie waited a few seconds for a reply, which wasn't forthcoming.

'Can you remember where you went after finishing your lemonade? Did you stay in the garden? Did you go to the field behind your house?'

Florence had a blank look on her face. She was giving nothing away with her expressions and was clearly not currently inclined to provide any verbal responses. Gillespie persevered.

'Do you remember leaving your garden? Perhaps you went somewhere else, I hear that the park is quite nice.'

Gillespie was making brief handwritten notes, or annotations to the list of questions she had prepared, but clearly nothing of any substance was being added to the paper at the minute.

'Whilst you were outside playing, did you see anyone else? Perhaps Aunty Pauline or Uncle John. You play at their house sometimes, don't you?'

Florence nodded.

'Did you see them?'

This time she shook her head. Gillespie was happy that she was eliciting a different response to a head nod.

'Okay. Did you see anyone else?'

Florence pulled herself closer into her mum's embrace and snuggled her head into her chest, desperately looking as though she wanted to be anywhere else but there right now.

'Florence? Did you see anyone else? Anyone that you know, anyone from the village, or perhaps a stranger?'

Callum was seated at the kitchen table across from Calvert and Jackie Macallan. He was eager to enter the lounge and see what was going on himself, but Aileen had made him promise that he would remain outside of the room. Callum, she had noted previously, was inclined to add unnecessary stress to any situation. He had conceded that point about his personality traits.

'This DC Gillespie, she looks about eighteen. Are you sure she knows what she's doing?' Callum asked, perhaps searching more for reassurance than actually needing to know.

Calvert smiled.

'She's got youth on her side that's for sure, but…yes, Callum, she is more than qualified. Me, I catch bad guys and put them behind bars, she is trained to interview minors following certain incidents or ordeals that they may have been through or witnessed. I'm not local, as you know, but as best as I know, she has been a police officer for eight years, of which the last three have been spent in this specialist role.'

'Aye, okay.'

'She is without doubt the most qualified person here. She will be a qualified Advanced Child Witness Interviewer, and also National Specialist Child Abuse Investigator.'

Calvert was quick to realise that his request for reassurance might not have done just that; reassure him. 'Don't worry, I'm not saying that anything like that happened, just answering your challenge about her being qualified.'

Callum forced a smile, trying immediately to forget the words *child abuse*.

'When someone has experienced a traumatic event, and this applies tenfold for, you know, children, they do tend to retrench into themselves. The mind tries to block out the events and prevent the person from constantly remembering any trauma. I guess it's a way of self-healing, or at least the start of that process. Anyway, depending on the event, blocking out the detail can sometimes be a good thing, or a bad thing. Arguably the professionals will tell you, irrespective of age, that it is always better to talk through the event as part of the healing process.'

Callum looked attentive, as though he was interested. Partially, perhaps.

'Anyway, in relation to Florence, we really need to fill in the gaps over those eight days. We need to know where she has been, and obviously, we need to know who she has been with. We need to know if she was taken against her will, and ultimately, we need to find and arrest them.'

'What if she can't remember?' Callum asked, 'or what if she won't say?'

'I'm sure that she will, Callum, in time. There's no rush. She'll talk in her own time. She won't be rushed. Trust me.'

'Aye, okay.'

'We'll find out all in good time, and rest assured, we'll be making arrests before too long.'

Having failed to elicit much of anything from Florence, Gillespie was still patiently attempting to draw something, anything, from her. Having watched Florence visibly retrench into her mum at the question of having seen any other person, Gillespie left that alone, for now.

'What can you tell me about where you have been for

the last few days, Florence?'

Florence shrugged her shoulders.

'Have you been staying with someone that you know?'

Again, at the mere mention of another person, she tucked herself tighter into her mum's chest. Aileen gave her a squeeze and kissed her on the top of her head before forcing a smile at Gillespie; a smile that Gillespie inferred to mean *I'm sorry* and *keep going, but gently.*

'Can you remember when you were found yesterday, Florence?'

She nodded.

'The landlord from the pub saw you walking near the harbour, just outside the pub, didn't he? Can you remember?'

Again, she nodded.

'Can you remember how you got to the harbour? Did you walk, or did someone drop you off in car, or a van maybe?'

Florence paused for a few seconds before she replied, with a not inconsequential answer, 'I walked.'

'You walked. Okay.'

A purposeful pause by Gillespie so as to not appear to be shooting quick-fire questions at her, then she followed up, 'it was about ten o'clock, I think, when you were seen at the harbour, can you remember where you had walked from?'

No reply.

'Okay, can you remember how long you had been walking for?'

Florence shook her head.

'That's okay, Florence, that's okay.'

Gillespie was regularly reassuring her, especially and ironically when Florence was either unwilling or unable to provide any response. She had potentially uncovered a huge breakthrough. Assuming that Florence was telling the truth about walking to the harbour, she had to have been within Kelvedie somewhere, at least immediately prior to that.

Yes, of course it was feasible that Florence had walked a fair distance from a neighbouring village, or even from the town of Tarbert, and yes it was possible that she had been dropped off in a car at the outskirts of the village, and had indeed walked towards the harbour as she had suggested.

But, just but, it was highly feasible if not probable that Florence had been held in Kelvedie for at least the hours preceding her release, or her escape.

'Do you need to take a break, Florence?'

She shook her head.

'Okay. I've asked you a couple of questions about other people, you know; did you see anyone else? Were you with anyone else? Do you remember?'

Florence nodded.

'I can see that those questions make you a little uncomfortable, don't they?'

Again, she nodded.

'Okay. I understand. I don't want to make you uncomfortable, Florence. That's the last thing I want. You've been great so far, really great.'

Gillespie paused for a few seconds before inevitably returning with *those* questions once again.

'I'm sorry about this, but I just want to ask again, did you see anyone else? Anyone that you know, anyone from the village, or perhaps a stranger?'

No reply.

'Whilst you have been away from Mummy and Daddy, have you been with anyone else? Has someone been looking after you?'

Gillespie really needed a response.

She didn't get one.

Gillespie smiled, firstly at Florence, then at Aileen. 'Okay, let's leave it there, shall we? Thank you, Florence, you've been really brave and really helpful.'

As DC Gillespie was closing her notepad and putting her pen back into the inner pocket of her jacket, Florence whispered something, initially barely audible.

She repeated it; 'Hayley.'

Gillespie looked at Aileen with a quizzical expression. 'Hayley.'

'Did you say Hayley, sweetheart?'

'Hayley was her sister,' said Gillespie confidently, having done her background homework before attending today.

'Yes, that's right. Hayley…' Aileen was interrupted by Florence.

'Hayley. I have seen Hayley.'

'Hayley?' repeated Aileen, 'what you do mean, you

have seen Hayley?'

'I saw Hayley,' she repeated.

Gillespie asked, 'Florence, over the last few days, are you saying that you have seen Hayley?'

'Yes.'

'Okay. And was this Hayley your sister, or another girl called Hayley?'

Neither Gillespie nor Aileen expected the answer they received.

'My sister Hayley.'

'Okay, sweetheart,' Aileen kissed her on her forehead, 'why don't you go upstairs to your room and put your TV on, I'll be up in a few minutes with some juice and a biscuit.'

Aileen waited until Florence had left the room and heard the bedroom door close, at which point coincidentally Callum and Calvert re-entered from the kitchen.

Callum could see Aileen looked a little shaken. 'What's wrong? Is everything okay? Is Florence okay?'

'Aye, Florence is fine.'

'Okay, what's with the glum face then?'

Aileen took a few seconds before she replied, 'Florence has just told us that she has seen Hayley in the last few days.'

'Hayley? Hayley who? Our Hayley? Are you sure?'

'Yes, that's what she said.'

'Well, that's impossible. Okay, well not impossible but highly unlikely.'

'No, you were right the first time, that is impossible.'

'So…' Calvert interjected, 'when Hayley went missing Florence wouldn't have been born yet, correct?'

'Aye.'

'Okay. I'm relatively familiar with Hayley's disappearance as it was necessary for background information on Florence's disappearance. Hayley would be nineteen now, correct?'

'Aye, but…' Callum was interrupted by Aileen.

'Florence knows that she had a sister called Hayley. Obviously, there are many photographs around the house, and of course we spend time talking to her about Hayley. But the last photo we have is ten years old, there is no way that Florence could recognise Hayley, and add to that Hayley didn't know that Florence existed, she had gone missing before she was born.'

'Add to which,' Callum said, 'we have long assumed that Hayley is dead. We resigned ourselves to this fact a few years ago. I don't know who Florence saw but it wasn't our Hayley.'

Silence filled the room for a few seconds, no-one really knowing what to say next, however improbable Florence's statement.

'Where was this?' Callum asked.

'She didn't say. Aside from mentioning Hayley by name, she didn't say where she had been, or with whom. That was the key thing that we couldn't get Florence to confirm.'

'Did she say anything else?'

'Not really, no.'

'She did say that she had walked to where she was found, at the harbour,' Gillespie confirmed.

'Walked?'

'Yes, but she couldn't say where from or how long she had been walking for. I dare say that Florence will start to feel more at ease over the next few days, she will remember more and be more open to discussing some of the detail.'

'Agreed,' Calvert confirmed, 'if it's okay with you, Callum, Aileen, let's let her settle for a while, and perhaps we might pop back for another chat tomorrow?'

Tomorrow? Aileen was hoping that he would have suggested a week or two. Clearly not.

Aileen and Callum agreed that Calvert and Gillespie would call again twenty-four hours later, but Aileen did retain the right to veto this if she felt that Florence wasn't up to it. Calvert reluctantly agreed.

CHAPTER 21

Calvert had been summoned to see Superintendent Talloch, and she had requested to meet him at Greenock police station. He was unsure whether this was a travel concession made by her to accommodate him, or she might have been in Greenock anyway.

Either way, whilst the journey from Kelvedie to Greenock was longer than that of Greenock to Glasgow, the former did mean that Calvert did not need to navigate the Monday morning traffic into the centre of Glasgow. The early morning drive from Kelvedie along the coastal route of the A83 provided Calvert with a relaxing, stress-free and enjoyable journey, and the two and a half hours passed by in a flash.

'Ah, Paul, come in.'

Talloch greeted Calvert warmly and had since the very

first day, in the main, called him by his first name rather than his rank. She had always been mindful and grateful that Calvert had stepped in to head this investigation and had done, and was still doing, the local force a really big favour.

'Morning, ma'am.'

'Sorry to pull you away from Kelvedie for a few hours. How are you?'

'Very well, thank you, very well.'

'Please, take a seat.' Talloch gestured towards the more informal twin sofas rather than the chairs either side of the desk.

'Well, let me start with congratulations, Paul. We have Florence Findlay back home safe and sound.'

'Back home, yes, but I'm not sure how much we affected the outcome, ma'am. It's perhaps more by luck that she's back home again.'

'Perhaps, but she is back home, safe, and it will definitely go down as a successful misper recovery.'

'Yes, as you say, she's back home, so that's all that matters in the end.'

'Aside from finding out where she has been for those eight days and who, if anyone, abducted her,' Talloch replied.

'Well, yes, there is that, of course.'

'Do we have any leads on her whereabouts during that period?'

'No, not yet, she hasn't really been in a talkative mood

since her return.'

'Okay…'

Talloch was interrupted as Siobhan brought in a tray with two coffees and a handful of biscuits.

'I'll just lay these down here and get out of your way.'

'Thanks, Siobhan.'

'Thank you.'

'There were two pieces of… well let's say interesting information that we did manage to glean from Florence.'

'Okay, what were they?'

'Firstly, you are aware that she was found wandering near the harbour, just outside the local pub, The Plough.'

'I am, yes.'

'Well, she said that she had walked to that point.'

'Walked?'

'Yes, but unfortunately, we couldn't get her to expand on that, you know, walked from where, walked from what house, how long had she been walking etcetera. All being well, and if her parents confirm that she is up to it, we plan to go back later this afternoon for a follow-up chat with her.'

'Okay, great. It's great that she's been found safe and sound, but we really need to know where she has been, if she's been held captive, and who by.'

'I know. Only half the job done to date. We're still on it.'

'I know you are, Paul, and I continue to appreciate your support.'

'The second part,' Calvert said, 'is a little more interesting.'

'Go on.'

'Well, as I said, little Florence wasn't giving much away during the chat, but she did say that during the time she has been missing, she saw Hayley.'

'Hayley? Hayley who?'

'Hayley, her sister.'

'Hayley Findlay? Florence said that she saw Hayley Findlay whilst she was gone. Did Hayley abduct her?'

'Not sure, ma'am, all the details are sketchy at best. Well, truth be told, there are no further details. Florence simply said that she saw Hayley, and that it was her sister.'

'It can't be possible, can it?'

'Improbable, ma'am, but not impossible I guess.'

'Well, if Hayley is alive, and Aileen and Callum are unconnected to Florence's disappearance, she might well be the one responsible for abducting Florence.'

'Seems unlikely, in my opinion, but yes, it is possible.'

'So, let's say she is telling the truth, we now have another dimension to the investigation, and a potential sighting of a long-term misper.'

'Ten years.'

'Okay, bloody hell, that's just ramped up the pressure, and the workload.'

They both paused for a few seconds, taking several sips of their coffee.

'With that in mind, I wanted to let you know that

Detective Chief Inspector Geary will be back tomorrow.'

'Ah, good. His son has recovered I assume and they're back from Jamaica?'

'Indeed. Anyway, DCI Geary will be picking up this investigation as SIO from tomorrow onwards.'

'That's fine, ma'am.'

'Can I ask one more favour of you? Just one more before you finally switch off and enjoy that relaxing holiday that brought you up here in the first place.'

'Of course. What do you need?'

'Do you think that you could stick around for a further twenty-four hours to brief DCI Geary, bring him up to speed and provide an active handover?'

'Yes, or course.'

'We'll continue to pick up the cost of your accommodation.'

'Yes, okay, that's fine. No problem. I'll brief the DCI and remain around for the next couple of days to get him up to speed and help fill in any of the knowledge gaps.'

'Great, thank you. I spoke to DCI Geary yesterday, he is aware that you have been leading the investigation as SIO, and also aware that Florence has been found. He'll take over with a view to discovering where she has been for those eight days, and with whom. This new information about Hayley is interesting too.'

'Understood, ma'am.'

'Thanks for all your help on this, Paul. You really were in the right place at the right time.'

Calvert smiled, 'my wife used to say that, or moreover she used to say the wrong place at the wrong time. It was a standing joke in our family.'

'Your wife?' Talloch had a sudden painful thought, 'your wife isn't here with you in Kelvedie, is she? She hasn't been here for the past couple of weeks whilst you've been working on the misper investigation?'

'No, she hasn't, I'm here on my own,' Calvert confirmed.

'Good. I had visions of a very pissed-off wife, annoyed that your week away had been ruined by you being seconded to the investigation.'

'No. My wife died six months ago.'

Now Talloch felt really bad. 'Oh, bugger, sorry, Paul, I didn't know.'

'It's fine, honestly, you weren't to know.'

'Will you stay on a few days, and actually start that walking holiday that you had planned?'

'I'm not sure, probably not. I think I might write this one off and perhaps plan another short break in a couple of months. If I do stay for a few days, I'm not sure that I'd remain in Kelvedie, it's too close to the family and the active investigation.'

'I agree, it will be good for you to get some distance.'

'I might return though, perhaps to another part of Scotland. I hear there are some nice areas around Edinburgh and some good walking around the Pentland Hills.'

'Indeed, there are. That's very much my neck of the woods. Listen, look me up if you make it back up to

Edinburgh and we'll grab a drink together.'

'Will do, sounds like a plan.'

'Good, and in the meantime, I'll be putting a good word in with your Chief Superintendent in Humberside.'

'Never hurts, ma'am.'

They said their goodbyes and Calvert left; he didn't expect that he would see Talloch again, despite the offer of a social reunion sometime in the not-too-distant future.

Calvert arrived at Lochgilphead station just after lunchtime and walked through the door to find Sergeant O'Brien and Constable Davidson sitting at two of the desks, frantically tapping away at their respective computer terminals.

'Afternoon.'

'Hi, guv.'

'Guv. Not sure that we'd see you again,' said Davidson, 'I hear Geary is back tomorrow.'

'Detective Chief Inspector Geary,' Calvert replied with the intended tone of correction, 'is indeed back tomorrow and will be taking over as SIO. So, the news has reached you already then?'

'Aye, we don't miss a trick out here, guv.'

'No, I'm sure you don't, constable.'

'Is this your last visit then, guv, have you brought cakes and the like?'

Calvert smiled, 'no, I haven't brought bloody cakes. I'll still be around for the next couple of days if that's alright with you, constable?'

After taking off his jacket and filling a mug with steaming hot coffee, Calvert pulled up a chair in front of them both. It had the intended effect as they both stopped clattering the keyboards and looked in his direction.

'What updates do we have since yesterday?'

'Well, we've struggled with the question of where Florence was before she was seen at the harbour at ten o'clock. There is no CCTV coverage around the village as you know, but we are reaching out to each and every resident again today to check if they have their own security cameras or doorbell cameras that might have captured something.'

'Good.'

'I guess we might have something one way or the other within twenty-four hours.'

'Let's try and make it by the end of the day, shall we?'

'Sure, if you find us an extra dozen pair of hands, guv.'

'Okay, let me see what I can do.'

'It is feasible that she could have been held many miles away, and potentially dropped off that morning by a car. There's no CCTV as we've said.'

'Agreed. It's just as feasible, although I'm sure that the community would be aghast to admit it, that she might have been held within the village for those eight days.'

'Look…' started Calvert, '…our biggest breakthrough in this case has been the safe return of Florence. Aside from the successful end to a misper investigation, she holds the key to unlocking the next stage of the investigation. We really need to get some answers from her.'

'Any progress from yesterday?' asked O'Brien.

'A little. She confirmed that she had walked to where she was found near the harbour, but we were unable to get her to elaborate further in terms of where she had walked from, or how far she had been walking for.'

'Shame. As you say, it looks like she holds the key to any progress.'

'Hopefully we'll be back later today for another chat with her. We'll keep plugging away, sensitively, and hope that we get a breakthrough.'

'Aye, here's hoping.'

'Right, I'm off to Kelvedie. If I don't speak to you later, I'll see you back here tomorrow, eight-thirty sharp. Remember DCI Geary will be back.'

'Hi there, Callum, can I come in?'

'Aye, away on in.' Callum stood aside and allowed Calvert to lead the way through to the kitchen where he found Aileen preparing lunch.

'Sorry, have I come at a bad time? Looks like you're about to eat.'

'No, no, it's fine. Sit yourself down and I'll put the kettle on.'

'Okay, thanks. I didn't know if I would find you to be honest, I thought that you might have returned to work, well, especially you, Callum?'

'No, not yet. My boss has been quite understanding and given me as much time as I need.'

'Aye but compassionate leave comes with fifty percent of the bloody salary though, so he's not that understanding,' Aileen said.

Callum just shrugged his shoulders.

'Well, that doesn't seem fair,' Calvert replied, 'would you like me to have a word with him?'

'That's nice of you to offer, thank you, but it won't do any good. He sent us a copy of the employment contract that Callum signed when he first started there. It clearly says that he's only entitled to fifty percent for periods of authorised extended leave. Anyway, it is what it is. It's more important that we are both here for Florence, for a while.'

'Okay, if you're sure.'

'Here's your brew.'

'Thanks. Well, I've come for a couple of reasons. Firstly, to let you know that I will be stepping back as the senior officer.'

'Oh dear, have you done something wrong? Are you in trouble?'

Calvert smiled, 'no, not at all. No, the local senior officer, Detective Chief Inspector Geary will be back tomorrow and will be assuming the role of senior investigating officer. If DCI Geary had been here at the time of Florence's disappearance, then he would have been involved from the start, and to be honest, you probably wouldn't have met me at all.'

'Okay, Geary, you say?'

'Yes, DCI Geary.'

'What's he like?'

'Haven't got a clue. Sorry. Never met the guy, but I'm sure that he's good at his job. The one thing that I've seen whilst I have been here is that the officers are very good at their respective roles. I'll be sticking around for a couple of days, just to brief him and support a handover.'

'Okay.'

'I expect that he will want to come and see you both. Florence is back home safe and sound, which is great obviously, but we still have an open and active investigation, and I know that he will want to continue with that. I'm not sure what he's got planned but I expect that he might want to come tomorrow, or the day after latest. Is that okay?'

'Aye, sure.'

'Okay, good. Has Florence spoken any further, you know, since we were here yesterday?'

'No, not really.'

'Do you think…' Calvert paused mid-sentence. It wasn't a good idea, but after brief reflection he decided to take the chance '…that I might speak to her, to Florence?'

'I'm not sure,' Aileen replied.

'Yes, of course.'

Callum looked at his wife. 'Look, we need to find out what happened, and, well, I don't think that she is going to open up to us.'

'She might, in time.'

'Yes, she might, and she might not. We have to find out if someone took her, where they held her, and…' now Callum paused, almost choking on his words '…if anything was done to her.'

'She's up in her bedroom watching TV. I'll go and see how she is feeling and if she feels up to it.'

'Okay.'

CHAPTER 22

Calvert had chosen to remain in the kitchen, and with Aileen finishing off the lunch preparations, it felt as relaxed as it could be. Calvert sat at the kitchen table together with Florence and Callum.

Aileen brought across plates of tuna mayonnaise sandwiches and crisps, and to his surprise, Calvert was presented with a plate too.

'Oh, thank you very much.'

He winked at Florence.

Aileen joined them at the table, and they ate in silence for a few minutes, broken eventually by Calvert.

'Florence…you remember speaking to one of my colleagues yesterday, Detective Constable Gillespie?'

'Kenzie? Yes, she was nice,' Florence said.

'Yes, she is nice, isn't she? Do you think that I could

ask you a couple of questions?'

Florence just shrugged, but then a broad smile took over her face and she turned to her mum, who noticing what Florence had seen, shared her smile.

'What?' Calvert asked.

Aileen pointed to the side of her mouth, and Calvert, not seeing anything untoward, eventually cottoned on and reached for his own. He picked a small piece of tuna from the side of his mouth and put it down on his plate.

Well, he thought, *that lightened the mood anyway.*

'Yesterday you said that you saw Hayley, can you remember?'

'Yes.'

'Your sister Hayley?'

'Yes.'

'Okay. Hayley went away before you were born, didn't she, and so I guess that she has never seen you?'

'No, I guess not.'

'Okay. How do you know that it was your sister Hayley? How come you are so sure?'

'She said so,' Florence calmly replied, like his question was the stupidest one she'd ever heard.

'She said so?'

'Yes. She said that I looked like her when she was my age. She told me her name was Hayley.'

'What else did she say, Florence?'

'She asked where I lived. I said, Kelvedie. She said that's where she lived too, although she hadn't been home for a long time.'

'Okay.'

'She asked if I lived with my mum and dad; I said that I did, and she asked me their names.'

Florence paused for a few seconds, staring straight ahead into her own personal abyss. 'I told her it was Callum and Aileen and she started to cry.'

As Callum saw a tear fall from Aileen's eye, he took hold of her hand and squeezed as tightly as he dared.

Florence continued, 'she told me that was the name of her mum and dad too, and that her name was Hayley, and she was my sister.'

Aileen rose from her seat and went over to hug Florence. They remained that way for several minutes, Florence never quite fully cognisant of what she had just told her mum and dad.

'Can I ask you a couple more questions?' asked Calvert. She nodded.

'Okay, thank you. Do you remember anything from the day that you didn't come home?'

Calvert was conscious not to say *went missing* or *disappeared*. From Florence's perspective, she had done neither.

'I was playing in the back field near the woods. I had just been back inside for some lemonade. When I went back out, I saw a man. He said hello…'

She paused, searching for her next words.

'…I don't know what happened then.'

Again, she paused.

'...I woke up in a dark room, and I had a headache. After a few minutes I heard some noises and I thought someone else was in the room with me, but it was very dark, and I couldn't see anything.'

There were so many gaps to fill but Calvert was heartened by Florence's willingness to talk.

'After a while a man came in and lit a candle on a table in the corner of the room. The candle gave a little bit of light, and then I could see the other girl, Hayley...but...I didn't know it was Hayley then, she told me later. He gave us both a sandwich and put a plate on the floor in front of us, with a plastic glass with some water in. I didn't really feel like eating; my head was hurting, but Hayley said that I needed to eat and drink it all up and we wouldn't get anything else for the rest of the day.'

'Could you move, Florence? You know, get up and walk around?'

'A little, yes. One of my ankles was chained to the wall.'

Calvert had ascertained this from the information provided by A&E consultant, Doctor Isla Sutherland. She couldn't be sure exactly what had been clasped around Florence's ankle, but she was sure that it had been some kind of restraint.

'We could stand up and maybe walk one step but no further because the chain stopped us.'

'Did the man say anything to you? Did he speak when he came in?'

'No. Well, he said a few words, sometimes, but it was

never a conversation. He blew out the candle and left. I started screaming but Hayley told me to stop as it was a waste of time, and no-one could hear us. She had done it for so long and given up.'

Aileen stepped in with a question. 'Did you have the conversation about being sisters straight away?'

'No, it was ages. Most of the time we were sitting in the dark. It was only when he came in with some food and water, he lit the candle and we had some light, then we could see each other. It was a while before she said she recognised me and told me that she might be my sister, Hayley.'

'You said that you were chained to the wall, Florence,' said Calvert, 'is that right?'

'Yes. I tried to pull it off, but I couldn't, I wasn't strong enough.'

'Did you get yourself free eventually, or did the man release you?'

'Release me?' she said with an astonishment belying all of her nine years, 'no, he didn't release me.'

'Okay, how did you manage to free yourself?'

'He came into the room and lit the candle as usual, and he said that he wanted me to do something for him.'

Aileen took a firm grasp of Callum's hand, fearing what was to come.

'Did he say what he wanted you to do?' asked Calvert.

'I don't know…err, no. He came over to me and started to release the chain that was around my ankle, and as he started to stand up again, I hit him over the head with a plate. He fell back to the ground again and I stepped over him and ran through the open door and up some stairs.'

'Okay. It sounds like you might have been in a basement, Florence.'

'A basement? I don't know what that is.'

'It's okay, never mind. How did you get out of the house?'

'At the top of the stairs I saw a door. I ran towards it and tried the handle, but it wouldn't open. It was locked…'

The tension in the air was palpable; with hearts pumping and pulses racing, both Callum and Aileen could have been watching a thriller on television. But this was real life, their life.

'…there was a key, so I turned it and opened the door. Then…then, I just ran. I kept running. I wasn't sure where I was, or where I was running to.'

'And then you ran to the harbour?'

'The harbour? Yes. I stopped and I was at the harbour. That man…'

'Gordon. The landlord of the pub.'

'Yes, he found me.'

Florence started to cry, 'I left her there, I left Hayley there with him, I left Hayley.'

'She'll be fine, sweetheart,' reassured Aileen, 'she's obviously strong, and what you've told us…well…we'll be able to find her now and bring her home, won't we?'

'But he'll be mad at her and will hurt her.'

'Don't worry, Florence, we'll find Hayley as soon as we can.'

Calvert spotted a freshly baked apple pie on the kitchen worktop. 'I'll tell you what, why don't we ask your mum if we can have some of that apple pie, eh? Let's have a break from talking for a while, and we can come back to that after our pie. How does that sound?'

Florence wiped away the tears falling from her eyes and looked at her mum. Aileen smiled.

'Go on then. Custard?'

'Yes please.'

After their dessert had been finished, including second helpings for Florence, Aileen cleared the table. Calvert had politely declined a further portion, despite it being probably the best apple pie he had tasted for as long as he could remember.

'Can we talk again, Florence?' he asked.

She nodded, feeling a little more confident and at ease now, having opened up a little earlier.

'What can you tell me about the man?'

'Like what?'

'Well, did you recognise him? Have you seen him before?'

'No.'

'Okay. Did he have an accent? Perhaps English like mine, or Scottish?'

'Scottish.'

'Scottish, okay. Was the candlelight good enough for you to see his face?'

'Not really, no.'

'That's okay,' reassured Calvert, despite hoping for much more.

'He was quite old though, you know, about seventy.'

'Seventy years old?'

'Well, I don't know. Sixty or seventy. He was old anyway.'

'Okay, that's good.'

Calvert pointed towards Callum. 'He was definitely older than your dad, then?'

She nodded, 'yes, loads older.'

'What else do you remember about him? Do you remember the colour of his hair, perhaps?'

'Not really.'

'It was dark, yes?'

'Yes. He would stand in the darkness, you know, out of the candlelight, so I didn't see him very much.'

'That's okay, Florence, that's okay.'

'But…'

'Yes…'

'I don't know if it matters, or I can say it.'

'Go on, Florence, just say what's on your mind, it's fine.'

'He was white,' she mumbled a little less than confidently.

'White? Alright, that's good, that's useful. Why did you think that you couldn't tell us that?'

'Well, it's racist, isn't it?'

Aileen smiled at her. 'No, sweetheart, it's not racist. When you are describing the colour of a person's skin, you can call them white or black. Those are the right words to use.'

'Ah, okay.' Florence dropped her shoulders and relaxed again.

'Is there anything else that you can think of, Florence? For example, did he have any scars that you could see, or any tattoos? Did anything about his teeth stand out to you? Was he wearing glasses?'

'No, not really. I don't think so.'

'That's fine, that's okay. What about his clothes, was there anything that you remember about his clothes?'

'I don't know. It was dark, and I didn't see much of him.'

'That's okay, Florence. What you've told us has been great, really useful.'

She turned to her mum. 'Can I be excused now, please?'

'Aye, sweetheart, of course you can.'

Calvert signed off with, 'thank you, Florence.'

After hearing Florence retreat to her bedroom and the door close behind her, Callum turned to Calvert and asked, 'can the other girl really be Hayley, our Hayley?'

'It's a good question, Callum. Well, she is still registered as missing. What I mean by that is that there has been no body found, and the records do not indicate any confirmed sightings of her since her disappearance in 2011. So, yes, it is feasible.'

'We have to find her.'

'Yes, yes, of course,' confirmed Calvert, 'our investigation remains the same; we are focussed on finding where Florence has been held, and also finding the man that abducted her.'

'Good…and Hayley?'

'Yes, of course. Locating the other girl and bringing her home to her family, whoever and wherever that is.'

Calvert was consciously generalising his words and not referring to the girl as *Hayley*, thus not inflating Callum and Aileen's hopes and expectations, potentially to be cruelly dashed.

'With this new information from Florence, I dare say that DCI Geary will want to step up the investigation. Hopefully that might mean more resource available. Trust me…we will find both him and the other girl.'

CHAPTER 23

Calvert was the last one through the office doors of Lochgilphead station, but it was seven fifty-five, and he was arguably still early.

As he entered, he saw Sergeant O'Brien, Constables Davidson and Crossman and Detective Constables Waller and Taylor. As the door closed behind him, it sprang open again as Jackie Macallan walked through. He wasn't the last in…but he *was* still early.

After acknowledging the team and exchanging some initial pleasantries, any further conversation was stifled as a man whom Calvert assumed to be DCI Geary stepped out of the office and walked towards Calvert.

With hand outstretched, 'DI Calvert, I assume?' he enquired.

'Yes, sir. Nice to meet you.'

'Likewise. Step this way.'

Calvert followed Geary into his office and closed the door after being beckoned to do so.

DCI Geary was what some people might call *a mountain of a man.* He stood at least six foot six tall with broad shoulders that filled every inch of his crisp white shirt. He wore his hair shaved and short at the back and sides, tapered up to a fairly severe flat top that would not look out of place in the 1980s. But none of those features where what defined him, none of those features were generally used to describe him, and none of those features were more prominent than the scar.

Detective Chief Inspector Blair Geary had been nineteen years old, and yet to join the police force, when he and his mates got caught up in a fracas outside a Glasgow bar. The incident hadn't been instigated by Geary or anyone of his fellow teenage companions, in fact it was a terrible case of mistaken identity fuelled with more than a skinful of Tennent's and Jägermeister. After being separated from his friends, Geary was assaulted by one of the two warring parties. Despite suffering a broken arm, fractured cheekbone and three broken ribs during an initial brutal assault, his attackers clearly thought that a more meaningful lesson on respect needed to be taught.

On the verge of consciousness, Geary was grasped by his arms and held up straight, whereupon one of his attackers withdrew a Stanley knife from his pocket. With a quick but purposeful strike, the blade entered at the top left-hand side of his forehead and was rasped down to his chin. The cut was eight inches.

After standing back and admiring his handiwork, and with blood pouring down his victim's face and onto his shirt, Geary's attacker did exactly the same on the other side of his face.

Nineteen-year-old Blair Geary spent seven days in hospital and had a total of sixty-four stitches across a V-shaped wound that came together just under his chin.

The subsequent thirty-one years of summer holiday sunshine and general rugged ageing had obviously helped to lessen the visual impact of the scars, but it had to be said, they were still both prominent and striking. Ironically, Geary's physical image had only served to bring to mind, if not initially create, a persona of a tough Glaswegian copper who would-be gangsters would do well to avoid.

'How's your son? Is he fully recovered?' Calvert asked.

Geary was a little taken aback, surprised at Talloch's lack of confidentiality, although it mattered not in the grand scheme of things.

'Aye, he's fine now, thank you. A bit of Delhi belly I think…or whatever the Jamaican version is. Either way, it resulted in me being delayed in Jamaica for a few days longer than expected.'

'Good holiday otherwise?'

Calvert was hoping that his son's stomach upset was not the defining moment in what should have been an otherwise unforgettable vacation.

Geary smiled, 'aye, thank you. Up until that point it was a great holiday. Good to get away and unwind, you know.'

'Yes, I certainly do, guv.'

'So,' started Geary as he leant backwards in his chair, 'let me start by thanking you for stepping in, especially in light of the fact that you came to Scotland for a vacation, I understand.'

'It's no problem, and yes, I did.'

'We appear to have had a bit of a gap in our senior investigation team over the last couple of weeks.'

'So I understand,' replied Calvert, 'yourself and DCI Mason?'

'Aye. To be honest, I'm a bit pissed off with Talloch, signing off concurrent annual leave for both me and Fraser Mason. Anyway, I guess no-one expected events to unfold as they did.'

Calvert recalled how Talloch had mentioned the very same thing, and she herself had wondered how concurrent annual leave had been signed off for her two most senior detectives. Perhaps she had done so, perhaps she had not. Calvert chose not to mention Talloch's apparent lack of clarity on the subject.

'It's fine, guv. Right place, right time.'

Geary smiled; familiar with the saying, he reminded Calvert of the contradiction, 'aye, or the wrong place at the wrong time.'

'Story of my life, guv.'

They shared a knowing smile.

'So, I received a brief from Talloch a couple of days ago, and then a further update last night. I believe that you're sticking around for a couple of days?'

'That's up to you, guv. It was just a suggestion, perhaps to help with an initial handover and support any ongoing lines of enquiry. I'll leave that decision with you, guv. I can fill my time with hiking and whisky drinking.'

Geary smiled again. He took an immediate liking to Calvert. His kind of man.

'A couple of days might be helpful; at least today, perhaps tomorrow.'

'No problem. The hiking and whisky can wait a little longer.'

'Okay, let's see if we can't get you back home, or at least rambling within thirty-six hours.'

'Sounds good,' Calvert confirmed, 'to what level of detail did Talloch brief you, guv? Shall I provide a brief now?'

'Let's do it outside with the team,' Geary said, 'let's have a general recap, then bring us up to date. You lead.'

'Yes, guv.'

'Morning, all.'

'Morning, guv,' came the response from most.

'Well as you know DCI Geary is back with us, and I have ceded the role of SIO to him. I'll probably stick around for twenty-four hours or so just to manage a handover and fill in any gaps on information on the investigation.

So, I do have some fresh information that came to me late yesterday. It doesn't help us directly with the Florence Findlay investigation, well a little perhaps, but as you'll hear, it is connected and potentially provides new evidence in an old and still open misper investigation; add to which I expect it to spur us on somewhat. First of all, a quick recap.'

Calvert took a gulp of his coffee, wetted his lips and commenced.

'As we know, nine-year-old Florence Findlay went missing eleven days ago, and after an extensive search we came up empty-handed. Fortunately, she turned up three days ago, found wandering near the harbour in Kelvedie. She was subsequently reunited with her parents. Talking of her parents, we interviewed Callum and Aileen Findlay, albeit as potential suspects whilst Florence was still missing, but they were unshakeable in terms of their respective stories.'

He paused for another sip of coffee.

'Whilst it is great news that Florence turned up alive, what we do have, or more importantly what we don't have, are answers to two questions. One, where has she been for those eight days? And two, who has been holding her captive?'

'What's the latest from yesterday, guv?' asked an impatient Crossman.

'Yep, just getting to that point now. As you all know, Florence was interviewed by our specialist, DC Gillespie, a couple of days ago, and whilst she opened up a little, we didn't really get the answers to those two questions. I called to see the family yesterday and asked to speak to Florence, and well, let's just say that she was in a talkative mood. Less scared, more relaxed, and we had a half-decent conversation.'

'What did we learn, guv?'

'Well, hopefully I've not built this new lead up too much, because we still don't know where she was held, or who had been holding her.'

There was an audible frustration from the team and a collection of disappointed faces in the room.

'What we now understand though, is that there was and still is a second girl being held hostage at the same location.'

That got everyone's attention.

'Florence told us that when she awoke she was in a dark room, no natural light, but as she regained consciousness, and over the subsequent minutes and hours she was aware of another girl in the room. They were both chained to the wall via some kind of shackle to their ankle, and with very little free movement. She noted that their captor, a male, would enter the room periodically to give them some food and water. It was at this point that he would light a candle in the room, and for a brief period of the time, the girls would see each other.'

Calvert paused for a second '…but that's not even the most surreal new information we have.'

'Really, it seems bloody weird to me.'

'Well…try this on for size…Florence told us that the other girl was her sister, Hayley.'

He paused again to let that sink in.

'Didn't Hayley go missing about ten years ago?'

'She did. Similar circumstances. She is still documented as a misper, with no communication over the last decade, and no body found anywhere.'

'It seems a bit farfetched, guv, a bit unlikely if you ask me,' remarked DC Waller.

'Hundred percent agree,' Calvert confirmed, 'but Hayley, as we'll call her for the purpose of this conversation, was adamant that she recognised Florence, and that they were sisters.'

'Florence hadn't been born when Hayley went missing,' noted O'Brien as he tried to recall some of the details and chronology of the investigation from the recesses of his mind.

'Correct. She recognised herself in Florence.'

'Still sounds dubious.'

'Perhaps, but then Hayley mentioned the name of her mum and dad, Aileen and Callum.'

Geary, who had been quiet until this point, stepped in. 'Either way, whether it is Hayley Findlay or not, it doesn't matter for the moment. Thanks to DI Calvert we now know that there is another girl currently being held captive somewhere. So that, if nothing else, is our added incentive to find this location and find this bastard that has…and I can't believe that I'm saying this…has potentially been holding a girl captive and against her will for the last decade.'

After a brief pause where everyone took time to reflect on the latest update, Geary stepped up, and Calvert took his cue to take a seat.

'Suspects…' he started, '…talk to me about suspects, from those that are obvious to any left-field ones that we might not have considered.'

'To be honest with you, guv, we've really struggled with suspects. We all know that most child abductions are perpetrated by the parents or members of the wider family. As DI Calvert mentioned, we hauled in both Callum and Aileen Findlay during the period when Florence was missing, but he had an alibi at the garage where he worked, right up to the point where he received the phone call to say she was missing.'

'And the mother?'

'Well, she called it in to the station. She doesn't have any alibi, but, well, I just don't see her being involved. She was beyond overjoyed when Florence returned home safe and sound. For me, guv,' said DC Taylor, 'this looks like a stranger abduction.'

'In the absence of any verified alibi, and the fact that most child abductions are in some way connected to a family member, let's keep her as a person of interest for now. What about a wider family member? What do know about brothers, sisters, aunties, uncles, grandparents etcetera?'

'No siblings for either Callum or Aileen, guv, and as to grandparents, Callum's have both passed, and Aileen's live in Lennoxtown, just to the north of Glasgow.'

'I assume that we have spoken to the grandparents?'

The embarrassed silence from the room was deafening.

Calvert stepped in. 'No, guv, we haven't.'

'Can I ask why? Did we not think it remotely conceivable that one or either of the grandparents could have abducted the young girl, or perhaps the mother, Aileen, concocted a plan in which the grandparents are complicit in some way?'

Geary was just about to seemingly blow his top further, no doubt citing the blindingly obvious lines of enquiry and incompetent leadership, when Calvert quietly and assuredly replied, 'they are both in their nineties, live in assisted accommodation, suffer differing degrees of dementia and regularly soil themselves. I spoke to the housing shelter manager; Aileen hasn't visited in over twelve months, and aside from stretching their legs in the garden, neither of them has been out of their accommodation for about the same period.'

He paused.

'We can follow it up, guv, if you like, but I deemed it to be a waste of precious time and resource.'

'Okay, let's leave it on the backburner for now,' Geary confirmed, capitulating slightly more easily and quickly than Calvert had expected.

'Right, next, talk to me about forensics. Tell me that we found some forensic evidence from Florence, or her clothes, when she was picked up.'

'Nothing, guv. Nothing that helps us narrow down our investigation.'

'Elaborate for me.'

'Well, she was found in the same clothes that she went missing in, so as you might expect after eight days, her clothes were covered in dirt, but nothing special, nothing unique. We have no foreign bodies, no human ones at least. No hair that didn't belong to Florence, and her fingernails were generally bitten short, so there was little if anything there, but again, general dirt.'

Calvert picked up the back end of the conversation. 'I'd like to say that we found traces or petrol, paraffin, kerosene, some special unique scented oils or the smell of smoked herring, but we have zero forensics that help us in identifying where she has been held captive.'

'Jesus fucking Christ, we are certainly in need of some kind of breakthrough,' Geary exclaimed.

'Okay, right, when did we conduct the door-to-door in Kelvedie?'

'Shortly after her disappearance was reported, guv.'

Geary turned to Calvert. 'What's your gut feeling? Was she being held, and do we find the second girl locally within Kelvedie, or further afield?'

'Difficult to say, but my gut feel tells me that it's local.'

'Aye, me too.'

'It sounds like a basement,' piped up Crossman, 'you know, from the information provided by Florence as she was escaping. She said that she fled out of the room and up a flight of stairs, then she opened the door and fled the house. So, the room where she was being held captive was below ground level; thus, probably a basement.'

'Aye, sounds plausible to me,' said Geary.

'Do we know the construct of the houses in Kelvedie?' Calvert asked, 'are they likely to have basements?'

'Not sure, but it has to be our primary line of enquiry from this point onwards.'

'How will we know?' asked Davidson, 'some of those houses are old fishermen's cottages that were built two or three hundred years ago. We aren't going to be able to find any plans.'

'Plans?' puffed Geary, 'we aren't looking for plans, we are going to do a house-to-house across Kelvedie. Gain access to and search every house. How many did you say there are?'

'Thirty-five- I think- in the village, then two or three more a little further afield.'

'Okay, well that's doable,' Calvert said, 'we probably need a couple more pairs of hands, guv, if we are going to get in there and get this done swiftly.'

'Agreed. Let me see if I can rustle up a few more bodies to help.'

'What about a warrant, guv?' asked Crossman, naively trying to be helpful.

'Warrant? We don't need a warrant. Following receipt of the latest information gathered by DI Calvert, we now know that there is another girl currently being held captive and that itself provides authority for us to enter homes and undertake a search.'

Geary went away to make some phone calls, trying to secure some resource at short notice.

'Have you ever done this kind of search before, guv?' asked Crossman.

'What? Searching an entire village, house to house?'

'Yes.'

'No. I've done many house searches, with and without a warrant, as I'm sure have you, but never descended on an entire village mob-handed to enter and search every house.'

'Should be interesting.'

'Aye, that's one word for it.'

CHAPTER 24

After receiving final approval from Superintendent Talloch, and a further eight uniformed officers to help, DCI Geary confirmed that the wholesale search of every one of Kelvedie's properties would commence this morning. Unfortunately, it would do so without Geary at the helm.

DCI Geary had been admitted to Mid Argyll Community Hospital in the early hours of the morning with suspected deep vein thrombosis, and was due to be transferred to the larger more specialist Inverclyde Royal Hospital. Initial assessment had surmised that the ten-hour flight from Montego Bay, Jamaica to Glasgow had been the trigger and primary cause.

Geary was expected to be out of action for a least a couple of weeks, after which he would be assessed and further decisions would be made. To say he was pissed off would be an understatement.

Either way, DI Calvert found himself back in the driving seat once again as SIO.

Calvert and the team mustered outside of The Plough, in front of the harbour. Including himself, there were fourteen officers ready to undertake a mass door-to-door and property search, the likes of which had rarely been seen across the north-west of Scotland. For sure, houses were raided all the time in Glasgow for example, but not generally en masse to the tune of thirty-five over a continuous period of activity spanning a little less than five hours.

The team were advised that they would enter the houses in pairs and would not under any circumstances enter a house on their own.

With some preparatory work done, each officer was paired and provided a list of five houses they were tasked with gaining access to and undertaking a thorough search. Their primary objective was the location of a girl, approximately nineteen years old, although they should factor in a tolerance of two of three years either way. Their secondary objective, in the absence of any girl, was to ascertain if the house had a cellar or basement, gain access to it and look for signs that someone might have been held captive there.

They were advised to look for chains or shackles, or even fastenings on the wall that might have held chains.

Old mattresses, old or dirty clothing, unwashed plates, and even slop buckets were on the list to keep an eye out for.

'When you knock at each house, try and be polite and try to gain entry with the consent of the occupier,' Calvert told them, 'tell them very briefly that you are investigating the disappearance of a girl and that you have reason to believe that she may be being held within one of the properties in Kelvedie.'

'Warrant?' asked one of the newly seconded officers.

'Don't mention it unless the occupier does, but if they do, simply say that we have probable cause that a crime is being perpetrated right now and that there is an immediate risk to life, and that means that we do not require a warrant to enter and search the house.'

'And we are going to say that to each of the thirty-five homes? We're going to piss a lot of people off.'

'Yes, quite probably, but I'm prepared to piss off thirty-four people in the hope that we find our missing girl within the home of the thirty-fifth.'

'Fair enough,' conceded the young officer.

'Hopefully the residents are understanding about this, and we are able to gain access to their house with their consent, but be under no illusion, we will need to gain access and search every house, irrespective of their consent or not. Are we clear?'

There was plenty of head nods in acknowledgement.

Within five minutes, each of the assigned couples were on their way towards their first house.

Calvert, and seconded officer Constable McDougall, found themselves at the gate of their first house, 4 Everard Avenue.

Calvert rapped his knuckles four times on the blue composite door. They waited no longer than ten seconds before it was opened.

'Hello,' said the middle-aged woman as she greeted the strangers.

'Hello there. I am Detective Inspector Calvert, and this is Constable…' He couldn't recall her name.

To be honest, they'd had less than half a minute to say hello and introduce themselves; nevertheless, Calvert was a little embarrassed that he couldn't remember her name.

'McDougall, Constable McDougall.'

They both extracted their warrant cards and held them aloft for a few seconds for visual inspection. The occupier chose not to inspect them any closer; after all, one of them was wearing a police uniform, so the other must be a copper too. Her rationale was relatively sound.

'Can I ask your name?'

'Mary. Mary Dunscombe,' she replied.

'Hello, Mary. We are investigating the disappearance of two girls, both of whom are local to the village.'

'Yes,' she said, 'I heard about young Florence. Terrible situation, terrible.'

'Yes, indeed.'

'But you said two.'

'That's right. Florence has been found safe and sound,

but we are concerned about the whereabouts of another girl, perhaps slightly older.'

That was about all Calvert was prepared to give away.

'We have reason to believe that she may still be in the village, and we are searching every building, every house.'

'In the village? Oh dear.'

He paused for a second before politely asking, 'would it be okay if we came in for a few minutes, Mary? We want to search your house. I'm sure you've nothing to hide, so I bet we'll be in and out within five minutes.'

'Search my house,' she challenged, 'whatever for?'

Calvert was just about to repeat his last sentence, when Mary confirmed that they should enter.

With Calvert noting the importance of a basement, he directed Constable McDougall to check the first-floor rooms whilst he started a recce of the ground floor.

Constable McDougall reappeared at the foot of the stairs at the same time as Calvert came out of the kitchen. No basement, no girl, and no signs of anyone having been held captive. As Calvert had expected when he crossed the threshold into Mary's home.

One down and four to go for Calvert and McDougall.

Sergeant O'Brien and fellow uniformed officer Constable Allison were having a little less luck and were greeted with significantly less cordiality at their first house.

'Fuck off,' was their greeting.

'Sir, we are searching for a missing girl, and are instructed to search every house and building within

Kelvedie. I understand that you might view this as an inconvenience, but I would ask you to look at the bigger picture here. Help us to find this missing girl.'

'Well, you're not going to fucking find her in my house, so no, you can't come in.'

'Sir, we have authority to enter and search every house, so at some point I will change from asking you politely, to telling you. I would rather do it with your permission.'

After a further five minutes of verbal wrangling, and O'Brien on the cusp of arresting the occupier for obstruction, tensions finally cooled, and the two officers walked into the hallway.

'Where does this lead?' asked O'Brien, pointing towards a small door under the stairs.

It wasn't a full-sized door, and he was fully expecting to be advised that it opened up to reveal some under-stairs storage. But it didn't.

'The cellar. Well, basement. We don't really use it to be honest,' he was told, 'it's a bit damp and smells, and it's generally kept locked.'

O'Brien tried the handle. No joy.

'Can you unlock the door please?'

'Why? I've just told you that no-one has been down there for years.'

'That's not what you told me. It's damp and smells, that is what you told me. Now please be kind enough to go and find a key.'

'I'm not sure where the key is.'

'Well, I'm having a look in that basement, so you can either find a key or I'll come back in ten minutes with a crowbar, a sledgehammer and whatever else I need to gain access. It'll no doubt leave a hell of a mess, but just consider that you were given an opportunity to cooperate.'

Unsurprisingly, the guy returned momentarily carrying a key. O'Brien took it from him and opened the door, and as he did the smell hit him. It was a stale and fusty odour, a quite oppressive smell of stagnant air and O'Brien couldn't imagine anything or anyone living down there.

To his surprise the light switch did work, and a single bulb flickered into life as he made his way down the concrete steps. Constable Allison chose to remain at the top.

As O'Brien reached the bottom of the stairs, the initial open space that revealed itself was a room about four metres by six metres, but it was empty. No tables, no chairs, no mattress, and certainly no shackles or captive teenagers.

The far wall had a door to what looked like another room.

O'Brien shouted back up the stairs, 'are there two rooms down here? Does this door lead anywhere?'

'Aye, there are two rooms,' came the reply, 'but as I've told you, there is nothing down there.'

O'Brien walked over to the far wall, took hold of the handle and opened the door in towards the next room.

Nothing. A second room with nothing.

'Bollocks,' he quietly said to himself.

'All that fuss for nothing,' was the greeting he was met

with as he reached the top of the stairs, 'I told you so, didn't I?'

'Have a nice day, sir, thank you.'

In a little over four hours, the police search teams wandered back to their assembly point outside The Plough. Gordon and Angie were waiting with two large urns, one tea and the other coffee.

As the officers reconvened, they chatted over their hot drinks, retelling encounters with a particularly difficult resident, or elaborating on the questionable décor of some of the homes. In the main though, they'd found the residents to be helpful, understanding and generally willing to open their homes to be searched.

Calvert's open debrief, where he invited each pair to provide a brief update and any pertinent details, fell somewhat short on expected results, or hopes at least.

For sure, no-one had found a girl being held hostage, nor any evidence of there being one, let alone two long-term abductees. Furthermore, only two houses had basements, and nothing was found at either.

It appeared that the teams had been unsuccessful in gaining entry to five of the thirty-five houses, and this was solely due to the occupants not being at home. The officers had chosen not to force entry, despite the urgency of the search, and Calvert had agreed with their decision, at this point.

With five houses left to search, Calvert confirmed to

the team that this would be managed over the following hours by a number of the local officers. He thanked them all for their work, especially those seconded from different stations, and confirmed that they could all leave.

As the officers started to disperse, Gordon appeared with a mug of coffee which he handed to Calvert.

'Your lads haven't searched the pub,' he said, 'I assume you'll be wanting to give it a once-over?'

'Yes, thank you, Gordon, we will. We need to be thorough in our search of the village and that includes each and every building. Is that okay?'

'Aye, nae bother, of course it is.'

'Great, thanks.'

'Will I get one of your boys to come back inside with me?' Gordon asked.

Calvert didn't reply directly to Gordon but shouted over Sergeant O'Brien.

'Sergeant, I don't think that we included The Plough and the B&B, Shallowbrook Lodge, within the allocated buildings to be searched. I know it seems highly unlikely, but can you take one other officer and complete a search of both premises before we knock off, please?'

'Aye, of course, guv.'

O'Brien tapped Constable Crossman on the shoulder as he walked past, and with a wiggle of the finger, invited him to follow the landlord into The Plough.

'Are you buying the beers, sarge?'

His question wasn't met with any kind of response.

Having overheard, Calvert smiled. Then his mobile phone rang.

'Hello, you.'

'Hi, Dad.'

'Are you okay?'

'Me? Sure. Just checking in, seeing what you are getting up, and if you are finally relaxing.'

'Well, I just participated in the consecutive search of three dozen homes looking for another young girl.'

'Another girl?'

'Yes. It's all connected to the first girl, we got her back safe and sound, but she told us about another girl that was being held captive. We just searched a number of houses looking for her.'

'Any joy?'

'No, I'm afraid not. Not yet anyway.'

'Have you had any time to rest and relax? And when are you coming home?'

'Well, the local DCI is back at work now, so he should have stepped back in as SIO.'

'Should have?'

'Yes, unfortunately he was admitted to hospital sometime last night with suspected deep vein thrombosis, probably connected to his long-haul flight back from Jamaica. Anyway, the cavalry arrived and went again, so I might be here for a few more days.'

'It's not good, Dad, they are taking advantage of you.'

'They are doing nothing of the sort. If I didn't want

to be here, to help, I wouldn't. And besides, it's what I do, I'm a police officer.'

'Four hundred miles away, Dad, you're a police officer four hundred miles away.'

'Ah, semantics. Look, I'm fine, I'll be home soon. I'll write this week off and rearrange another week of hillwalking and whisky drinking, perhaps in a couple of months' time.'

'You'll not get any more time off work.'

'I'll get this week again. I'm down as working at the minute. An arrangement between respective superintendents.'

'Oh, that's good,' she said with some surprise, 'I thought you were working on your own holiday time.'

'Nah, I'm not that bloody daft, lass. Anyway, how are you and how's things at home? You haven't burned the place down yet then?'

'Ha, ha. Yes, all good. I've been throwing debauched parties every night, drinking Cristal champagne and sniffing coke off the chiselled chest of a male escort.'

'Good stuff, as long as you're enjoying yourself.'

Lisa could tell that he had now switched off and his mind had wandered elsewhere. 'Right, I'll let you go. Call me tomorrow please.'

'Will do. Love you.'

'Love you too.'

Before putting his phone away, Calvert decided to call Aileen Findlay.

'Aileen, hi, it's Detective Inspector Calvert. Just a quick one, I mentioned a couple of days ago that Detective Chief Inspector Geary would be back at work and stepping into my shoes as it were.'

'Yes, I remember,' she replied.

'Well, just wanted to let you know that there's been a little bit of a setback. DCI Geary has been taken ill, so I'll be remaining with you for a few more days.'

'Okay, I can't say that I am too disappointed. I'm happy that you're still on the investigation.'

'Thank you.'

'Do you have any update on Hayley?'

'I know that you've pinned your hopes on this girl being Hayley, but it's highly unlikely.'

No reply.

'We are doing all we can to try and locate this second girl, and to find the person, or persons, responsible for taking Florence. As soon as we have something to share, you'll be the very first to know.'

'Evening, Paul, another tough day at the coal face?'

'There aren't many easy days, Brian,' Calvert replied as he walked towards the reception desk at Shallowbrook Lodge.

'Can I get you a wee tot?'

Calvert checked his watch; five past six. 'Better make it a beer, Brian.'

'A beer it is, coming right up. Sit yourself down in the snug and I'll bring it through.'

'Thanks.'

A moment or two later Brian came through with a pint of chilled Tennent's, which he handed over, and watched as Calvert took a deep refreshing gulp. .

'Ah, that hits the spot. Thanks.'

'You're welcome. We had a couple of your mob here an hour or so ago, wanting to look around the place.'

'Yes, sorry about that. We are searching every building in the village.'

'It's nae bother, Paul. I showed them around and they left about fifteen minutes ago. I'm surprised that you didn't run into them as you came in.'

'No, I didn't see them.'

'They seemed happy enough anyway.'

'Well, Brian, unless they found a young girl being forcibly detained and chained up in one of your rooms, then yes, I'm sure all is well…here anyway.'

'I once spent a rather enjoyable evening at a party where a young naked man was chained to a wall, consensually of course.' Brian's face lit up with the memory.

'Of course.'

'Hmmm…on that interesting note, I'll leave you to enjoy your beer in peace. Will you be staying for dinner later?'

'I will, thanks, Brian.'

Resting his head back on the chair, Calvert began to

relax and was only stirred when he received a text message. He looked at his phone and immediately a broad smile spread across his face. It was from Sarah.

Hi, she started, *I know we said that it was just a fleeting encounter, but I've been thinking about you these past few days. Anyway, just wanted to say hi, again, and check that you've made it back to Hull ok. X*

He continued to smile as he read through the message, and despite the joy that it brought to his face, he paused for a second, pondering whether to send a reply. After all it was he who had said that the timing wasn't right, and had it been twelve months later…

He decided to reply.

Hi, nice to hear from you, Sarah. No, I'm afraid that I'm still in Kelvedie. Long story. Expanding scope of the investigation and illness for my replacement.

He chose not to add the kiss. He was fifty-six years old, what would he be doing adding kisses to a text message sent to a stranger; well, a partial stranger.

Having placed his phone back into his jacket pocket, he immediately it retrieved in order to answer a call. Sergeant O'Brien.

'Sergeant.'

'Guv, just a quick one. Confirming that we completed the search on both the pub and the B&B, and nothing to report.'

'Okay, thanks. I'm back at the B&B now actually.'

'Crossman says to tell you that you've got a messy

room, and you need a tidy-up.'

'Ha, cheeky bugger.'

'What are we going to do about the five that we missed today?'

'We'll tackle them first thing tomorrow morning. Just me, you and probably Crossman.'

'Sounds like a plan. Goodnight, guv.'

CHAPTER 25

Calvert's phone had rung three times whilst he was in the shower. He towelled himself dry and sat on the bed expecting his phone to ring yet again. It did.

'Hi, inspector, it's Aileen.'

'Hello, Aileen. Is everything okay?'

'Can you come over?'

'Yes, possibly. Why? What's wrong?'

'Florence has said something that we think might be important when you're looking for the man who abducted her.'

'Right, okay. Give me ten or fifteen minutes and I'll be there.'

Calvert arrived and was ushered through to the lounge to find Aileen and Florence sitting on the sofa. He declined the offer of a coffee and was eager to hear from Florence.

'Tell Inspector Calvert what you told me earlier, Florence. Go on, it's okay.'

Although Florence appeared to be a little hesitant at first, eventually she said, 'the man from the house…' She paused again.

'It's okay, Florence,' Calvert said, 'take your time. Do you remember something about him?'

'He talked funny,' she said.

'Talked funny?'

'Yes.'

'Okay. That's great.' Calvert paused for a second.

'He didn't speak much, but when he did, he spoke funny.'

'When we spoke a couple of days ago you said that he had a Scottish accent, yes?'

'Yes, but that's not it,' she confirmed.

'Okay, what do you mean *funny*?'

'When he said some words, they sounded funny. The words sounded funny.'

Calvert was a little confused, but then came the clarity.

'When he said words with an *S* in them, he sounded like a snake talking.'

'What words, Florence?'

'Like *shut up*.'

Now it clicked for Calvert. 'Did it sound like, *thut up*?'

'Yes.'

'Ah, he had a lisp.'

'Is that useful?' asked Aileen, 'will it help find the man?'

Calvert knew that it wouldn't help in short term, certainly not in identifying the location, but eventually when they had their suspect in custody, that could well be a key point in tying him to Florence.

'It's very useful, yes. Thank you, Florence.'

Florence left to play in her bedroom.

'Are you any closer to finding Hayley and finding out who took them both, inspector?'

'A little, Aileen, a little. We make constant progress by ruling things out, and this drives us towards the right answers, the right places, the right people. We'll get there. Soon. Trust me.'

'Okay.'

'With that in mind, do you mind if I nip off now, we've got some important activities this morning.'

'Yes, of course, sorry to have pulled you away. I thought it was important that you knew what Florence had told me.'

'It was, Aileen, thank you.'

CHAPTER 26

Sergeant O'Brien and Constable Crossman were tasked with numbers 9 and 15 Harbour View, whilst Calvert said he would take Dorsal Cottage and Abbeydale Cottage. These four were the last remaining buildings, let alone homes, to be searched in Kelvedie.

Neither search party was particularly optimistic about their chances of finding Hayley within one of these remaining houses; after all, they had searched thirty-one homes and two businesses already. Why would they have any success at these last four?

Either way, Calvert remained sure that Florence had been held captive somewhere in Kelvedie, but this was based on a number of assumptions and probabilities, and not on any real factual evidence.

With no joy at Dorsal Cottage, nor any as reported

by O'Brien at 9 Harbour View, Calvert moved on to his last house.

Abbeydale Cottage was an old fishermen's cottage built around 1850 and located twenty metres from the shore of Loch Fyne. Constructed of natural limestone mined from the local area, it had no doubt experienced and survived many storms over the last one hundred and seventy years, and despite what looked like a partial replacement of the roof tiles, it appeared to have weathered well over this period.

The owner was a guy called Michael Macaulay. Calvert knew this because he had researched the owners of the remaining four homes. He had not done so at the start of the mass search of the initial thirty homes but having some spare time on his hands combined with idle curiosity, underpinned by his unsubstantiated and unproven confidence that Florence had been held captive in Kelvedie, he was now overeager to bring this investigation to a close. That would mean arresting the abductor, and of course, God willing, finding the second girl alive and well.

The cottage itself was relatively small but was set in a large garden to both sides. As Calvert approached the gate, he saw a man sitting a few metres away from a stream that ran adjacent to the westerly border of the plot. He was perched on a small wooden stool in front of an easel and canvas.

Calvert assumed this to be the owner, Michael Macaulay, but wasn't sure. He opened his mouth to call out to him, but then chose not to. For reasons that he could not immediately explain or rationalise to himself, he decided not to make his presence known, but to walk up to the cottage and enter, if he could gain access of course.

He tried the handle on the front door. It turned, and he had gained access.

Through the door and off to the right was the lounge, and immediately off to the left were the stairs to the first floor. In the space under the stairs there was a door. It could, of course, be a storage area, or it could be stairs leading down to a cellar.

Having grabbed the handle and eased open the door, he found it to be the latter. With a deep inhale and a palpable mix of expectation and trepidation, he started down the steep stone steps using the light on his mobile phone to shine the way, albeit little further than three steps ahead.

Thirteen stone steps later, he reached the bottom. Obviously, there were no windows and thus no natural light, and as best as he could see there didn't appear to be any artificial light either, certainly not from any ceiling-hung bulb.

His phone light did catch a small wooden table upon which stood a lamp. He recalled Florence mentioning that her abductor would light a candle when he entered the room but didn't recall any mention of a lamp. The lamp had a mains cable that was plugged into the wall; he had nothing to lose, so tried the switch.

It worked, although the spiral-shaped energy-saving

light bulb was clearly taking its time to reach full illumination. Or was it? Was it simply poor?

Either way, it provided Calvert with some further light that supplemented that given out by his phone.

The stone floor was partially covered by a threadbare rug that would offer little by way of either warmth or comfort if sat upon.

As his eyes grew accustomed to the poor light he saw a set of chains, heavy duty chains with shackles on one end. The other his eye followed to the wall where they were fastened to a large iron hoop partially buried in the wall itself. The floor was further littered with some old clothes, although in their current state, they looked more rags than clothes.

Just off to the left of the rug was a metal bucket. The smell emanating from the bucket immediately informed Calvert that it was a slop bucket, but this was for human excrement.

'Hello.'

The voice was faint but still sufficient to startle Calvert.

'Hello,' he replied, 'where are you?'

He heard the clanking of iron chains dragging against the stone floor and out of the darkness slowly emerged a girl.

He had found Hayley, she was alive…well her identity was to be determined, but whoever the girl was, she was alive, and was now safe.

Calvert beckoned her to come out from the dark

corner. 'It's okay, you're safe, I'm a police officer. You're safe, you can trust me.'

There wasn't much slack on the chains, but what there was allowed her to reach forward and attempt to throw her arms around him. He reciprocated, and down on his knees he took hold around her waist, hugging her tightly.

They held each other for a while.

'Right, let's get you out of here.'

She wasn't about to let go any time soon. She didn't know this man. In fact, this was only the second man she had seen in a long time, but she trusted his word. He said he was a police officer. His presence, steady and strong, reassured her that she was no longer alone, vulnerable or trapped. The fear and tension that had consumed her were replaced with a tentative hope that her ordeal was truly over. Was she safe now?

'Where is he?' the girl asked.

'He? The man holding you here?'

'Yes,' she confirmed.

'He's outside. I sneaked into the house without him seeing me.'

'How did you know I was here?'

'I didn't, but since we found Florence, we've been looking all over for you.'

'Florence.' Her face lit up. 'Is she safe?'

'Yes, yes, she's back with her parents. She's safe and well.' Calvert confirmed.

The girl didn't reply but maintained the broad smile

across her face.

'Those parents,' said Calvert, 'might be your parents, I'm led to believe.'

A simple 'yes' was her reply.

Despite tugging at both the shackles and the ring attached to the wall, there was no budging either.

'I've tried and tried, every day,' she said, 'but I can't get out.'

'It's okay. Not to worry. Listen, I have to leave you for a while. I…'

'No, please, no,' she quickly interrupted.

'It's okay, you're safe. I need to find something to break these chains, or probably call a colleague to bring something that will break them or cut them.'

He gently and reassuringly took hold of her shoulders. 'Trust me, you're safe. We'll have you out of here in no time.'

She reluctantly let go of his arm, but her eyes never left his.

'I have to go. I'll be back, I promise. Trust me. Hayley, isn't it?'

'Yes.'

'Trust me, Hayley. I'm not going to leave you. I'm not.'

As expected, there was no mobile phone signal down in the basement, so Calvert made his way back up the stone steps to the ground floor. He wandered briefly around the four rooms on the ground floor trying to get his bearings but also looking for something that might help him free the girl from the chains. He lucked out on the latter.

Having settled for a second in the kitchen, he peered out of the window to see Macaulay still sitting on the wooden stool with paint brush in hand. Yet again, he couldn't rationalise with himself why he simply didn't confront him, arrest him, then free the girl. It seemed the rational and logical steps to take, but no, he was steadfast in his own mind that he needed to focus on getting the girl free and to safety. Macaulay would still be there in an hour, or tomorrow, or the day after.

'Sergeant, it's me, Listen…'

'What are you whispering for, guv?'

O'Brien didn't give Calvert any time to respond before following up with, 'we've had no joy at either 9 or 15 Harbour View, so…'

Calvert interrupted him, 'never mind that. I've found her. I'm at Abbeydale Cottage. This is where Florence was being held captive, and I've found the second girl.'

'Hayley?'

'Yes, well, her identity remains to be proven either way, but, yes, for the sake of argument, Hayley.'

'Fuck me!'

'I know, right! Anyway, I found her in the basement chained to the wall. I can't free her, I need something to cut the shackles or the chain, or perhaps something to prise the iron fastening away from the wall.'

'Okay.'

'It's quite heavy duty.'

'Understood. Not sure what I can get and from where, but I'm on it. I'll be there as soon as I can. Have you called it in? Do we have backup and an ambulance on its way?'

'Not yet, no.'

'Do you want me…'

'No, not yet. Let's focus on releasing the girl and then we can take it from there.'

'Okay.'

'Oh, and by the way.'

'Yes.'

'Macaulay is here.'

'What do you mean, here? Is he there with you now? Is he cuffed? Assume you've arrested him?'

'Well, no, no and again, no. He's in the garden sitting on a stool in front of a canvas, looks like he's painting something.'

'Painting? Fucking painting!'

'Sergeant.'

'Sorry, guv. Why haven't you arrested him?'

'Let's get the girl free from the chains, out of the basement and to safety, then we can worry about Macaulay.'

'Right, okay, if that's what you want to do.'

'Anyway, if you can, try and enter via the back door of the cottage and if at all possible, try and do so without Macaulay seeing you. You'll see him on the west side of the cottage, near the stream that runs adjacent. I'll be at the back door waiting for you.'

'West, stream, back door, okay got it. Right, let me see

what I can find to help with those chains. I'll be there as soon as I can, guv.'

'Good man.'

'Abbeydale Cottage, did you say?'

'Yes, it's the further of the two cottages that was on my list. It's about three hundred metres from the harbour, heading north-west.'

'Got it.'

Calvert waited patiently for the first ten minutes, but as the time nudged closer to twenty, he started to become concerned that his stealth plan was not going to work. He had tasked Sergeant O'Brien with a challenging request to say the least – small village, no motor repair garage, no B&Q, no idea where to acquire heavy duty bolt cutters from. Perhaps he should call in the cavalry and be done with it, less of the lone ranger approach.

Macaulay had moved during these twenty minutes, albeit just to stand and stretch his legs. He had looked over his shoulder and back towards the cottage, something that caught Calvert holding his breath and moving back away from the kitchen window, but he returned his focus to his canvas.

He had popped back down to the basement to reassure the girl, Hayley. He must start calling her Hayley, after all this was how she referred to herself, and of course she must know her own name. He had returned to reassure Hayley that help was on its way and that she would be free of the chains and shackles in a matter of minutes. Although these *minutes* continued to march on.

'Stay with me,' she pleaded, 'please stay with me.'

It was almost enough to break his heart. This poor girl had been taken from her family ten years ago and had, probably, seen most if not all of those years chained to the wall in this numbing, unlit and chillingly depressing stone basement with nothing but the well-worn clothes on her back and a threadbare rug to keep her warm.

He gave her a hug and reassured her that he would be back again, within minutes. She held on tight, steadfastly refusing to let go.

'Trust me, Hayley. I'm not going to leave you.'

'Bloody hell,' said Calvert, 'where have you been?'

'I hope you're winding me up,' replied O'Brien as he strode through the door with a pair of bolt cutters to hand.

'Where did you have to go to find them?'

'Well, the pub, The Plough.'

'The pub?'

'Yes, aside from the B&B it's the only other business in the village, and with the relatively short notice and urgency of the request, I thought, and hoped, the logical place to go. Well, logical to ask anyway.'

'And Gordon had these, did he?'

'He sure did.'

'What a bloody result. Remind me to buy him a beer or three.'

'Let's see if they work first, eh?'

'Right,' commenced Calvert, 'I need you to remain here and keep an eye on Macaulay.' He pointed out of kitchen window towards the figure still sitting in front of the easel and canvas.

'Aye, I spotted him on my way in.'

'Good. Keep out of sight for now and watch him. Let me go and free Hayley, hopefully, and we can get her to safety.'

'Now there are two of us, tell me again why we don't simply arrest and cuff him now, then free the girl?'

'It's a good question, but I want to focus on Hayley. He will still be here when we have freed her and taken her to safety.'

'Okay, your call.'

Calvert made his way down to the basement and back to Hayley.

'Hey, I'm back. Let's see about getting you out of here, shall we?'

He lifted the bolt cutters and Hayley presented her wrists; with the end suitably aligned Calvert made two sharp movements and both shackles fell to the ground.

Hayley lunged forward immediately, taking Calvert by surprise as he dropped the bolt cutters and reciprocated the hug.

'Thank you.'

The juxtaposition of pain and relief was etched on her face. Yet again she held on tightly, refusing to break the hold.

'Come on, let's get you out of here.'

Calvert took hold of her hand and slowly led her up the stairs. Her steps were slow and laboured, so Calvert didn't force the pace. They moved as quickly as she was able.

The chains, he noted, had been long enough to allow her to stand and thus exercise her legs a little, but Calvert guessed that it was likely to have been a very long time since she walked more than a couple of steps.

She struggled, but with Calvert's steadying hand, was determined to make it up the steep steps.

Sergeant O'Brien had requested an ambulance, even before he had met Calvert at the cottage, and had asked that it arrive as quickly as possible but without the lights and sirens, and remain out of sight down the road. They had complied with the unusual request.

As Calvert and Hayley came out of the cottage and into the direct sunlight, Hayley faltered. It wasn't overly sunny, but it was the first and only natural light her eyes had seen for ten years.

'Close your eyes,' he told her.

Calvert steadied her as they walked towards Sergeant O'Brien. Hayley had tears streaming down her cheeks, but not a word or sound passed her lips as Calvert handed her over.

As O'Brien took Hayley towards the waiting

ambulance, Calvert set about the next task, apprehending Michael Macaulay.

He was still in front of the canvas but was now standing. Calvert approached from the rear of the house and from a direction that Macaulay would immediately recognise hadn't originated at the front gate.

Macaulay turned upon hearing noise behind.

'Hello, can I help you?'

'Detective Inspector Calvert,' he replied, holding aloft his warrant card and identification, 'we've met before. I assume you recall?'

No response.

'I'm investigating the abduction and false imprisonment of two young girls.'

'Two girls, you say. Local, are they?'

'Yes, very much so.'

'Right. I'm not sure how I can help though.'

'How you can help?' Calvert replied, 'well, releasing the girl that you are holding captive in your basement would be a good start, I would have thought.' Direct and straight to the point.

No reply.

'Actually, scratch that. I've already freed her. She's safe and on her way to hospital, and you're nicked.'

Macaulay threw down the paintbrush he had been holding and tipped over the easel as he started to run towards the stream.

Really? thought Calvert, *aren't we a bit long in the tooth for this?*

Despite his silent protestations he knew that he had to follow him, and follow him he did, across the remaining lawn, down the slight embankment and into the stream.

Macaulay had reached the halfway point across the gently flowing crystal-clear water when he was brought down with a rugby tackle. Both men rolled in the water for a few seconds before finding their feet once again.

'For fuck's sake,' exclaimed Calvert, 'now look at me, pissing wet through. Could you not have run across the lawn or something?'

Calvert took out his Hiatt rigid folding handcuffs and placed them on Macaulay's wrists.

'Michael Macaulay, you are under arrest for the abduction and unlawful imprisonment of Florence Findlay, and the abduction and unlawful imprisonment of Hayley Findlay. You do not have to say anything, but it may harm your defence if you do not mention when questioned something which you later rely on in court. Anything you do say may be given in evidence.'

'Having fun, guv?'

O'Brien appeared just as Calvert was escorting Macaulay up the bank and back to the lawn area. Both were wet, head to toe, and dripping as they squelched forward with each step taken.

'Oh, yes, having the time of my life.'

Pushing Macaulay towards O'Brien, Calvert said, 'get this piece of shit out of my sight.'

CHAPTER 27

'Callum, hello, it's Detective Inspector Calvert.'
'Aye, hello.'
'We've found her, Callum, we've found the girl.'

'You've found Hayley?'

'Well…'

Calvert could hear Callum shouting to Aileen that the police had found Hayley and was beckoning her to come to the phone.

'You're on speaker now, inspector, myself and Aileen are here.'

'You've found Hayley?' blurted Aileen. Overexcited but totally understandable. 'Is she okay?'

'As I was just about to say to Callum, we've found a girl, and yes, she is alive and safe. It is possible that the girl is Hayley, but obviously I can't provide a definitive ID, we will need to ask you to do that.'

'Aye, aye, of course. We can do that, can't we, Callum?'

'Aye,' Callum was heard to agree.

'Where is she? Where is our Hayley?'

'She is at the Mid Argyll hospital.'

'Hospital? Is she okay? Injured? Ill? Sick?'

'Calm down, Aileen, calm down. She's safe now, that's the main thing. The doctors are checking her over, no doubt running some tests.'

'Can we see her?'

'Well, yes, of course, that's why I called you. We still need to definitively identify her, so if it's okay with you, that'll be the first thing that we need from you. Is that okay?'

'Right, we're on our way now.'

'That's fine. I'll meet you at the main entrance.'

Hayley had been taken to Mid Argyll hospital and had been seen by the same doctor who had treated Florence, A&E consultant Doctor Isla Sutherland.

'Hi, Hayley, how are you feeling?'

Doctor Sutherland took a position at the side of Hayley's bed, clutching a digital tablet.

'I'm okay.'

Doctor Sutherland wasn't overly convinced by her reply, and expected that an intense adrenaline rush creating the relief and happiness of being rescued and now being safe was masking any true thoughts and feelings that Hayley had. Physically she wasn't in a great place, but emotionally, whilst mental health wasn't Doctor Sutherland's area of expertise, you could take the knowledge of a first-year medical student to understand and expect that Hayley had years of mental health recovery ahead of her.

'Hayley, I understand that your parents are on their way in, but as you are an adult now, would you be okay if I talked some things through with you?'

'Sure.'

'We can wait for your parents if you would prefer.'

'No, it's fine. It's okay.'

Hayley didn't feel much like an adult. She had been taken when she was nine years old, and her transition to adulthood, whatever that now meant, took place whilst she lay in a cold damp cellar. Nineteen years old. *Fuck!*

Doctor Sutherland was pleased that she had agreed; after all, irrespective of the medical facts, Hayley and her parents would have other things on their mind, and other topics of discussion no doubt.

'Right, so, we have the results back from some of tests that we did. You have what we call osteomalacia.'

'Osteo…what?'

'Osteomalacia. In essence it's an adult form of rickets. It's a softening of the bones that most often occurs due to a lack of vitamin D, and vitamin D helps your body absorb calcium. Your body has suffered from lack of vitamin D and direct sunlight for a sustained period of time, and needs calcium to maintain the strength and hardness of your bones.'

'Okay. Is that all?'

'No, I'm afraid not. It won't come as any surprise I'm sure to learn that you are also suffering from malnutrition, but also possibly from something called sick building syndrome.'

'Did you say sick building syndrome?'

'I did, yes. To be honest, it's quite subjective and not a firm diagnosis, but being cognisant of your environment for the last, well, decade, it's a possibility. Sick building syndrome is sometimes used to describe a situation in which the occupants of a building experience acute health issues or comfort-related effects that seem to be linked directly to the time spent in the building. Symptoms such as headaches, blocked or runny nose, dry, itchy skin, dry, sore eyes or throat, cough or wheezing, rashes, tiredness and difficulty concentrating. Do any of those sound familiar?'

'All of the above.'

'Okay. I'm more concerned with your weight at the minute, and any potential damage done to your body through malnutrition.'

'Will I recover?' Hayley asked tentatively.

'Yes.'

'Fully recover?'

'Yes, hopefully. We need to do some more tests to check any long-term damage to your organs, and perhaps your eyesight, with the right nutrition and perhaps some supplements in the short term, both coupled with an exercise plan to rebuild some of your lost weight and strength. It's going to be a long road, Hayley.'

'I understand.'

'You'll need to be patient and allow yourself plenty of time to heal, okay?'

'Okay.'

True to his word, Calvert was waiting at the main entrance to the hospital as Callum, Aileen and Florence arrived.

'Hi, Florence, how are you?'

'Okay, thanks.'

'Good. Good.'

His attention turned to her parents. 'Right, shall we go inside?'

He didn't receive any verbal replies, but it was accepted all round to have been a rhetorical question.

'Before we do though,' he stopped in his tracks, 'at the risk of being a little direct and clinical, what I need at the very outset is confirmation one way or the other that this girl is your daughter, Hayley.'

'Aye, of course.'

'Just bear in mind that it has been ten years since you will have seen her, and she has grown up and matured outside of your view. She will have changed considerably, I guess. Don't be quick to make any decisions either way.'

'Aye, we understand,' replied Callum.

'I'll know,' Aileen added.

'Yes, Aileen, I'm pretty sure that you will. We will be doing a DNA test just to confirm, you know, as she has been away for so long. We all want to be sure, don't we?'

Calvert thought that the mention of the DNA test might annoy them, Aileen especially, but it received little more than a nodding acknowledgment. For sure, they were only interested in reuniting with Hayley, their daughter from whom they had been separated for a decade.

As the four were walking up the hall towards the ward, Callum asked, 'so how does this work then?'

'What do you mean?' Calvert asked.

'Well, you are wanting us to identify her. I assume we have to do this…I don't know…from behind a window or something, you know so she can't see us.'

'No, Callum, this isn't a formal line-up of suspects. Although, to be fair it's a good question. As a matter of fact, we spoke to her about the need for absolute clarity on identification, and the fact that we had called you and asked you to attend hospital. As you might expect, this irked her a little. She is adamant on her own identity, which I understand of course.'

'And…'

'Well, she said that you should just come into the room and see her, and I quote, it will be what it will be.'

'That sounds like Hayley,' said Aileen, 'she's always known her own mind.'

'Listen, I'm torn between saying it's just a formality and don't get your hopes and expectations up, you know, just in case it isn't Hayley. It has been ten years.'

'Aye, let's just get on with it, shall we,' said an increasingly vexed Aileen.

With Calvert leading the way, they stopped abruptly outside of a room. They were still within the A&E Department, but it had two separate treatment rooms that provided a little more privacy than the screens that separated patients on the main ward. This was one of them.

Calvert opened the door inwards and gestured to Aileen to enter. She did so with Callum and Florence close behind. As she rounded a partition screen that blocked any immediate view, she found herself at the foot of the bed.

Their eyes met and they both knew immediately. Aileen had changed a little, but to a daughter, there's not much difference between Mum at thirty-two or Mum at forty-two years old. As Calvert had pre-warned, and of course as Aileen had expected, Hayley had changed considerably.

During her brief time at the hospital, the staff had helped her shower and wash her hair. With ten years' growth, you wouldn't argue against a much-needed cut and blow dry, but the wash and brush through had made her appearance far more presentable than when she had initially arrived.

Her face had a hollow, sunken look, with her now prominent cheekbones being a standout feature of her face, and not in a good way, not in a way that young teenagers aspire to when fawning over images of Bella Hadid or Cara Delevingne.

She looked all of her nineteen years, and probably a dozen more.

Aileen rushed towards Hayley and they flung their arms around each other, gripping tightly and neither wanting to let go. But let go they did, eventually, with tears falling down their cheeks, Aileen stepped aside to allow Callum to hug his daughter.

As he did so, Aileen looked at Calvert and simply nodded. Words were not necessary. Calvert took his cue and closed the door behind him as he left the room.

'Hello, princess.'

'Hello, Dad.'

'We've missed you. Mum and me. We've missed you so much.'

Callum started to cry, which whilst completely natural and understandable considering the circumstances, was the first time that Aileen had seen him cry for almost two decades, since the day Hayley was born.

As Callum stepped aside, Florence went rushing in and flung her arms around Hayley. Aside from the time spent together in the basement, she had never met her sister. She had a sister! Overwhelmed was an understatement.

Hayley hugged her back.

'You made it out,' she said with tears streaming down her cheeks, 'you're safe.'

'Yes, and you too,' Florence replied, 'and I have a sister!'

They laughed, and hugged each other so tightly.

'So, what have I missed?' asked Hayley, ever so tongue-in-cheek.

They all smiled and laughed again.

'Well…' started Aileen.

Callum slipped out of the room to see DI Calvert.

'Inspector…'

'Yes, Callum.'

'We don't know many details about where Hayley was found.'

'I understand. Is now the right time though?'

'Probably not, but I need to know. Where was she found? Within the village?'

'Yes.'

'Yes?' repeated Callum.

'Yes, Hayley was found within Kelvedie,' Calvert confirmed.

'Where?'

'Sorry, Callum, I can't tell you that. I can't give you any more details at this stage. I'm sorry.'

'But she had been close, that close, for all those years?'

'I'm not sure how long she had been at that specific

location, Callum, but it is certainly within half a mile…'

He was interrupted.

'Within half a mile of our house! For the last ten years? Oh – my – fucking – God!'

'Quite possibly, yes. Listen, we will learn more over the coming days and weeks as we interview the suspect and start to piece together the picture for both Florence and Hayley. I promise, we'll get you the answers that you're looking for.'

Callum turned away somewhat dejected, frustrated, and angry, and he started back towards the door.

'Callum.'

He stopped and turned to face Calvert.

'Best not mention anything to Aileen at the minute, eh? Let's wait until we have the facts. Yes?'

'Don't worry, inspector, I won't be the one telling Aileen that our daughter has been less than half a mile from us for the last decade whilst we thought she was dead.'

Calvert didn't reply. There were no words. He simply nodded and Callum disappeared inside to be back with his family.

CHAPTER 28

Calvert was at Lochgilphead station bright and early that morning. Today was going to be a long day, and dependent on how things went with the Michael Macaulay interview later that morning, it could prove to be a very successful day. A pivotal one in the investigation no doubt, although Calvert knew that his absolute defining day had to be finding Hayley, alive. Slightly ahead of discovering Florence was safe and sound, there was little better feeling than having rescued Hayley from a decade of being held against her will in the basement of Michael Macaulay's house some eight hundred metres from her own family home.

That was particularly galling to say the least. Calvert reflected on the missed opportunities by the investigating team a decade ago and wondered if a more thorough search of the local area had not been undertaken. Perhaps it had, perhaps they had searched all of the buildings, including Macaulay's house. Perhaps Hayley had been moved several times during her forced internment.

Either way it was a mixed bag of feelings throughout the team at present; joy, relief, anger, surprise, astonishment, and for some, embarrassment and a little unease.

Calvert's record on the successful retrieval of mispers, as acknowledged by Superintendent Talloch during their first meeting, was almost without equal anywhere across the regional police forces of Great Britain. But recovering Hayley Findlay had to be his standout moment, his Everest peak. All he had to do now was nail the bastard that had robbed her of ten years of adolescence.

As the investigation was scaled back now that Macaulay was in custody, all of the uniformed officers were returned to their normal duties. Only Detective Constables Taylor and Waller were still assigned to support Calvert, and hopefully DCI Geary when he eventually returned to duty, to close out the final elements before handing the case over to the Crown Office and Procurator Fiscal Service.

As the clock tipped eight-thirty, both Taylor and Waller entered the incident room. Calvert came out of the DCI's office to greet them.

'Morning.'

'Morning, guv.'

'Do you two share a ride in?'

'No, guv, just coincidence.'

'Okay. Right grab yourselves a coffee, bacon sarnie, whatever, I want to start in ten minutes. Let's catch up on all things Macaulay related before the interview later this morning.'

'Yes, guv.'

'Right, tell me about Michael Macaulay.' Calvert's question was expectant of significant details, especially as he had tasked them both late yesterday to come prepared on this very subject. DC Waller riffled through his notebook and started.

'Michael James Macaulay, aged forty-nine, resides at Abbeydale Cottage, Kelvedie, where he has been for twenty-three years according to the electoral role. He's not employed, or at least he's not registered as employed and paying income tax, he's also not registered as claiming any benefits either.'

'I've got something on that,' said Taylor, 'I'll chip back in later.'

Calvert smiled.

'Macaulay is a widower. He was married in 1999 to Catherine McNulty, later Macaulay, but his wife was killed in a road traffic accident in 2010.'

'Okay.' Calvert knew that Waller wasn't yet done with this thread.

'Also involved in the accident, and also deceased, was his daughter Caitlin. She was ten years old. Prior to 2010 he was a deckhand for a local fisherman, but from what

I can gather, after the death of his wife and daughter, he never returned to work.'

'Just moving on from the RTA in 2010, guv,' Taylor noted, 'and pulling together the employment piece, I'll been able to confirm that the Macaulays had some life insurance that covered each other. He received a payout of £225,000 from the life insurance.'

'Wow, that's enough to keep you in clover for a few years,' replied Calvert.

'Yes, but that's not all. Their daughter, Caitlin, was not covered under their life insurance policy, but the car accident they were in was not their fault, so Macaulay, or rather, the legal eagles from the insurance company assigned to the cost recovery, obtained a payout for the loss of life. Caitlin's loss of life.'

'Go on then, how much?'

'£293,000.'

'Fuck me! Wow that's a lot of money.'

'It is, guv, but the argument at the time, which to be honest is a valid argument at any time, is that their ten-year-old daughter had her whole life ahead of her, and obviously, whilst no amount of money would ever compensate for such a loss, the insurance company was penalised where it hurts, in the pocket.'

'Do we know what happened to the other driver in the accident?'

'No, guv, I didn't look. Do you want me…'

'No, it's fine, it's not important, I was just interested.'

'So that's £225,000 and £293,000,' Calvert paused for a second whilst he completed his mental maths, '£518,000.'

'Aye, that's what I added it up to also.'

'That's bloody lottery-style figures.'

'Okay, so he's been living off the insurance payout since 2010 then?'

'He has, yes, guv. Well, that's what we assume. Also, you recall when you collared him, he was in the garden painting?'

'Yes, he was sitting on front of an easel with a large canvas. Looked like he was doing some kind of water colour, some landscape of some form.'

'That's right. Apparently, he's quite good. Well, as an artist. He sells some paintings at the Wednesday market in Tarbert.'

'How good is good?'

'I'm not sure that I'm best qualified to judge if his paintings are any good, but I was told that he sells pieces for between one hundred and five hundred pounds, size dependent.'

'Okay. Interesting. Anything else, background-wise?'

'No, that's about all we have, guv.'

Calvert looked at them both with a look that conveyed the message of *you've forgotten something*.

Then it finally dawned.

'Oh, aye…and he has no criminal record, not even a caution. As far as I can see he's never been on the radar of the police, for any reason.'

'Right, okay. Thanks, both.'

Coffees refreshed, Calvert brought the conversation up to date.

'Any overnight issues to report?'

'None, guv, quiet as a mouse apparently. The custody sergeant didn't hear a peep from him all night.'

'Okay,' Calvert looked at both DC's, 'which one of you has got more experience interviewing suspects of serious crimes?'

Waller's shoulders visibly sank; he knew that his three-year tenure as a Police Scotland detective constable was dwarfed by Taylor's eight years.

'He does, guv, he has more experience,' confirmed Waller.

Taylor nodded.

'Okay, they you're with me, DC Waller, as we interview Macaulay.'

Now Taylor's disappointment showed through his body language. It wasn't very often that serious crimes like these occurred across this patch, so of course either one would be naturally disappointed not to be involved in the interview.

By the time DC Waller had collected Macaulay from the holding cells and brought him to the interview room, it was ten past ten. Macaulay was shown where to sit, and

Waller took a seat opposite him. They waited on Detective Inspector Calvert.

As they waited, Macaulay surveyed the room. It was about as bland and uninteresting as it could be. Ten feet by six feet with enough space for a small table and four chairs, with magnolia emulsion walls and a light blue check carpet.

A few minutes later Calvert arrived, closed the door behind him and took a seat next to Waller.

'Good morning, Michael, how are you?'

'Aye, nae bad.'

'Good. Good.'

'So, I understand that you don't want a legal representative.'

'Aye, that's right.'

'Are you sure?'

'Aye.'

'Okay. I'll ask you again in a few minutes, just for the formalities of the recording. Okay?'

Calvert nodded at Waller, and he in turn pressed the record button on the digital recorder. They waited, as usual, a few seconds for the initial beep to end.

'The time is ten twenty-two on Thursday the twenty-ninth of July 2021 and this recorded interview is taking place at Lochgilphead police station. Present are Detective Inspector Calvert, and…'

'Detective Constable Waller.'

'And…say your name please.'

'Michael Macaulay.'

'I must remind you, Mr Macaulay, that you are still under caution. You are not obliged to say anything but anything you do say will be noted down and may be used in evidence. Do you understand?'

'Aye.'

'You are also entitled to legal representation during this interview. This is something that you have declined. Is this correct?'

'Aye.'

'Do you have a solicitor?'

'Have one? A solicitor?'

'Yes, do you have your own appointed solicitor? Just want you to know that we can arrange for a duty solicitor to attend the interview if not having your own is the reason for declining any representation.'

'No, I don't need any solicitor.'

'Okay, that's understood, we'll continue on that basis, but if you change your mind at any stage, just say so.'

Macaulay nodded.

'Right.' Calvert opened a buff-coloured folder and turned to the first page. It was blank, although Macaulay didn't know this. 'Tell me a bit about yourself, Michael.'

'Tell you a bit about myself,' he repeated, 'what is this, a job interview?'

'No. I thought we might ease ourselves in, Michael.'

Macaulay just stared at him. He didn't reply.

'No? Okay, let's dive straight in at the deep end. Twenty-four hours ago, we found Hayley Findlay in your basement, chained to the wall like a dog. She had been reported missing ten years ago and had been assumed by everyone, including the police and her parents, to be dead. You abducted her ten years ago, correct?'

This was a pivotal moment. Would Macaulay admit and cooperate through the course of the interview, or would there be a continuous flow of *no comment* and denials?

'I don't recall how long ago it was, to be honest. Time flies.'

'Indeed it does, but probably not if you're chained to a wall and your liberty and freedom have been taken from you. Do you not think?'

No reply.

'Had you held Hayley there since her abduction?'

'Yes.'

'Did you know her, you know, at the time of abduction?'

'No, not really. I knew of the family, but we hadn't really spoken. I don't think.'

'Take me back to that day in May 2011, where did you take her from?'

'The park.'

'Talk me through the events of that day. What led up to you taking Hayley?'

'I've no bloody idea. It was ten years ago. I'm not a bloody memory man.'

'Not a memory man,' Calvert replied, 'surely that date has to be the most prolific, the most dramatic, the day that sticks in your mind over all others in the last decade. No?'

No reply.

'Okay. Why did you take her?'

'I don't know why.'

'Yes, you do. Why did you take Hayley from the park on that day back in May 2011?'

After a long pause, Macaulay replied, 'company, I guess.'

'You wanted company?'

'I guess.'

'Are there not a million other ways to get some company? Perhaps call in to The Plough on a weekend and share a few beers with your fellow villagers. You could have invited some of them back to your cottage for drinks or dinner, or even a barbecue. You could have started a darts team, a dominoes team or a bowls team!'

Macaulay sat and stared at him, motionless, expressionless.

'Hell, if it's female company that you needed, I'm sure that you could have found that, perhaps online, or if not in Kelvedie then further afield.'

There was a further long pause whilst Calvert brought his heart rate back down again.

'You wanted the company of a girl, didn't you, a young girl?'

'I'm not a paedo,' came the stern reply.

'Are you not, Michael?'

'No. I despise men that treat girls like that.'

The irony of his comment wasn't lost on either detective

as Waller's raised eyebrows towards Calvert showed.

'Tell me about your little girl, Michael.'

It took a few moments for Macaulay to respond, clearly not eager to open up about his family. Eventually he did.

'Caitlin died in a car accident a few years ago.'

'2010 wasn't it?'

'Aye, the twenty-third of December,' he replied, 'she died in the same accident as my wife.'

'Twenty-third of December you say? That was about six months before Hayley was abducted.'

No reply.

'Did you take Hayley to try and fill the void in your life, left by the death of your wife and your daughter?'

'Don't know…possibly…probably.'

'Did you not think about her parents? How worried they might be, and eventually after all the years passed, they assumed that she was dead.'

No reply. That was becoming a common theme for the avoidance of difficult and awkward questions.

'You're not saying very much, Michael. Help us try to understand and make some sense of this.'

'There is none.'

'What?'

'Sense. It's nonsensical.'

'We've already established, I think, that you took Hayley to fill the gap in your life after the death of your wife and daughter, and whilst that doesn't make sense, well, not to any rational man anyway, that was your motive.

Correct?'

No reply.

'Were you ever going to release her?'

'It's hard to say.'

'Hard to say. Why? Based on what?'

Again, no reply.

DC Waller chipped in at a timely moment as planned with Calvert as part of their all-too-brief planning discussion prior to the interview.

'So, you abduct and hold Hayley captive for the best part of a decade… tell me about Florence. Why take her?'

Macaulay was again silent, but this time he at least looked pensive as though he was formulating some kind of response.

'Why take her?' Waller repeated, 'was it purposely and targeted, you know, her being Hayley's sister, or opportunistic and a coincidence?'

'I'd been watching her on and off for a while, from a distance. She liked to play in the park, or in the woods at the back of her house.'

'Okay, and…'

'And… I wasn't sure if the older one would be around for much longer.'

'What do you mean by that?'

'She was looking really ill.'

'Why do you think that might be, Michael?'

'She was really thin. Not really eating much.'

Calvert re-joined the conversation. 'Let me be

absolutely clear. I am not in any way condoning what you did. Abducting and imprisoning a young girl is abhorrent in my mind…but… would it not have been in both of your interests if you had looked after her better?'

'Looked after her better? You mean like, fed her better, dressed her better, or perhaps let her come upstairs and eat with me at the table every evening?'

'Well,' said Calvert, in his finest sarcastic tone, 'preferably you could have released her so she could do all of that at home with her family.'

'Florence didn't quite go to plan, did it?' Waller took up the lead once again, 'she escaped, didn't she? How did you let that happen, Michael?'

No reply. Macaulay was clearly irked on the subject of Florence.

'She was found wandering in Kelvedie. By the way, she is safe and well now. Well, physically anyway.'

Again, no verbal reply, but Macaulay was visibly irritated over any mention of Florence's name, or the fact that she had escaped.

'You took two girls from their family, one for just over a week and one for a decade. Do you have any regrets? Any remorse for the suffering that you have caused?'

No reply.

Throughout the interview so far, Calvert was aware of Macaulay's lisp; his 's' became 'th', and it supported the comments made by Florence that her captor had the very same speech impediment.

Calvert thought about continuing the interview and further elaborating on the abduction of both Hayley and Florence, but he had what he needed to be able to charge him, he had his confession for both abductions; that and the fact that Hayley was found in the cellar of his house. Calvert was confident that the charges for both Hayley, obviously, and for Florence also would stick. The Procurator Fiscal would never turn this away for lack of evidence, and the jury… well the jury would have him hung, drawn and quartered within two minutes of the opening statements.

CHAPTER 29

'Hi, Hayley.'

Doctor Sutherland entered the room.

'Hi.'

'How are you feeling?'

'Tired,' then after a large exhale she said, 'and I've got a headache too.'

'Yes, that's understandable considering what your body has been through, and especially now as we work towards reversing the muscle wastage and returning you back to general good health. Try and rest. Rest is the best medicine you can give yourself at the minute, Hayley.'

Doctor Sutherland looked and smiled at Hayley's three guests, her mum, her dad, and her sister. She was unsure that Hayley would get much quality rest with those three semi-permanently camped at her bedside, although conscious of the family circumstances, she would not begrudge them this time together, nor would she ask any of them to leave.

'I'll check your pain meds again shortly.'

The doctor picked up the medical chart and looked at her watch. She smiled and placed it back down, happy that the requested hourly observation had been undertaken and recorded by the nurses. Nothing untoward to note.

'And how are you feeling, Florence?'

Florence looked up from her seated position. 'I'm okay, thank you.'

Florence's ordeal might have only lasted a week or so, and her scars were significantly more mental than physical, but Doctor Sutherland made a point of checking in with her too.

'Good. Good. I just want to speak to your parents for a second. Would it be okay if I took them outside? Florence, perhaps you could stay here with Hayley. Okay?'

'Sure.'

Aileen and Callum followed the doctor outside.

'Is it bad news?' asked Aileen immediately after the door closed behind them.

'Relax, Aileen. Relax. I just wanted to update you on the psychiatric assessment that we carried out earlier this morning, just before you arrived.'

'Psychiatric assessment?' Callum looked slightly confused.

'Aye, Callum,' Aileen said scornfully, 'we were told about this.'

'Okay. So, the psychiatric assessment confirmed what we suspected. Hayley is suffering from anxiety and, whilst it is too early for a definitive assessment, quite probably PTSD, as well as the obvious physical ailments.'

'PTSD?' Callum challenged, 'don't soldiers get that in battle, you know, from seeing dead bodies and such?'

'Well, yes, kind of, Callum. It probably became more well-known to the wider public as a result of the conflicts in Iraq and Afghanistan where many soldiers were diagnosed with PTSD, but that was probably also reflective of a better understanding and diagnosis. But everyone, anyone, in everyday life can suffer PTSD following a traumatic event. The person may have nightmares and flashbacks vividly recalling the traumatic event.'

'Aye, okay. I see that.'

'Hayley definitely, and possibly Florence to a certain degree,' she paused; 'we'll have to keep a watchful eye on Florence too. Anyway, as Hayley starts to adjust back to normal life, she may experience bouts of paranoia and depression. It is likely that she will have panic attacks when reminded about her experience; you may notice an irritability or potentially aggressive behaviour. In the main, I think that she will struggle with lack of sleep, or disturbed sleep and she will find it hard to focus or concentrate, perhaps on simple everyday tasks.'

Doctor Sutherland paused for a second, wanting to

ensure that they were both absorbing the information as best as they could.

'I mean, well,' Callum started, 'it's obvious that she will be suffering from some kind of mental illness, I could have told you that.'

'Indeed,' confirmed the doctor, 'but it requires confirmation of the medical diagnosis as this helps with the initial and ongoing treatment and support. You need that initial diagnosis in order to be able to access a range of support services throughout the NHS.'

'Okay, we understand.'

'Her PTSD is likely to last for years to come, and she may never full recover, whatever *recover* looks like.'

'So, how do we help?'

'Is exactly the right question, Callum,' the doctor said, 'she is going to need long-term support. As I said earlier, it's a very early assessment and she will be closely monitored over the next few weeks, after that, the therapist may recommend something like cognitive behavioural therapy to help Hayley come to terms with the events and help manage the distress. She will live with PTSD and in time, hopefully, she will use coping mechanisms and learn how to manage it. When I say that she will need long-term support, I'm not talking about, you know, a full-time carer, it's not like that. Her PTSD will be ever present, but may lie dormant over several months, or even years. It's immediate and short-term help and support to help her understand her PTSD and provide her with the tools to manage it. And in the longer term, it's just being there for her, providing that loving stable support network.'

Aileen smiled, 'we can do that, doctor, we can do that.'

The doctor returned her warm smile.

'When can we take her home?

'Well, Hayley will be moved up to a ward later today, so she will transfer from my care to that of another team, so I can't be one hundred percent sure, you'll really need to ask them after the transfer.'

'But…' said Aileen expectantly.

'But, probably somewhere between seven and ten days. We will want to see some weight gain, however small, and we will want to see Hayley starting to take some regular food. She also has some large, and obviously very painful, sores on her bottom and thighs. We will continue treating those, and again expect to see those well on their way to healing too.'

'Okay.'

'Don't worry, she'll be home in no time at all, then you can fuss over her all you want.'

'The doctor says that you'll be moved to a ward later today. We'll have you home soon,' Aileen told her daughter.

'Yes, she told me too.'

'Everything's going to be alright, sweetheart.'

'So,' Hayley started, 'just what have I missed?' She appeared jovial, certainly outwardly positive even if she was suppressing any true thoughts and feelings.

'Well, you have a sister!' Florence jumped in.

'Yes, I saw that. I always wanted a sister.'

'Me too.'

Aileen started to get upset and tears that were welling in her eyes were now rolling down both cheeks.

'I can't tell you how much we've missed you. We thought you were dead.' Aileen took hold of both Hayley and Florence and squeezed them tight.

'I'm never letting either of you out of my sight again.'

Callum suppressed all urges to tell Aileen that they had both been held within the village, only a few hundred metres away. He knew that this would come out at some time, and he further knew that this would burst Aileen's bubble of joy. There was no way that this fact would not send her spiralling into a melting pot of anger, disbelief and self-criticism. She would need to know…but not today, and perhaps not for many days to come.

Neither Hayley nor Florence could confidently and accurately say where they had been held captive, and this would, ironically, help to supress the issue with Aileen, for now at least.

'We'll have you back on your feet again soon,' she repeated.

Aileen had so many things running through her mind like a freight train; *eight years of missed school, if and how does she catch that up? Puberty and periods – OMG, how has she managed and navigated this, on her own, over the last few* *years? Teeth, boys, school, puberty, clothes, health – mental and physical, driving, walking, her sister, the impact on her sister. OMG – don't lose sight of Florence and her own thoughts and struggles…..*mind blown!

CHAPTER 30

'Hang on a second, let me just pull over to the side of the road.'

Superintendent Talloch had caught Calvert whilst he was driving toward Lochgilphead station that morning.

'Sorry about that.'

'That's fine, Paul. Pulling over is the sensible thing to do.'

'And the legal thing,' he added.

'Of course. Listen, I understand that you are heading back home later today.'

'Yes, ma'am. I'm just off to Lochgilphead now, then I'll be going home in a couple of hours I guess.'

'Okay, well I wanted to thank you for your sterling work on these two mispers, Paul. Finding both Florence and then Hayley after all this time, and alive and well, was truly remarkable. Truly remarkable.'

'Thank you. I appreciate the kind words, but you know as well as I do that it's a team effort. I worked with some great officers of yours over the last couple of weeks. They're a credit to Police Scotland, and to you, ma'am.'

'Thank you, Paul.'

'Wouldn't say it if it wasn't true, ma'am.'

'Yes. Yes, I firmly believe that to be so. Anyway, safe travels back to England. If you find yourself back up here anytime, work or pleasure, do drop me a text and we'll catch dinner or drinks perhaps.'

'I'll make sure and do that, ma'am.'

'Oh, and there will be a letter of commendation wending its way to your superintendent. It will probably arrive in Hull before you do.'

'There was no need, ma'am, but thank you.'

'Goodbye, Paul.'

'Bye, ma'am.'

Walking into the incident room at Lochgilphead station, Calvert saw that only Sergeant O'Brien was in, and greeted him warmly upon walking through the door.

'I'm good, thanks, guv,' O'Brien replied, 'what are you doing here? I thought you be halfway down the M74 by now.'

'I will be soon enough. I just wanted to call here first

to check that there's nothing outstanding, no loose ends, nothing left behind…'

'And to say goodbye of course?'

Calvert smiled, 'yes, of course. But it looks like that might be only you. Where is everyone?'

'They're all out this morning, and to be honest you've only just caught me. I'm off out in five minutes.'

'Okay, well in that case,' Calvert stepped forward with his hand outstretched, 'it was good to work with you. Thanks for all your help on these two mispers.'

'Aye, likewise. Good to meet and work with you too, guv. If you're ever back up here again…'

'I know…look me up.'

O'Brien smiles at him. 'You've heard that a lot then?'

'Once or twice.'

'Is there anything else that you need from me before I leave you?'

'I don't think so, guv. All the paperwork is squared away, the case is with the Procurator Fiscal and Macaulay's first court appearance is tomorrow. You'll be needed to return when it comes to trial, I guess.'

'Possibly, but that all depends on how Macaulay pleads tomorrow.'

'Aye, of course it does. Well, if his interview is anything to go by, I don't see any plea other than guilty.'

'Yes, me too, but my experience tells me that sometimes, just sometimes, these guys just want their day in court.'

'Agreed. I've experienced the same, but for me, Macaulay is more of an introvert, I don't see him wanting his day in court and courting, if you'll forgive the pun, the media attention.'

'Yes, I'm with you there. Anyway, you take care, and you never know, our paths might cross again in the future.'

'Aye, safe travels, guv.'

'By the way,' Calvert paused as he was leaving, 'how is Inspector Mason? I had completely forgotten about her, until this very minute. How weird. She fell and broke her ankle when we undertook the initial search a couple of weeks ago.'

'She returned to hospital after a couple of days and had an operation. It all went as expected and she's back at home convalescing until she's fit for duty again.'

'A few weeks, I guess?'

'Aye, I don't think that we'll see her back for another six or so.'

'And DCI Geary? Is he still in hospital with suspected deep vein thrombosis?'

'He is, although it's not suspected any longer, it's confirmed DVT.'

'Ouch. Bloody hell. Triggered from his Jamaica flight?'

'That's what it is being blamed on, aye. Dependent upon the severity and resultant treatment, he should be back on duty in a few weeks' time.'

Calvert smiled. He didn't know why.

'Take care, see you anon.'

A little after noon, Calvert had returned to Kelvedie on the next stop of what he himself was now calling his *Elton John Farewell Tour*. This stop was going to be short, but important.

Having parked his car behind the B&B, Calvert walked the short distance to the Findlay house. As he approached, he could see Aileen in the garden with Florence playing swingball. In the fifteen seconds it took Calvert to reach the garden gate, Aileen had missed the ball with two attempted swings and Florence had thoroughly clattered it twice, accelerating the ball around the post at a ferocious pace.

They paused when they saw Calvert.

'Don't stop on my account,' he said.

'No, no, it's fine. It'll give me a quick breather,' Aileen replied, 'will you come in?'

'No, I won't, thanks, Aileen. I just wanted to let you know that I'm heading back home, and to say a quick goodbye.'

'When do you leave?'

'As soon as I leave you, I'll be going home.'

'Where do you live?' asked Florence, completely unaware of the circumstances that brought him to Kelvedie, or the personal sacrifice he had made whilst on his holiday.

'Hull.'

'Hull?'

'Yes, have you heard of it?'

'No,' she replied.

'It's a city in England, in Yorkshire.'

'So, you don't live in Scotland? You don't live near here? Glasgow or somewhere like that…'

'No, Florence, I don't. I came to Kelvedie two days before you went missing. I came for a bit of a holiday. I came to do some walking, and just relaxing.'

'Oh, I'm sorry.'

'There's nothing you need to be sorry for, Florence.'

'We are very grateful that you were here, inspector,' interjected Aileen, 'will you be back, perhaps in the future? Perhaps to take that walking holiday?'

'Will I be back? To Scotland, yes, definitely. To Kelvedie? Unlikely.'

'Okay, well thank you for all your help. Thank you for returning my girls, both girls, back to me.'

Aileen walked over and gave him a big hug.

'Safe travels back home.'

'Thank you, Aileen. Say goodbye to Callum for me will you, and of course to Hayley.'

'I will.'

'And you,' he turned to Florence, 'you look after your mum, you hear?'

She didn't reply but smiled at him.

'And you enjoy getting to know your big sister.'

That brought an even bigger smile to her face.

'I will. Thank you.'
'You are very welcome. Bye.'
'Bye.'

Two stops left, he thought to himself as he walked back down the hill, and back towards Shallowbrook Lodge, the B&B where he was almost part of the furniture. His seventeen days there had been far longer than he had anticipated, albeit the cost for the last ten days had been met by Police Scotland.

Despite there being a general lack of holiday rental accommodation both in Kelvedie and neighbouring Tarbert, Calvert was pleased that he had landed at Shallowbrook Lodge. Both Brian and Antonio were great characters and wonderful hosts, and he would miss their warm welcoming company, the cosy fireside chats, and their hearty Scottish breakfasts.

Having collected his bag, and with one foot outside the open door, he looked back into the room and smiled to himself. He was pleased to be returning home, finally, but would miss Kelvedie. He surprised himself with his sentimental thoughts of room 5; after all he had spent very little time in there over the last seventeen days.

'Paul. Paul. Paul,' announced Brian as Calvert reached the front desk.

Calvert placed the room key on the reception desk. The small brass key that was attached by key-fob style connector to the six-inch wooden baton with the words

'Shallowbrook Lodge' burnt into the wood. The wooden baton that had started much conversation when it was handed to him upon first entering the B&B.

'I have refrained from hitting anyone over the head with it,' said Calvert.

'Glad to hear it, Paul. Although I wouldn't have minded if you had hit that Macaulay fella over the head once or twice.'

Calvert smiled.

'So, I guess that's you checking out then?'

'Yes, I'm afraid so. Back to the motherland as they say.'

Calvert took his wallet from his jacket pocket and extracted his credit card. 'How much do I owe you, Brian?'

'Nothing.'

A puzzled Calvert asked, 'what do you mean, nothing? If the superintendent was good to her word, they were going to pick up some of the tab, but I need to pay for the first few days.'

'Your superintendent was good to her word, and then some.'

'Explain.'

'Well, earlier this morning I received a call from a lovely young lady from the police informing me that she would be emailing a purchase order over, and that I should raise an invoice against that order.'

'Okay, understood, and…'

'And… she told me that it would be for the whole amount. The entire cost of your stay here.'

'Really?'

'Yes, really?'

'Bloody hell.'

To say Calvert was pleasantly surprised would be an understatement. 'I tell you what, Brian, if I'd have known that from the beginning, I would have been on steak every night, followed by half a dozen Taliskers.'

'I know. I think I would have been recommending the most expensive dish every night too.'

They both smiled and Antonio entered.

'What are you two smiling about?'

'I'm just happy to be getting out of this dump and going back home,' Calvert replied.

Antonio looked confused, partially because he was unsure of the word *dump* and thus its context, but also wondered, due to the reference to home, if Paul had not enjoyed his stay with them.

'He's only pulling your leg,' said Brian.

'Am I?'

Calvert and Brian laughed, with Antonio still none the wiser.

'Well, listen, guys, you have a wonderful place here, I have thoroughly enjoyed my time at Shallowbrook Lodge. You can rest assured that I will be singing its praises back in Yorkshire and will recommend you to as many people as possible.'

'That's extremely nice of you, Paul. You are welcome back here any time.'

'Thank you.'

'Do you think that you might be back again, perhaps next summer?'

Calvert smiled, knowing that this was the third time that he had been asked this question, and it was probably unlikely to be the last.

'I'm not sure, to be honest. Maybe. If I do find myself in this part of the country, you can bet that I'll be here, taking up residence in one of your rooms.'

'As I say, you are welcome any time.'

'Thank you.'

Calvert shook hands and hugged both Brian and Antonio before loading his bag into the boot of the car.

Hoping that he would find a parking space towards the harbour, he set off towards his fourth and final stop, The Plough Inn.

Having checked his watch, one pm, he decided that he could not stay longer than ten minutes before he needed to get on the road.

Opening the door to the snug he found it to be empty, which wasn't surprising considering the time of day. Everyone, he thought, would be at work.

Taking a seat at a bar stool he waited for a minute, but there was no sign of either Gordon or Angie.

'Oi,' he shouted, 'there's a fire in the snug, come quick, there's a fire.'

That appeared to do the trick. Firstly, Gordon appeared, then Angie hot on his heels, only to find Paul Calvert perched on a bar stool grinning at the pair of them.

Gordon couldn't stop himself from looking over Calvert's shoulder and panning left to right, just to make sure that he was actually joking.

'Aye, you're a weird sort, you, Paul.'

'I needed to get your attention, I'm dying of thirst here.'

'We thought that you'd be well on your way by now. You're leaving today, right?'

'Today? Yes, I am.'

'A wee dram to see you on your way?' asked Gordon.

'Tempting, but no I shouldn't. Give me a soda water, please.'

As Gordon poured the bottled soda water into a glass, he said, 'you'll be missed around here, Paul, you certainly made an impact during your visit.'

'Yes, I guess so. I would rather have had a quieter time here, if you know what I mean. Fell walking, whisky drinking, that kind of thing.'

'Aye, for sure. But those two wee lassies are now safe home with their parents thanks to you.'

'Not just me, Gordon, there are dozens and dozens of officers that were involved and played their part.'

'Aye, but under your leadership, Paul.'

'Will you…'

Calvert interrupted him, 'don't ask me if I'll be back.'

'You've been asked already then?'

'Yes, once or twice, and that's just in the last couple of

hours.' Calvert laughed, mainly to himself.

'Scotland, perhaps,' he said, 'but I'm not sure that Kelvedie will see me any time soon.'

'That's a shame. Have you also been told that you are welcome back any time?'

Again, he smiled, 'yes, that as well.'

'Well, if it's an incentive you need,' Angie said, 'we'll throw in a few free pints when you're next here.'

Gordon glared at her. 'Steady on, girl, have you gone mad?'

Calvert held out an outstretched hand towards Gordon. 'You'll never know, Gordon, how much I appreciate the fact that you had a bolt cutter in your pub.'

No other explanations or elaborations were necessary.

'Don't ever change, will you, either of you,' Calvert remarked as he regarded them both for the final time.

Calvert drained the remainder of his glass and bade his fond farewells to Gordon and Angie before making his way back to the car.

'Hi, Lisa, it's Dad.'

'Hi, Dad. Have you set off yet?'

'Just. I'll be back in about seven hours. Have the kettle on, eh?'

THE END

Printed in Great Britain
by Amazon